Wishing on Raining Stars

Destinee Hardwick

First Printing, 2015

ISBN-13: 978-0692386378 (The Mayhem Castle)

ISBN-10: 0692386378

www.themayhemcastle.com

Dear beloved,

This is for you.

Prologue

It was the same as ever. A dream filled with laughter and happiness. His black hair swung lightly in his eyes as his lips turned up into a sly grin. It absolutely made my heart melt with glee. He was perfect in every way.

Yet it seemed that every time I went to touch him I would suddenly awake. My body covered in sweat, my nightshirt sticking to me uncomfortably. I would swipe my hair out of my face and get up to peer out of the window, looking for him somewhere in the darkness, knowing how foolish I was acting.

He was only a figment of my imagination.

I would disappointingly crawl back into bed, squeezing my eyes shut, hoping for a different dream. I was becoming obsessed with an imaginary man. Yet how could I not?

The dreams were getting out of hand and I knew this. I knew I had to stop. Perhaps I was sick; a lot had been going on. But I knew deep down this was not the case. There was something spectacular and spooky going on in my mind that scared and delighted me all at once.

Perhaps I was right in thinking I was going insane. That was the only thought that kept me from telling my mother about the reoccurring dream. What would she say? Would she send me away?

I need not stress her any more. She was already at wits end over my father's death. To learn that her daughter was obsessing over a man that did not exist may send her over the edge.

So with that thought I would drift into a dreamless sleep every night around the same time, hoping that by morning I would forget his face.

One

Autumn was in full swing. Leaves were scattered on the ground in rich shades of red and orange, and the grass was the color of straw. The earth crunched under my black boots as I descended the hill towards town.

My mother was still staying holed up inside her room, not daring to come out to take care of her children. The loss of my father had hit her hard. She seemed to act as if no one else in the world mattered. Not even the people she pushed from her womb.

I pulled my shawl tighter around my shoulders as a gust of air went zooming past. By the time I got to my destination I knew my cheeks and nose would be a lovely hue of pink.

But never mind any of that. I hadn't been sleeping well. I knew the people that passed me on their horses and on foot could tell. There were dark patches under my eyes that I couldn't make go away. I had tried everything, even Juniper's absurd suggestion to put my head in a bucket of ice water.

Nothing seemed to work. He was haunting my dreams more often now. His dark eyes looking through me while his icy fingers grasped my wrist.

I couldn't shake him, no matter what I did. I couldn't tell anyone of the dreams, of this I was certain. They would call me mad. I may even be sent away. That was not an option while I had two younger siblings to take care of at home.

I shook the thoughts from my mind. I was feet away from the General Store and didn't need to worry Mr. Barton. He already seemed upset enough over the apparent disappearance of my mother.

I pushed open the wooden door. A bell overhead chimed and Mr. Barton immediately appeared with a smile on his face from the back room. A smile that quickly dissolved once he saw me without the company of my mother.

"How is she doing?" he quickly asked. His voice was soft and caring, with a tinge of hope.

"She still has not left her room. I have tried everything I can think of." I sighed, stepping further into the small store.

"Juniper and Honour? How are they holding up?"

"Surprisingly well. They are exceeding in their learning. Juniper is the main attraction as always anywhere we go, and Honour is still rambunctious as always. I can't seem to keep her out of the trees lining our house." I smiled at the thought of my younger sisters.

He smiled back. "Good, good. At least they are holding up. And you, dear? How are you? You seem tired."

"It's a lot of work to keep up with two young girls." I grinned. "Sleep is a distant memory as of late. But I needn't talk much longer. I should get my things and go. Juniper and Honour will be hungry and I suppose my mother will be also."

He smoothed his hands over the brown vest he was wearing. "Yes, yes. What will it be today?"

I gave him the list of items I needed and he hurriedly filled a brown sack with herbs and household necessities. I left with a small wave and hurried my way back through the town, up the hill to my house.

Dusk was closing in and I didn't like being about at night. Not at my age with drunken men lingering around. I was back at my house in mere minutes, slightly out of breath from my journey uphill.

The house was not anything special. In all honestly, it was falling apart. There were no men around to help keep it up and my mother didn't have the money to hire someone to fix it. It consisted of three bedrooms, a living area, a bath, a study, and a kitchen.

As I said, nothing special. A far cry from the homes that surrounded it. Three stories high with countless bedrooms and baths. I envied the people I attended school with for their luxuries.

Honour must have been watching out of the window because as soon as I could be seen over the hill, she bounded out of the front door, running as fast as she could to meet me.

Her golden hair swung down her back, rippling in the wind, while her blue dress that was far too big for her small frame almost tripped her. Yet a smile lit up her entire face to see me back so soon.

She caught up to me, her chest rising and falling rapidly. "I thought you would be gone longer than that!"

"I told you I only needed a few things." I replied, smiling down at her.

"There was a man here." She replied excitedly.

I stopped abruptly, almost dropping my sack of goods on the cold ground. "Who? Why?"

She struggled to recall his name, tapping her finger on her chapped lips. "He said his name was William... William..." a puzzled look crossed her face then brightened. "William Cundy! Yes, that's it. He asked for Juniper's hand in marriage, but she told him he would have to come back another time because you weren't around. Isn't that lovely, Reyenne? Juniper asked to be married! How romantic."

She swayed back and forth a bit thinking over the prospect of love and marriage, but I was livid. There was no way a man would come knocking for Juniper unless she had been seeing him without my consent or notice.

"Where is Juniper?" I asked, handing the sack of goods to Honour to put away in the kitchen.

"At father's grave I suppose. You know how she goes there every time she's faced with a big decision."

I strode off without another word and headed towards the field on the right side of our house. My thoughts were filled with malice towards my younger sister. How dare she go spend time with men of God knows what age when she herself had just turned fifteen. And behind my back!

No, this would not do.

She was kneeling in front of the stone slab that bore our father's name and dates of birth and death. She wore a long white gown with her light brown hair in a loose braid down her back. She also wore my slippers I saw with another surge of anger.

I approached unheard and stood directly behind her. She sat still like a small, frail statue on guard.

"Juniper."

She turned, obviously startled. "Oh. Hello, Reyenne."

It wasn't hard to see why men pined over her. She carefully swiped rouge on her cheeks that she made herself and enhanced her green eyes with a piece of charcoal. A light sweep of freckles spotted her nose and cheeks, and her lips were forever in a full pout.

Truth be told, I envied her.

I crossed my arms, looking down on her. "Who is this William Cundy I hear visited today?"

"Just a man." She shrugged, her cheeks turning a slight shade darker.

"If he is just a man then why has he asked to marry you?" I asked with a slight edge to my tone.

She stood up, only slightly smaller than me in stature. "He is just a man! I foolishly thought I could spend my life with him but I cannot. It didn't feel right when he asked me. He isn't the one. It is in the past now."

Her eyes shifted slightly to the ground then back up to my face. A sure sign that she was lying. "You are not being honest with me. Honour told me you sent him away to come back when I was around to give my consent. When have you seen him before?"

She twiddled her thumbs nervously. Then, in the smallest voice she could muster, she replied, "Every night."

I stood shocked. "Has he..." I couldn't think of how to form the question politely, like a lady. "Has he touched you?"

Her eyes opened wide and she shook her head vigorously. "No, no. It's nothing like that, Reyenne! We walk through the streets and talk, and sometimes stop for a bit of tea when we are too tired to walk further. I love him..." She trailed off, looking down as if it was a shameful act to love someone.

I didn't know what to say. I had never experienced this except in my dreams. I was plain and didn't put much effort into my appearance. Men seemed to look straight through me. I was not prepared to handle something of this sort.

It should have been my father questioning Juniper and approving William. Not me. Not at my age with another sibling to watch over, and a mother who rarely moved.

"Please don't send him away, Reyenne, please." She begged, tears glistening in her eyes.

I thought over things for a moment then dropped my arms to my sides. "When he calls again I will talk with him then make my decision. Although I think you are far too young to marry. Leave me now so that I can talk with our father in peace."

She scurried away with a glint of hope in her green eyes. I sighed, dropping to my knees in front of the grave.

Truth be told, I missed my father a great deal. He always seemed to have the answers to my questions, and when he didn't, he would use all his energy to help find a solution.

I ran my hands over the stone, silently pleading him to help me with the choices I must make and the tasks I must do. Suddenly, the air became somewhat cooler. I hugged my arms around my body and shivered.

A whisper drifted on the wind. It was so faint that at first I mistook it for the sound of leaves swaying to the ground, their crisp edges catching on each other.

But no.

It was my name.

Someone was whispering my name.

I shot up, looking around. Could it be? Could my father be back to speak with me? Juniper had sworn she saw him mere days after he had passed, but ghosts were not something I put faith into.

I swiveled around, looking in every direction. Would I be able to see him? Would he be a mist, a shadow, an apparition?

Something caught my eye, I peered in the direction. Something had surly moved behind the tree I was staring at. I stood still, pretending to look in another direction while still watching the tree from the corner of my eye.

Yes, there it was. Something was definitely moving behind the tree, stepping side to side, much too tall to be an animal. I quietly made my way towards it as my heart beat wildly against my chest.

I was mere steps from the tree when he emerged. My breath caught in my throat, a scream almost made it out but stopped leaving me choking and grasping for words.

My eyes had to be wide in fear and trepidation. This could not be, it was impossible.

Yet, it must... it must be him.

"Reyenne?" he asked timidly.

I still couldn't seem to catch my breath. I felt as if I had been running for miles. Questions zoomed through my mind faster than I could keep up.

Finally, I stammered, "This cannot be... you are not r-real."

He smiled, his black hair a stark contrast to his pale skin. He was alluring. "Oh, but I am."

The smile never wavered from his face. He didn't seem to be phased by my reaction in the slightest. In fact, he seemed to be expecting it.

"H-how?" I questioned.

"I am real just as you are. I was brought into this world just as you were. We are no different, the two of us."

His response seemed to be conveying some cryptic message. A warning or threat, I hadn't a clue which. But before I could even begin to ask one of the many questions I felt I needed to, a shout echoed from the distance.

"Reyenne!" Honour yelled across the field.

I turned for an instant and when I turned back... he was gone. Vanished into thin air. I looked around for a few moments before shaking my head and walking back towards my father's grave.

I was going insane. There was no explanation other than that. I had watched my aunt suffer the same fate I was heading towards and it scared me. I saw as she slowly lost her ability to think and began to talk to people that were not there.

I had caught the same disease she had. I was going to die talking to strange beings that did not exist and babbling to myself in my sleep.

"REYENNE!" The shout was louder, she was worried.

"I'm c-coming!" I stammered, finding myself unbalanced on the hard ground. I somehow made it back to the house swiftly and faked a smile at Honour who disappeared back through the door.

I skipped dinner, checked in on my mother, and made my way to my bedroom. Sleep was what I needed. I didn't bother with lighting a fire or changing into a nightshirt. I simply pulled off my boots, wrapped my blankets and shawl tightly around me and fell into darkness.

Two

The dreams abruptly stopped after that day. Two weeks passed without me seeing his face. I was hurt, yet relieved. I missed him in some strange way.

Things were beginning to look up though. I wasn't given much time to ponder over my lost imaginary man. My mother had begun to move around again, she was taking responsibility for her children at last. She had even approved of William; my sister was to be married the following spring.

I was happy and yet felt saddened at this news. Juniper was younger than I and already going to be a wife. What would the townspeople say? Would they fake sympathy and laugh behind my back? Or maybe think something was terribly wrong with me?

It quite frankly bothered me; the opinions of others. My mother above all else was my worst enemy on the subject of marriage it seemed. She constantly dropped hints about things being easier for me with a husband on my arm.

I began to feel numb to the world around me. Every day was exactly the same. I would wake up, put on whatever was clean, make sure Juniper and Honour were ready, and trudge off through the snow to the schoolhouse.

In school I was taking my last year. I would not be back. I didn't feel my classes helped me with much anymore. I could read, write, and recite certain poetry. These things didn't help me much in my daily life.

What I didn't know was that my world was about to be flipped upside down yet again.

On a Monday morning, the first week of November, I woke up and got ready the same way I did day after day. I pulled my dress on, fastened all the laces of my bodice, and buttoned my boots up.

Honour sat at the kitchen table eating a slice of bread and Juniper still sat in their room swiping charcoal under her eyes. My mother sat in our living area sewing my new dress I had wanted for so long. It overjoyed me to see the gray fabric moving under her bony fingers.

"Reyenne, after school today could you please stop by and see Mr. Barton for me? He has some gold buttons waiting that I ordered." My mother called in from her chair.

"Yes, mother!" I yelled back, grabbing a slice of bread for myself and a bit of milk.

Honour smiled sheepishly up at me. "I found fairies in the forest."

I raised a brow at this statement. Honour seemed dead set on the idea that mythical beings frolicked in the forest near our home. Day after day she came in holding some contraption she had made calling it a fairy repellent or a fairy home.

I sat across from her at our uneven kitchen table. "You did? And how do you know?"

"I know because he gave me something." She grinned.

"He? There are male fairies?" I questioned, grinning back at her.

"Oh, yes. How else are they supposed to have children? They work just as we do, he told me. They have mothers and fathers, and people they love. The only difference is they have huge wings that come out of their backs when they want them to." She was practically jumping out of her seat while telling me this. Clearly she was very excited about her newfound imaginary friend.

"Ah, I see. And what did this fairy give you?" I took a rather large bite from my bread and had to wash it down quickly with milk.

She dug around in the pocket of her peplum jacket and pulled from it a small wadded black cloth. Her tiny fingers fiddled with the cloth for a moment then produced a vial with gold residue on the inside. "He says it's usually filled with tears but this one has already been used."

I held out my hand and she placed the vial in it carefully. As if the small glass bottle was a delicate treasure. I spun the vial between my fingers, absorbing everything about it. I had seen this somewhere before. I racked my brain, trying to recall the place I had last seen this bottle.

I handed it back still pondering. "Are you sure a fairy gave this to you?" I asked.

"Yes, yes." She nodded while folding the cloth back up and stashing it in her pocket. "He told me not to show anyone or tell so you have to keep it a secret. His society is very secretive, yes. If they found out he had even talked to me he could be banished."

I stared amused down at my sister. What I would give to go back to her naïve age. Where fairies existed and no harm was ever done in the world.

Before I could ask any more about this secretive fairy world, Juniper appeared from their room.

I sat in the back of the room as normal with the other older students. Honour sat two rows ahead of me and Juniper right in front of my desk. The room was abnormally chilly, the furnace had not been lit. Miss Hadley was late which was also abnormal. Especially since she went on about punctuality every chance she got.

Juniper flipped her wavy hair over her shoulder and turned around to look at me. Ever since her engagement to William she had a certain gleam in her eye that never seemed to vanish. "I wonder where Miss Hadley has run off to."

I glanced at the door then back at my sister. "Perhaps the snow has slowed her down?"

Juniper rolled her eyes. "Yes, but Miss Hadley has a coach! Surely snow wouldn't slow her down too much. We're here on time every day and we walk to school."

If there was a person who loathed the rich more than I it was Juniper. She hated having to walk past women with beautifully embroidered bodices and long skirts with no tattered ends. It seemed every chance she got she would insult someone based on their social status.

"I heard the wheels sometimes get stuck in drifts and it takes hours to dig them out. She does live in a valley; the snow is bound to build up around her home." I replied casually resting my chin on my hand.

She pondered this a moment before saying, "I say it's no excuse. If I had a coach I would have enough servants to get it out of the snow, mud, rain... whatever, as fast as possible! Especially if I had such an important job to do every day. The young are the future! Isn't that what she's always raving about?"

Before I could reply the door swung open and in stepped Miss Hadley formal as ever. She was an extravagant woman with expensive taste. Many whispered her budget was the reason men would not dare ask for her hand in marriage, but I always wondered if it was her own doing that she did not have a husband.

It took me a moment to realize Miss Hadley was not alone. A man wearing a black cloak stepped into the room behind her. He lingered at the side of the desk with his head down and snow lightly coating his shoulders while she bustled about getting the furnaces heated.

After several minutes she resumed her place behind her desk in the front of the room and smiled cheerily at her awaiting students. "Good morning! I am terribly sorry for the delay this morning but as you may have noticed we are joined by a new student today." She paused, beaming, then directed her attention to the man. "If you would please remove your cloak and hang it on one of the pegs."

He shuffled to the right side of the room where a neat line of jackets and overcoats hung on small wooden pegs, and with a sweeping motion pulled his cloak off. His hair was jet black and hung almost to his shoulders; this was the first thing I noticed.

Next, was his attire. Not unlike what most men wore but somehow different. It consisted of the usual black shoes, pants, vest, and long sleeved shirt. For a reason unbeknownst to me, the mere appearance of his back kept me on full alert.

Miss Hadley drew my attention back while he fumbled in his pocket for something. "Yes, now, while our newest addition is getting situated I would like you all to take out your English assignments you were to do and please pass them forward."

I opened my small bag and removed my latest essay about our progress as a society. As much as I liked to write, I had to admit it wasn't my best. I passed it forward to Juniper with a sigh and closed my folder again.

Miss Hadley collected the papers and turned just as the man did. I stifled a gasp the best I could. It was him. The man of my dreams, or should I say, in my dreams. His pale skin as always a shocking contrast to his black hair and clothing, his dark eyes gliding over the many faces, and his mouth forever set in a casual smirk.

A few girls to my left giggled and whispered, no doubt as enchanted as I was by his beauty. The class went silent, all except for Honour who shrieked and stood up. "Miss Hadley, this is a terrible mistake! This is not a man but a fairy!"

The class laughed at her outcry, a few people loudly whispered about intelligence not running in our family. I sunk down into my desk not wanting to be associated with the child screaming about mythical beings.

"Miss Montgomery, if you would please return to your seat." Miss Hadley sternly said, "Unless you would like to stay after class is over today and write lines about not making such a fuss."

A few more giggles swiped through the room and then settled. Honour's shoulders sank as she placed herself once again behind her desk. Juniper quickly turned to me and rolled her eyes then faced the front of the room.

"Now, as I was about to say, students, please welcome Ember... um..." she leaned over to him and whispered in his ear, he whispered back and she beamed. "Sky! Ember Sky. He will be with us the rest of this learning term. He has just transferred from out of town."

Another murmur swept through the room, he shoved his hands into his pockets and smiled. My heart skipped a beat. I was in shock, that was the only viable reason I was staying so calm. Miss Hadley pointed to the vacant desk to the right of me and he strode to it, placing himself silently in the chair.

I sat stiff as the lesson continued. I didn't dare look at him while we went through our usual routine of literature, math, and other boring tasks. My hand barely moved as my hand flew across page after page of notes. I hated having to dip my quill each time in ink, for it resulted in my having to shift my entire arm.

At last, the lesson ended and we were dismissed. I gathered my things swiftly hoping to make a dash for the door and home, but in my haste I knocked my ink bottle onto the floor. It landed with a thud and with a shatter of glass, the contents spilled on the wooden floor, soaking into the floorboards.

I glanced up, noticing the only people left in the room were myself, him, and Miss Hadley who was wiping the chalkboard off. She turned at the noise and frowned. "I expect you will be cleaning that mess up, Reyenne, and locking the door on your way out. I must be going. Do have a good afternoon." She pulled her things together and made an exit.

I glared at her back as she went, silently cursing her for leaving me alone with this man. I made my way to the back of the room, making sure I didn't step into the now small trail of ink making its way across the floor and pulled a few towels out of the cupboard.

On my way back I made sure not to look up at him, but instead closely examined the bottom of my skirts. I knelt next to the spilt ink and began wiping it the best I could. A black stain would permanently be seen by whoever sat at my desk in the future.

I felt him kneel across from me, could see his shadow dance across the floor in the little sunlight there was. My fingers were red and numb from the cold, the furnaces already extinguished and the winter air was creeping in.

"Need some help?" his voice was not deep but not high, a perfect octave. The voice you would imagine the man of your fantasies having. But I had heard this voice countless times before, at night in my bed, with my covers wrapped snuggly around me.

I suddenly was tired and fed up. I was angry and hurt. All my protected feelings of the past few months seemed to be now channeled to him. I looked up into his bottomless eyes,

13

suppressing my desire for him. I let the rage wash over me. I wanted to hate him. "Who are you, exactly? Or rather, who do you think you are? You show up near my house unexpectedly and vanish, you plague my dreams, and now you arrive in my place of learning? You, sir, owe me explanations."

I stood, dropping the stained cloth, and placed my hands firmly upon my hips. My words must have sounded ludicrous; I was losing my mind, accusing random men of plaguing my dreams. I blushed but held my ground nonetheless.

He too stood up, a good foot taller than I and smirked. My anger boiled. How dare he smirk at me as if he finds me amusing. How dare he act like every other man I had ever come in contact with when I had such an intimate bond with him.

But what was I saying?

Did I have an intimate bond with him?

"I am truly sorry I ran off so quickly those few months ago. I... became nervous." His cheeks flushed a light pink. I gawked at him. Nervous?

"Nervous? Nervous about what, exactly?" an edge of anger still lingered in my tone.

"Is it not obvious why a man would be nervous in your company? Your beauty outshines most. I have been too many places and have never laid eyes on a woman such as you." He once again shoved his hands deep into his pockets.

My hands fell from my hips to dangle limply in utter shock. Me? Beauty? Those two words have never been used together except by my mother and father. But who really ever counted the compliments given by their parents?

I blushed yet again. "I am very flattered, I assure you, but your antics do unnerve me. I live a quiet life without disruption and I intend to keep it that way. If you plan on bounding into it with eccentric ways, I am uninterested."

I dropped back to the floor to scrub the ink stain thinking the conversation was well over. I yelled at my own mind for bringing up the dreams when I first addressed him. He surely thought I was out of my head accusing a man I had only now met twice for intruding on my sleep.

But instead of walking away like I assumed he would, he too resumed his place on his knees across from me. His pale hand reached across the stained floor and grasped mine, stopping it as it clutched the cloth grazing the floor.

My entire body went rigid. No man outside my family had ever dared touch me before. Except, of course, the occasional accidental brushes. Electricity seemed to sweep through my bones. Before I could register what he was doing he had my palm facing up and had pushed the sleeve of my jacket away from the wrist.

There lay across the peach skin a darker mark. It was straight and a brutal white. It moved with the blue and green veins like a ripple in a river. Heat flared across my cheeks and neck. No one had ever noticed this mark before, or its twin on my other wrist.

My mind grasped for words. An explanation, an excuse that would make him quit staring at it with questioning eyes.

Finally, I found my voice. "An act of cowardice and desperation, nothing more, my stupidity obviously did not work and it has caused me great shame to look upon this mark ever since, so if you would plea-"

Before I could say more, he brought his lips down upon the grotesque slash and kissed it. I did not know how to react. I was repulsed and yet... felt a connection to him greater than any I had ever had in my dreams.

Here, this man, had lovingly embraced my weakness.

He pulled back letting go of my wrist which I hastily placed back on the cloth. His eyes danced up and down my face before settling on my own. "An act of cowardice?" he whispered. "Why, that is the strongest battle scar I believe a person can wear."

I reddened at his words. They were easily the highest compliment I had ever been paid, on an insecurity nonetheless. "Thank you." I replied meekly.

I stood with the cloth in my hand, the ink now far too soaked in to be cleaned and walked swiftly across the room to the cupboard. He followed closely behind. I placed the destroyed cloth on a shelf and turned. We were almost nose to nose.

"I would like to see you in a setting where we can be alone."

I tensed thinking this over. It was against my better nature to be alone with men, yet here I was in a deserted room with no one but him. It flattered me even more, yet made me feel all the more uncomfortable. "I don't think that is the best of decisions." I admitted.

He shrugged. "Then I shall continue to randomly bump into you until you finally oblige."

And without a goodbye he turned and left, grabbing his cloak as he walked through the door. I leaned into the cupboard, my heart beating fast, air once again engulfing my lungs. I was blushing furiously, this I knew.

Yet my mind was blank. I simply didn't know what to think.

Three

The random encounters he had promised happened more than I originally thought they would. I couldn't leave my home without seeing him. He would ironically have to pick up things at the store the same time as I did, drop letters off at the post office when I did, and of course spend time at the school just as I did.

Juniper had of course noticed this strange behavior and had posed questions of her own, although she rarely voiced them. Honour, on the other hand, was still convinced he was the fairy she had visited with numerous times in the months prior to Ember entering our school.

Although she only admitted this in the privacy of our home, having been embarrassed by her outburst on his first day, Ember surprisingly played along with her twisted fantasies. He would talk in depth about the vial he had supposedly given her and I found him on more than one occasion with her running through the forest near our home with snow up to their knees.

It was charming but strange. But Honour seemed to have no complaints, she was deeply infatuated with him, voicing that if she was just a year or two older she would marry him without question. Juniper always found this amusing and enlisted her to help with the planning of her own wedding ceremony which was to take place in just a few weeks.

Our house was filled with white lace and silks that were far out of our budget as my mother constructed her wedding gown. The constant talk of our house seemed to be of nothing but guests, vows, and consummation behind the back of our mother.

William also visited on a daily basis, laughing loudly at things Juniper said and conversing quietly with our mother about his good intentions.

I couldn't stand any of it. I was not naturally a people person. I spent many days sitting in the snow in the field by our house as long as I could possibly take it, then running to the house before I lost my fingers to frostbite.

It was on one of these days when I could no longer take the stifling heat of conversation and bodies pressed together that I made my way to the field when spontaneously Ember also trekked through the snow with me. By this time I was used to him randomly showing up at the most opportune times.

I sat, letting the white slush engulf me and soak through my clothing, leaving my legs and bottom completely numb. He sat next to me, his shoulder against mine, his black clothing, a warning sign in the pure snow. They seemed to say, "Danger. Dangerous, beautiful man sits here."

He rested his elbows on his knees. It always was a wonder to me how he seemed so proper yet in no way acted like the usual gentleman. "It is beginning to warm up, although it doesn't much seem like it. The snow is melting." I voiced, striking up a conversation.

"Well, it is February. I would hope the snow was beginning to dissolve. But I have always hated this month. So gray. By the time March comes in I would be impatiently awaiting the sure signs of spring. Green grass, birds chirping, the smell of new life." He replied.

"I've never much liked spring, or summer for that matter. I like the cold, I like the mundane. Spring and summer simply mean to me heat. The sun bearing down on you while you try to go about your daily tasks, making you itchy and uncomfortable in your skirts."

He chuckled, and cast a glance towards me. "Yet another reason I find you so alluring. Your freedom of speech regularly exercised. It does not matter that I am a man and you a woman. Nor does it matter that you have been taught to act proper in my company. No, your conversation immediately leads to the unbearable heat inside your skirts during the summer months."

My eyes widened at his vulgarity. "You know well I did not mean it like that! How dare you spin my words on me like that. You should be the one that is ashamed, talking to a woman about such things."

I pushed him playfully and he fell onto his side in the snow. He shot a shocked look at me then shoved me back. I too fell into the snow laughing.

"Me? How dare you lay hands upon your superior. As a man we both know I am entitled to do whatever I wish, but you? No, you were born to the inferior sex and so shall your actions follow suit."

I rolled my eyes. "As if I care about such social structures when I am in your presence. I thought we were long past the days of formality. Now, if I was a woman of money and grace I would surely be singing a different tune. But you know best as I that I come from the land of barely making it."

A silence fell over us both. He came from money, loads of it, and I came from a home that scraped together coins just to eat. He did not like this fact, that I worked for the things I had while he had food with the snap of his fingers.

He opened his mouth to speak but I immediately cut him off. "I do not wish for you to be feeding me money like a mother feeds her infant. I am doing just fine on my own helping to support my family in place of my father. Thank you very much."

He frowned having heard this all before. This conversation was a staple in our communication with each other. Then, slowly, a sly grin spread across his face. "Yes, I know this. It is exactly why instead of, how did you put it? Feeding money to you, I have been feeding it to Honour who in turn has been giving it over to your mother." He chuckled at my shocked expression. "You didn't expect me to just drop the subject?"

"I did! I expected you to respect my wishes but clearly I am mistaken." I folded my arms, and tried my best to be angry with him.

"I know, I know." He waved a hand through the air exasperatedly. "I'm such a terrible man for wanting to see you, and your sisters and mother to be well fed and have a warm place to lay their heads at night. Please, by all means, yell at me and tell me I'm just like all the others."

I sighed deeply, defeated before I even got started. "Fine, thank you. You are very generous. But I am still angry with you for going behind my back."

"I can handle that." He smiled.

The snow seemed to evaporate overnight. It was covering everything in sight when I went to bed on a Monday in March and when I awoke for school the next day spring had arrived with a flourish.

I peered out my window at the green grass, the birds flying about, and the flowers that sprung up literally overnight and questioned the world we lived in for several minutes. It amazed and confused me that so much could change outside my window in a few hours.

And yet hadn't I had the same mixed feelings about my personal life recently? The wedding had been moved to our house by way of anonymous vote. Juniper was on edge constantly, and Ember had moved into my mother's room, due to him having nowhere else to stay, while she slept in mine.

Things seemed to be flipped upside down. The only one attending school anymore was Honour, Juniper and I both removing ourselves due to our age. Who really needed to finish their schooling when they were either getting married or becoming the head of their household?

Yet I still awoke every morning at eight to see Honour off. Walking with her as far as the end of our lane and then watching as she disappeared around the bend. This morning she seemed to have an excited air about her.

I glumly trudged my way into the kitchen and cooked some eggs for us both while she hopped around singing random tunes. "What has you so thrilled?" I asked, carefully watching the eggs to make sure they didn't burn.

She twirled in a circle, her hair and skirts billowing away from her body. "It's spring! Oh, it's lovely out! I was so tired of snow. And it's sunny and warm and it's just a miracle." She sighed, plopping down into one of the rickety chairs surrounding the table.

I dumped the eggs in the pan onto two plates and grabbed utensils out the drawer. I didn't speak again until I had sat across from her, watching her devour her eggs with haste. "Have you seen anymore fairies as of late?"

The topic of Honour and her fairies had become a normal conversation in our house. She seemed to find something new lurking in the woods on a daily basis. "No, yesterday the ground was too muddy so I didn't go out. I'm sure they wouldn't like it either, though. I haven't seen any except Ember for months though. He assures me they'll be coming! Especially, now that it's warm. Oh, I'm so excited!"

She bounced up and down in her chair, and shoved a rather large bite of egg into her mouth and chewed happily. I took her plate from her and stacked it on top of mine, throwing them lazily in the sink. "Shall we get going? You'll be late."

I pulled my boots on without bothering to button them and followed her out the door. It was ridiculously warm out to have been so cold the previous day. She ran ahead making sure to circle back around to me every so often.

Finally, we reached the end of the lane. She wrapped her arms around me swiftly, first making sure there was no one around to witness this affection, then ran off around the bend out of sight.

I made my way back up to the house, surprised to see Ember up and about walking around outside. He was plainly dressed and yet attractive all the same. He wore a white button down shirt that was undone on the top exposing his bare chest, and loose fitting black pants.

I walked over to him, noting how we would make an odd pair to any onlookers. Him disheveled and me in a simple gray dress with gold buttons.

He smiled at my appearance and began walking towards the field without waiting for me. I couldn't deny that we had grown extremely close over the past few months, almost as if an enchantment was cast on the both of us, making us inseparable.

There was barely a time when you would see me without him or vice versa.

I caught up with him and flopped myself into the dry grass on his right side. The sun was already beating down on us, making the top two buttons of my dress feel as if they were choking me with heat. I unbuttoned them and fell back onto my elbows, watching as the birds flew past.

"Ember..." I caught myself. What was my mind doing? Going before my better judgment, that was clear. I mashed my lips together trying to suppress the stupidity that was surely about to escape them.

"Yes, my darling?" he brought his hand up and pushed the loose strand of hair hanging on my face away and tucked it behind my ear.

"What would you say if I were to tell you I'm in love with you?"

I was silently screaming at myself to stop, my inner self was tearing her hair out in agony and yelling about how stupid of a female I was. Why did I say that? What had possessed me? Some force unbeknownst to me. I was not acting myself.

My stupidity had once again gotten the better of me.

But without missing a beat he replied, "I would say, I'm in love with you, too."

I did a double take, and smiled sheepishly to conceal my inner terror. What had I just plunged myself into? In one sweep I had created an instant romance that I loathed in the books I read. The same romance Juniper was well known for.

My inner self was tearing my outer self to bit as I smiled at him. How foolish. What a stupid, stupid girl. Charms and enchantments were not a real thing, but the lust I was letting take over my entire being was and how just... stupid! I could barely think over the raging in my mind.

Finally, I was able to ask, "Do you really? Or are you just saying that because I said it?"

Yet again he didn't miss a beat with his response. "No, I would never do such a thing. Reyenne, I'm in love with you. I would travel the world to tell everyone I am. I would shout it from the highest mountain, I would die to prove it to you if it came to that."

The voice in my head settled at this and true happiness engulfed me. Happiness I had never known until that point. "How can I be sure your words are true?"

He grinned and before I could protest or pull back, he had cupped my chin in his hand and kissed me. It was soft and rough and sweet and vulgar all at once. My thoughts clouded, shutting my inner self up, and I fell into bliss for a moment.

I had never experienced affection of that caliber. I would have surely fallen if I hadn't had already been on the ground. I released the embrace and peered into his hazed eyes. He smiled and lay back on the grass, watching as the clouds rolled by.

I felt enlightened; happy. But at the same time, unsure and uncomfortable. I didn't want to be the woman who gave herself over willingly to the first man to notice her. I didn't want to be the stupid girl in every novel who loved without question and entered relationships that didn't make sense.

I swiftly decided to love him to the best of my ability and tread carefully.

Four

Our bond strengthened in the coming weeks. Kissing became something shared privately between us several times a day. My feelings, against my own will, were growing stronger and stronger for him.

As the wedding drew nearer Juniper, Honour, and I spent more and more time together. The last days of being the Montgomery sisters.

Ember was helping with William's attire and vows, while we played like small children in the forest. Our feet were perpetually covered in fresh dirt and our hair never staying perfect for long.

Juniper and I sat under a tree in the shade while Honour constructed a flower necklace a few feet away. Juniper turned to me, dirt on her hands and a flush in her cheeks. "Are you going to marry him?"

The question took me off guard. I glanced at Honour then back to Juniper, my thoughts materializing. "I don't know." She looked at me as if I was lying. "Truly, I don't. He is lovely, but there is something about him that is off-putting. Do you ever get the feeling around him that he's hiding something?"

Honour piped up at this. "He is hiding something! He's a fairy!"

I rolled my eyes as did Juniper. "Men have their secrets, I assumed at sixteen years of age you would have figured this out, Reyenne." Juniper scoffed. "As always I am the only knowledgeable one when it comes to the opposite sex."

I grimaced. "I know, I know. Don't treat me like a fool. It's just unnerving around him sometimes. This air of secrecy."

"The only advice I give to you is get over it, my dear sister. That may seem harsh but it is the way of life. William has his secret affairs." I raised my eyebrows. "No, no. Not that kind! He has no mistress that I know of, but if he did? That is his secret to keep. Not mine. I am merely going to be his wife. I will accompany him to parties, business events, small dinners and I will support him in his wildest ventures. As much as I love him I know my place, and that place is as an object."

She knew I didn't agree with any of these views. I, in no way, thought women were an inferior gender, and I made this clear whenever I possibly could. "Yes, but-"

She cut me off. "Before you even begin on your tirade of objections, I am moving on to my point. You love Ember. This is just mere fact. And he loves you; you can see it in the way he looks at you when you aren't watching. Yes, I see these things. You need to let go of all these suspensions and your worries of moving too fast. I knew William a handful of weeks before he asked to marry me! We are entering fast changing times, things are moving ahead no matter if you are or not. You either jump at the chance or you miss it, because if you don't snatch him up, I assure you another woman will."

I stared at the ground pondering over what she had said. She had some very valid points. Especially about another woman taking him from me. I had seen firsthand the way women watched him as we walked through town and into shops, how they practically drooled all down the front of their expensive dresses.

Yet the questions were unyielding.

"I still can't help but question him." I admitted.

She stood, brushing her skirts off. "Then question him to death if you must!" she threw her hands into the air, clearly exasperated. "You're going to the Food Festival tomorrow, yes? Well ask away then! A public setting, he can't escape. But, the question is, what if you don't like his answers?"

I awoke early the next morning with Juniper's question still lingering in my mind. What if I didn't like the answers he produced? What then? Would we just walk away as strangers and never speak again?

For whatever strange reason I couldn't see my life without him anymore. Nor could I remember what it was like before him. He had become a vital part of my being, no matter what hidden devils he kept.

I pushed the thoughts from my mind, and got up, pulling my favorite black dress on and lacing up my newest black boots. I pinned my hair into a simple bun then went to wake Ember.

My favorite festival of the year had at last come around, The Food Festival. Vendors from all over the country came with the most absurd concoctions and exotic fruits from around the world. It was splendid.

I entered his room, or rather my mother's quietly, and pulled a fresh outfit out for him to wear. I folded it neatly at the end of the bed then opened the curtains to expose a sunny day. Finally, I shook his leg. "Ember! Come on! I want to go into town! Wake up!"

I knew from past experience I had to shout if I wanted him to wake quickly. He rolled over and sat up, his mouth opened into a wide yawn and he covered his eyes where the sun streamed across his face.

Once accustom to the bright light he looked around the room, his eyes fidgety until they finally settled on me. "Reyenne." He smiled.

"Good morning." I said simply, smiling back.

He reached his arm out as if to stretch but instead grabbed me by the waist and pulled me to him on the bed. The pins I had so carelessly put in my hair fell out, leaving my hair sprawled over his chest in great waves. My sleeve slid up my arm as I scratched at my wrist, he mechanically rubbed my scar as he had countless times before. It was something I had grown accustom to, his fascination with my attempted suicide.

Even though I had told him it was long ago. It didn't seem to matter.

"How are you this fine day?" he asked sleepily.

"Quite chipper now that you're up." I replied.

We laid there a few minutes in silence before I finally grew restless. I couldn't lie about anymore, I was too excited. "Get dressed. I want to go into town." I stood up as I said this.

"Tell me, what is so important in town today?" he asked.

I stood almost shocked. After I had talked about it for days I couldn't believe he had forgotten. "The Food Festival, of course!" I clapped my hands together, practically shouting in excitement.

"Ah, the Food Festival." He laughed. He had been laughing at me ever since I first mentioned it, exclaiming he had never met a woman who was as interested in food as I was.

I punched him playfully on the shoulder. "Just get up and get dressed, I'll be in the field."

I left without waiting for a response. I had flowers to tend to before we left. No doubt my mother was already outside picking vegetables. The gardens had been her safe haven ever since she came out of her grief induced coma.

Sure enough, as soon as I left the house I saw her bent over a patch of garden staring at some vegetable that was unrecognizable to me. She stood up and smiled. "Hello, darling!"

"Hello, mother." I replied, rolling my sleeves up and putting my hair back into a messy bun.

"Come to help me look over the plants?"

"No, not today. I'm going to look over my flowers then Ember and I are off to the festival."

She nodded approvingly and went back to watching over her treasured plants. I skipped merrily to my flowers and began picking the best ones for the vase in our house.

I had only been at this a few minutes with a handful of flowers chosen when I was abruptly swept into the air. My first instinct was to fight until a breeze of air sent his smell cascading over me. One I was extremely familiar with. I laughed and dropped my carefully picked flowers in the process.

He sent me down and I turned to face him. "Don't you ever do that again!" I smiled while trying to act stern.

"Oh, but why? You didn't seem to mind it."

"Ember. I swear. Sometimes I don't know why I'm with you." I replied.

"But what would you do without me?" he wrapped his arm around my waist. I was used to this gesture and my body followed suit, leaning up to kiss him, before my mind could react.

The moment was ruined by a glimpse of my mother staring at our embrace. I looked over his shoulder at her. "Mother, must you watch me so closely?" I asked, slightly agitated.

She grimaced at being caught. "Reyenne, you are my beloved daughter. I must see that Ember is taking care of you well."

I flushed at her response, not expecting it. The fact that my family was already acting as if we were married unnerved me in more ways than it should have. It should have pleased me, but I ended up only feeling queasy and unsure.

"Fear not, Ms. Montgomery, as long as I'm alive I shall take care of her," his voice boomed over the small space of yard.

This apparently was all my mother needed to hear because she smiled and went back to tending her plants without another question or comment. Ember stared into space in deep thought. I brought him out of it by saying, "I believe we should get to the festival."

He nodded then agreed, "I believe we shall, too."

We made our way into town, silently walking hand in hand until we got to the main street. Cart after cart and vendor after vendor were stationed along the road. Coachmen were having a hard time pulling their bosses through the chaos. Small children went running by carrying ribbons and toys that I was unaware existed.

Ember seemed at unease as I pulled him through the crowd to try the different foods. The entire day he would merely take small bites of things I handed him then throw the rest away, and I caught him on more than one occasion sniffing at the air as if he was suffocating.

But I didn't let his behavior discourage me. The festival meant more to me than I could ever describe to him, having been a tradition between my father and I. Not even the small sprinkles of rain that splashed now and then brought my mood down.

After hours of delicious, weird, and splendid foods I was ready to go home. The sun was beginning to fade and as always, I didn't want to be caught outside alone after dark, even if I did have Ember with me.

We walked once again hand in hand back to the hill where my house sat. The sun cast everything in a golden glow making the remaining patches of rain sparkle and shine. Ember stayed quiet, again in apparent deep thought.

I thought it best not to disturb him and so I stayed quiet until we got to my house where I launched into all the day's events to my mother who smiled and nodded. I couldn't deny the fact that I was in a great mood, a better one than I had been in a long time.

Ember, sensing this mood, decided to join in. Starting with a few innocent pushes, we erupted into a full on game of tag in our house. My mother yelled for us to go outside until finally Ember picked me up, swinging me around as he ran. "Ember!" I screamed laughing. He pushed open the door and took us outside where he set me down in the grass on our usual spot.

I was out of breath and laughing. Because of this I didn't notice his serious mood had returned until a few seconds had passed. I quit laughing and gazed into his eyes. Something was wrong.

He coughed, seemed to sputter, then said, "Reyenne, I must tell you something. Promise me you'll never tell anyone. Ever, I mean it. No one can know."

I searched his eyes for some evidence that he was merely pulling a prank on me. But no such laughter was there. My mood immediately dimmed. Then, I decidedly perked up. Perhaps this was just another game. "Ember, whatever it is, tell me! I can't live in the suspense any longer! It's absolutely killing me!" I laughed, thinking this all a joke.

He coughed. "This is quite serious..."

I sat up and looked at him. "Oh." It was all I could manage. Here it was, about to come out of his mouth, the secrets I knew lingered behind his façade. Did I want to know? Would Juniper be right? Were his secrets better kept? Should I flee?

All of these questions flitted through my mind but I sat and waited until he finally spoke again. "I am not like you." He stopped, seemed to gather his thoughts, then went on, "I mean, I am really not like you."

"What is that supposed to mean?" I asked, bewildered.

He looked to the house and then stood up, holding his hand out for me to take. I did and he pulled me up, setting off into the woods. I didn't speak, the air around us seem electrified with meaning and secrecy. I was afraid if I spoke I would somehow break this barrier and he would never tell me what plagued his thoughts.

After we were well out of view of the house, he stopped, and let go of my hand. His gaze lingered on the ground for a moment before he swiftly pulled his shirt off and let it drop to the ground. My breath halted. This couldn't be the moment could it? The ones mothers tell their daughters about, the thing girls giggle over?

No, not here. Not in the middle of dirty ground.

Before I could object, turn away, or stand my ground; he turned exposing his back to me. It was the first time I had seen his naked back in the months I had known him and what I saw terrorized me.

This perfect man should have had a perfect back. He shouldn't have had scars or wounds or anything of the sort to disrupt the canvas of his flesh. And yet on his upper back were two vertical scars that stretched halfway down his pale skin.

I covered my mouth with my hand, not wanting to gasp, afraid I would offend him. But it was a horror to behold. What could have possibly happened to him? Was he beat? Molested?

Thousands of possibilities swarmed my mind. But stopped when something seemed to be protruding from the closed wounds. Had he been in a train wreck? Was shrapnel stuck in his back still? Was this his big secret?

Before I could register what was happening, two large pieces of what looked to be metal sliced through the scars and caused me to stumble back. I fell onto my bottom in the dirt, my eyes wide, and gasped in alarm.

I couldn't make myself stand or look away. This was impossible. He surely was a freak of nature, something that belonged to a circus. Is this why his past had never come up? Was he some type of illegal experiment conducted by crude doctors?

He turned to face me, a trickle of... no, not the water of tears, but gold made its way slowly down his cheek from his left eye. Gold? Was he crying gold?

He spoke, which did not alleviate my fright. "I am not human; as I'm sure you can tell. I know you probably won't want anything to do with me ever again after this but at least hear me out. Please." He looked to me for some sort of sign that I wasn't going anywhere for now, I nodded and he continued. "I'm not some experiment gone wrong, which I know you're thinking, or some plain freak of nature. I am part of an elite race of being. One that is secretive and dangerous, although you have nothing to fear from me." He paused. "I am a Mayhem Fairy."

I didn't register what he had said at first, entranced by the wings flapping soundlessly behind him. They were huge and had the appearance of soft feathers, although from the sound they were making I assumed they were probably made of a hard material.

The word fairy brought me back and I began laughing. So this was all a joke after all. Honour had definitely put him up to this. I shook my head and stood up. He looked surprised to see me taking this news so lightly.

"This is a lovely joke and all but I would really like to go home and go to bed now. I am very tired from today's events. I admit, you had me. You and Honour must have put a lot of thought into this fairy nonsense. Now take those contraptions off and let's go to my house."

He shook his head. "This is not nonsense, Reyenne. Quit hiding behind laughter and jokes in the face of seriousness. I am not human. And Honour is not crazy or extremely imaginative. I did give her that vial and I have been telling her the ways of my people. It is normally against the law for us to converse with anyone outside of our species about what we are but since she is a mere child it is allowed. I am breaking so many laws right now to be speaking freely with you. You have no idea how long this secret has weighed on me!" he almost shouted the last bit.

I furrowed my brow then threw my hands in the air. "Are you delusional? Is this the issue? Have you escaped some mental institution and ran here? Because I do find it odd that I've never met your parents or that they allow you to stay here all day every day. And I do find it strange that you would go to this much trouble to convince someone that you're a fairy. Something as girlish as that! And, if it truly has been you that has been putting these ideas into my sister then you should feel ashamed playing with a young girls mind like that. But you cannot do the same to me! I am older and wiser than she is."

I was livid. How dare he come up with some game to screw up the happiness I had finally found. The happiness I had been searching for since the moment my father died and my house was thrown into depression. It was not his place to take my own joy away from me.

"What do I have to do to prove it to you, Reyenne? Because I love you. That is the simplest truth there has ever been in my life. I am going against everything I have been taught in my species by feeling this way, but I do. I love you. I will do anything to prove it to you."

He seemed to come up with an idea. He lifted his arm back behind his head and scraped the interior against one of the wings. He beckoned me forward, my feet followed suit although my mind screamed no.

Where he had just placed his arm was now an open wound leaking gold. It seemed the same consistency as blood but the odd color proved my assumptions wrong.

He was telling the truth.

Before I could even express this, the cut sealed shut as if it had never been there before. I looked into his eyes. I wanted to beg him and plead with him to tell me this was all some twisted joke and everything was going to go back to normal.

But the sorrow found within his eyes silently screamed it was fact.

I backed away without thinking. My back hit the tree and I clung to it like a lifeline. I didn't want to know anymore. This was some bad dream; I would awake at any moment. I pinched my clasped hands together trying to wake myself but I stayed rooted to the spot staring at him.

"I am not human." The words echoed all around me. I had fallen in love with something outside my realm of perception. I had let a creature such as this into my home and allowed him to sleep under the same roof as the people I held dearest to my heart.

I didn't know what to do. What was I supposed to think? Was I hallucinating? I put my palm to my head to feel for a fever and although I was sweating my skin was ice cold.

He put his hands out in front of him as if that would ensure my safety. As if that would make me feel like everything was perfectly fine. "Please, don't run away. I can sense it. You want to bolt and I don't blame you, but I'm not a monster..."

Tears welled in my eyes. "Before I go, tell me everything."

"Everything?"

"About you. You have exactly one minute before I leave."

His eyes scanned the trees like the answer he was looking for would suddenly appear out of thin air. "Well..." he was stammering, I was crying harder. "We have wings, we can flictate, which is our method of flying, we have a Queen, I have a Mother in Mayhem who taught me everything. We bleed and cry gold, and our diet consists of... organs." He looked down again. "Human organs."

I couldn't hold it anymore. I doubled over and threw up. All the foods I had tasted and enjoyed and laughed over regurgitated onto the healthily growing grass. He didn't make a move to help or comfort me. I didn't want him to.

I stood straight again, tears streaming down my face and onto my dress. I was trying to be brave. "D-don't you ever come near me or m-my family again." I tripped over my words in fright. "I don't ever want to s-see you around here again. Do you hear me?"

Without another word or glance at him I took off in a run towards my house. I tripped over roots and branches. How far had he brought me? I hadn't noticed in my happiness just a little while earlier. With a happy gasp of tears I broke through the trees and into the field. I sprinted the rest of the way, past the flower beds and my mother's plants, all the way to the front door.

Honour stood with a bucket obviously on her way out to the woods to play. She saw me, smiled, then faltered. But before she could ask any questions I grabbed her shoulders and sunk to her level. Her face was pure confusion. "Honour, you listen to me." I shook her shoulders slightly, she nodded. "Don't you ever go into those trees again, okay? Ever. If I find out you've been out there I will beat you bloody." Her eyes widened in terror at my words.

Tears still streamed down my face, no matter my efforts to stifle them. "Do you understand me?"

"Y-yes, Reyenne." Her voice was quiet and timid. Not the usual boisterous echo it usually was at all.

I stood up and began to walk into the house but stopped and turned around. "Honour?" she turned. "And don't you ever go around Ember again."

Five

I was paranoid. It wasn't something anyone had to tell me because I knew. I kept Honour at my side all hours of the day to make sure she didn't wander off and had deep discussions with Juniper about what had happened when I couldn't sleep at night.

Juniper was awestruck. She didn't believe me when I first told her, but as I went into further detail, puzzle pieces seemed to click and she became as scared as I was. She promised to keep the wedding in our fields and to make sure none of her guests wandered too far. And I promised to patrol to enforce this rule.

I started every morning by opening my window and observing the area around our house, then going to every room to make sure no one was harmed and the house hadn't been broken into. We thought it better not to tell our mother for fear that she would sink into another depression.

It was best if I just stayed as a guardian over her. Although I didn't know how I would prevent them from... eating her if they came.

But would they come? Would he bring others to attack me for abandoning him? These questions lingered on my mind at all times of the day, they were what I fell asleep thinking and the first thoughts in my head every morning.

I sat down at the foot of Juniper's bed while she put her usual face of makeup on in her small mirror. She turned on her stool and looked at me. "Reyenne, I'm sure everything is going to be fine." She placed her hand on my knee. "The wedding is tonight and all the guests will be arriving and we will have a splendid time! Nothing bad is going to happen. I promise." She held her pinky up and I took it with a smile.

"I'm going to help set everything up." I left to find my mother and Honour placing chairs near the garden. An arch of sorts had been built for this occasion by William's father and I had covered it in flowers.

It really was quite beautiful now that I took the time to absorb it. This only lasted a few minutes though. I quickly immersed myself in the task of getting things ready, all the while checking the trees for signs of anything abnormal.

The wedding began at exactly six that night. Twilight had fallen across the hill casting everything in purples and blues. Juniper had kept her promise of only inviting a couple handfuls of people. But even this small crowd made me nervous. Any one of them could slip by without my notice.

Despite my worrying Juniper looked beautiful. My mother had handcrafted the entire dress she wore. The bodice made her waist even smaller than normal and tiny flowers were embroidered into the entire skirt. The sleeves were long but made entirely of lace, and her shoes were small white boots.

I stood in the doorway of her room watching as she made the last few adjustments to her hair and face. She stood, took one last glance in the mirror, then drifted her eyes to me. "I'm going to throw up."

I laughed the first real laugh I had in days. "You are not going to throw up." I crossed the room and straightened her skirts. "You are going to strut out there like you have up and down the streets and through this house your whole life and capture the attention of every single person out there. Then you're going to marry the man of your dreams and live happily ever after as his little house wife." I grinned.

She hit my shoulder playfully. "Are there a lot of people out there?"

"No, only a few dozen. Our family is all here. Grandmother, grandfather, even father's parents. Aunts, uncles, cousins. The same with William's side. Immediate family, that's all you wanted, isn't it?" I raised my brow.

"Well, yes. But you know how mother can be sometimes. She gets carried away and invites everyone she knows. I was afraid the entire town would be sitting out there." She grinned nervously.

"Just those of us that care about you and love you, I promise. Now, shall we go marry you off?" I held my hand out for her and she took it, her palm sweaty in mine.

We made our way to the door of the house and I left her to assume my place next to William's brother, Colson Cundy. We stood at the ready behind Honour who was to be the flower girl.

The wedding proceeded without incident. Juniper and William were alight with excitement all through the ceremony and into the festivities afterwards. But as soon as dark erupted across the merriment I grew even wearier.

No one else seemed to notice my nervousness. I made my way around, saying hello to those I absolutely had to, and making small talk with those who it was necessary. Then I retreated to a chair set on the edge of the woods, watching all the while for a figure to appear.

My heart was racing sitting alone in the darkness, shouts and jeers of drunken fools calling from the house and gardens surrounding put me on edge. I was absolutely sure something would happen tonight. Ember knew all about these wedding plans and the amount of people who would be present.

It could be a feast. A massacre.

But the hours moved on and nothing happened. I was starting to come off guard. Perhaps I was anxious over nothing. Footsteps behind me startled me and I turned to see Colson Cundy wandering towards me.

I sighed deeply then plastered a fake smile to my face. This was the last thing I needed. He sauntered over, a glass of wine dazzling in his hand. He was quite full of himself.

He stopped next to my chair and grazed the forest with his eyes before resting them hungrily on me. "What is it you're doing out here all on your own?"

I tried to reply as sweetly as I could. "I just needed some fresh air, is all."

He nodded as if that was a sufficient enough answer. "I find you quite appealing."

Ah, so this is how it was going to go. I should have known from his arrogance that he wouldn't beat around the bush for too long. He was a man accustomed to getting the things he wanted when he wanted them, including women.

I kept up my act. "That's very nice of you."

He raised his glass and drained the rest of its contents. He held his hand out for me to take at the same time he dropped his glass to the ground. "Take a walk with me."

I hesitated unsure about leaving my post then decided it couldn't hurt to scope out some other areas of the woods. I took his hand and he helped me out of my chair. We strode down the path deeper among trees.

My eyes never lingered on one spot too long. Every branch snapping, every movement of an animal sent me on high alert. I couldn't allow myself to feel too comfortable. My defenses couldn't be penetrated.

"So our siblings married to each other. Quite lovely, isn't it? This makes us siblings in a way I guess." I could see his grin in the moonlight, his white teeth glinting under the faint light.

"Generally, just family, but if you insist, siblings it is." I replied still barely looking at him.

He didn't seem to notice my disinterest. "My family has quite an amount of money, you know. Your sister is going to live comfortably for the rest of her days."

I nodded. "Yes, and I am very happy for her. She deserves it."

"You aren't in the least bit envious? Jealous, even? That gets to have dresses made by the finest seamstresses and servants to do her every whim at every hour of the day or night?"

He was trying to get at something, what I was unsure. But it was irritating me. Of course I couldn't let this be known. My mother would have my head if I jeopardized my sister's marriage before it even began by fighting with her new relative.

I shrugged. "Not in the least. My sister has worked hard her entire life, just as Honour and I have. I am glad she no longer has to labor over making her own attire and mixing up her own recipes for rouge and other such necessities. I hope she lives comfortably the rest of her days." What I spoke was truth; I wanted nothing but the best for my sisters.

We stopped near a rather large tree and I placed my hand on it to steady myself. The ground was uneven and hard to walk over in the heels I was forced to wear. Colson lingered near my side, his grin ever present.

"That's quite a good quality in a woman. Modest, loving, unselfish. All things hard to find in a woman this day and age."

I glanced at him then back into the woods. "I suppose so." The conversation was going nowhere.

He sighed deeply, then pressed me into the tree. My back was flat against the bark, the wiring in my bodice dug into my flesh. He lips strayed to mine, stopping inches from their clear destination. "I'm going to be honest, Reyenne." He ran his fingers through my hair, pulling it out of its braid. "You really aren't much to look at, but my father is insisting I get married, and who better to marry than the sister of a woman we're already tied to?"

My breathing grew shallow. I didn't expect this kind of violence from a man such as Colson Cundy. He was always timid, shy even, he never talked much. A shadow behind his younger brother William. "I will marry who I choose, and that person is not you." I tried to shove him away, to escape, but he pushed me forcefully back against the tree.

"I thought you would say that. So I've devised this entire plan." His hand went from my hair to my shoulder and ran its way along my arm. "See, I don't know if you know this, but virginity is a virtue. Not so much in a man, but a woman? Why, it's necessary for marriage." His hand moved farther down to rest on my waist.

I had almost stopped breathing entirely. I had to remind my lungs to keep exhaling and inhaling, to keep pumping me the oxygen I needed in order to live. "I am afraid I don't see your point."

He laughed. It was light, whimsical. But the evil glint in his eyes didn't match the innocence found in his laughter. He grabbed a handful of my skirts and lifted them up to my waist. My heart began beating rapidly. How was I to get out of this?

Yet again I had acted stupidly and trusted someone I shouldn't have. Why did I go on a walk with him alone in the dark? "The basic logic I am seeing in this is if I take your virginity now, no other man will want you. So that would make you mine for the taking, wouldn't it? Soiled on the night of your sister's wedding. What a shame." He laughed again.

He let go of my skirts which only shifted a bit but otherwise stayed in place, exposing me for him to clearly see if he bent down. I was sniffling, tears silently wetting my face. He fumbled with his own pants, cursing in his drunken haze.

"P-please d-don't do this." I begged.

"You wouldn't talk if you know what's good for you. It's high time you learned women are in fact inferior to men. As much as you want to act like they aren't." He finally got his pants down and hiked my skirts up further. "You are an object."

I closed my eyes knowing well what was about to come. Tensing myself against all feeling, I tried to make myself numb. But he fumbled a bit more then... nothing. His grip loosened and there was a sudden gust of wind.

I didn't dare open my eyes. I stayed leaned against the tree whimpering, hoping he had changed his mind. A warm liquid splattered against my face and chest. The smell of rust lingered in the air and there was a thud on the ground at my feet.

I hesitatingly opened my eyes and looked down. Colson's body lay sprawled at my feet, his chest ripped open to expose his organs. I had never seen anything so grotesque in my life. I leaned to the side and threw up, emptying the contents of my stomach all over the tree roots.

When there was nothing left I looked back up, making sure not to let my eyes wander to the body below me. Ember stood, wings unfolded, eyes ablaze, staring at me. His hands and face were vermillion.

I started to scream, but suddenly his hand was clasped tightly over my mouth. A ring was lit around his pupil flaxen in color. He let go, letting his arm drop to his side. My face felt sticky from the gore on his hands.

"You're going to kill me." It was a statement not a question. I knew what was coming but couldn't make myself fearful. I had been awaiting this since the day I told him to leave.

A baffled expression crossed his face. "Of course I'm not going to kill you."

"But that's what you do, is it not? You eliminate the weaker race."

"Why are you challenging me?" he demanded.

I pushed my skirts down, realizing I was still exposed to anyone who wanted to see, then stepped forward. I was so close to him I could feel the cold air his body stirred. "I am not challenging you. I am putting it out in the open, what you do. You kill us, humans, in order to supply yourself with energy. We, I, am the inadequate race and sex. So do what you must. I am tired of living every moment with conflicted feelings about you. I am tired of being scared."

It was easily the bravest I had ever acted in my feeble life. I had never stood up to someone better, older, or bigger than me. But here I was questioning a creature far outside my spectrum of evil.

He exhaled. "I thought I made this perfectly clear. I would never kill you because I'm madly in love with you."

Six

I sneered. "Is this romantic among your race? Killing a man at the feet of your loved one then telling them sweet nothings?"

He looked appalled. "You're joking, correct? I just saved you from rape! I protected you! Now I have to somehow clean this entire mess up and hide the body of a very predominant man in this town because of you."

His wings sunk into his skin and his eyes went back to their normal nothingness. If not for the blood covering his upper body I would assume he was perfectly ordinary. "I did not ask for you to save me. I don't need some man, or whatever you are, to be my hero."

"Oh, forgive me. I hadn't realized you wanted to be defiled and debased by a man you barely know. Next time I'll let them have their way with you!" he roared.

At this I began to sob hysterically. The weight on my shoulders was too much; I sagged under its burden. I couldn't handle all of this. Ember wrapped his arms around me and pulled me to him. I didn't object, just shoved my face into his chest and blubbered like an infant.

He said nothing, but rubbed his hand down my back. Something clicked in my mind halfway through my wails. I stopped caring, completely and utterly. I didn't care that the man I stood so close to could kill me with one swift motion. I didn't care that another man lay dead at my feet. I didn't care that I was caked in blood or that my sister was not even a mile away ending the night of her wedding on a high note.

None of it mattered. I knew that by falling to him in my time of desperation I had just signed a slip of parchment that said I had just entered an entirely new world. A world I could never imagine or make up.

I had just sold my soul to the devil and he wore all black and had wings.

I pulled away from him, and shot a glance at the body of Colson Cundy. "What are we going to do?"

He too looked down. "You are going to go home and say you saw a wolf attack him."

I shook my head. "I can't do that. It's dishonest."

He sighed almost irritably. "Then what would you have me do? Bury him? I doubt his disappearance would go over well, especially on the same night your families were to be joined. And everyone there knows you and him both were not seen at the party. I can't let you be blamed for something I did." He sighed again. "Just this once you need to lie."

I shuffled back and almost tripped over the corpse of Colson. I caught myself and began sobbing. "Is this what I've gotten myself into? A life of trickery and deceit?"

He put his arm out as if to comfort me then recoiled. "I... I know it isn't easy, Reyenne. You can walk away right now and I'll leave forever, it'll be hard but I'll do it. I live every day under a blanket of secrecy and lies, but I won't pull you into it unless you are sure this is what you want."

I didn't know how to respond. What was I to say to that? I loved him, of this I was sure. I exhaled slowly, "Attack me."

"What?" he asked incredulous.

I placed a hand on my hip. "Do you want this to look real or not? I highly doubt a random wolf would attack one of us and not the other. I need some scratches, bruises, torn up clothing. And those could be a great deal of help," I waved my hands toward where his wings usually stood.

He hesitated, his mouth set in a grim line. "I could kill you if I'm not careful."

I steadied my voice and tried to act bold. "Well, then I guess you better be careful."

He motioned for me to stand still and shoved my arms down to my sides. His wings jutted out of his back with inhuman speed and I shut my eyes tight. In my mind's eye I was far away. As the first few slashes dug into my torso and arms I envisioned myself standing with my father, his chestnut hair rippling in a foreign breeze.

I looked to him for guidance as I had when he was alive. "Am I doing the right thing?"

He turned to me, smiling with an air of all knowing. "I don't know, are you?"

I didn't expect him to answer my question with one of his own. I pondered over it a moment before answering. "It's all so horrific. He slaughtered a man, father. And yet... I do not judge him for it. I realize it is only his nature and I accept it."

He tittered. "The first rule in the book of love is acceptance."

"Does this make me a bad person?" It was the question lingering on the tip of my tongue since the moment I realized what Ember was. If my love stayed intact, no matter my worries and fears, did that make me horrible? Retched? Inhuman?

He faced me, a gleam in his eye. "No, you will never be a bad person."

"A-are you sure?"

"Do not question your destiny."

I awoke with a start. It was completely black, wherever I was. I lifted my hand in front of my face and was greeted with the same blindness. "Daddy?" I called it out like a small child.

"Oh, Reyenne," cooed my mother from nearby. A wet cloth was placed on my forehead. Beads of water dripped down the bridge of my nose.

My body was on fire. Every inch of flesh felt as though I was being scorched and stabbed simultaneously. I couldn't remember how I had got here. What had happened? My mind raced under the damp towel. "M-momma? What happened?"

I tried to sit up but was blinded by a pain more ferocious than I had ever experienced. I dropped my head back onto the pillow and tried my best not to breathe. Every shallow intake was another dagger to my stomach.

"Oh, Reyenne." She removed the cloth. I listened as she dropped it into a water basin and brought it back out, ringing it of excess water and placing it back on my forehead. "You were attacked."

"A-attacked?" my voice was barely a whisper.

"Just a few hours ago... by a wolf." Clear as day my memory came back. Ember. Ember had attacked me. It was a set up. "You've been out for a few hours, dawn is drawing near. But don't you worry about that, you get your rest."

She made to stand up but I reached out and grabbed her arm. The effort left me breathless. It was a moment before I had enough air to speak again. "How bad are my wounds?"

She patted my arm gently and laid it back at my side. "They are..." she hesitated, "bad enough. Do not trouble yourself right now, Reyenne. As I have said, you need your rest. All is well and... everyone is safe. You just sleep now."

Her skirts swished softly and she exited the room, closing the door behind her. I once again lay still, counting the beats of my heart, steadying my lungs the best I could. The damage must be terrible. There was no other explanation for the excruciating pain I was in. He had really hurt me... he had gotten carried away.

I had to get up; I had to see for myself. I tried pulling myself up again, wincing in pain, and fell back onto the bed. "Get ahold of yourself, Reyenne." I whispered furiously.

I could and would do this. I held my breath and sat straight up, ignoring the stabs of pain and the sweat trickling down my face and chest. I slowly exhaled, and swung my feet onto the floor. The wood panels were ice cold... they felt good.

I sat like this for several minutes, postponing the moment I knew was about to come. Pain, no doubt, would wash through me once I stood up. I counted to three.

One...

Two...

Three...

I stood straight up and almost doubled over in agony. My body throbbed, my skin crawled, and tears found their way down my cheeks. I wrapped my arms tight around my body and step by step persisted until I was standing in front of my mirror.

I reached a trembling hand out to light my candle and almost dropped my tinderbox in the process. With an immense amount of concentration I brought the match to the wick and light washed over my exterior.

I dropped the box on the chipped wood and positioned my hands firmly next to it. I raised my head to the mirror and gasped in horror. I had been torn apart quite literally. Bruises lined my face on either side; a long white bandage was wrapped around my chest, and more around my arms.

In horror I reached up and unbuttoned my nightshirt, and let it fall to a heap in the floor. More bandages wound themselves around my stomach, my legs, there was a dark red stain leaking onto the chalky bandage located on my hip.

My skin was ashen, my eyes rimmed with dark circles. With haste I started unwinding the bandages one by one, revealing the ghastly lashes beneath. The dressings fell to the floor in ripples, pooling around my bare feet.

The wounds themselves were deep, jagged lines crisscrossing every inch of my body. Blood gurgled and spit as it trickled down my bare skin. I ran my hands across each and every one, smearing blood over my untouched flesh.

My hair matted on my shoulders, having been coated by the streaks of ruby. I pushed it back away from my face and collar bone. Blood splattered on the floor making soft plopping sounds in its wake.

How could he have done this? I began weeping then wailing. My shoulder shook heavily, rivulets streaked down my flushed face. And then the screaming began. My voice cracked, the noise reverberated throughout my entire fragile frame.

I hugged my arms to my chest, the wounds still bleeding. I was covered in blood, a victim of war waging in my own mind. I let myself drop to the floor. My legs folded beneath me, my blood and tears flowing freely to the planks beneath me.

Honour opened my door harshly, her eyes wild and frightened. Her hair and nightshirt were disheveled and the remnants of drool could easily be seen on the corner of her mouth. She wiped it away with the back of her hand and gazed down at me.

I must have been a sight to see, a broken doll crumpled in the floor, shaking with agony. Our mother appeared in the doorway, her hand clutched to her bosom. She gasped in alarm.

"Honour, dear, fetch the necessities," her voice was unnaturally tranquil. She made her way to me, trying her best not to step foot in the puddles surrounding my body. "Reyenne, can you stand?"

I threw a mauled arm towards my dresser and latched on, pulling myself up. I simply stared at her, watching her eyes sweep their way down and up my body several times before stopping at my face.

Honour reappeared holding a basket full of objects I could not see. My mother gestured towards the bed and I sat obediently. She sat the basket down next to me then herself and began pulling bandages, ointments, and other medical objects out.

"Honour, please go get some water and clean this mess off the floor and dresser." She didn't speak as she swabbed the slashes and applied generous amounts of cream before bandaging them tightly.

I had stopped crying by the time she was finished and my floor was back to a dull brown. Honour stripped the blankets and sheets from the bed and replaced them with fresh linens and my mother covered me gently.

Before leaving she pulled a small bottle of medicine from her basket and pried open my lips, dumping the contents into my gaping mouth. The liquid slid down my tongue and throat, foul tasting and smelling. I gagged but choked it down.

Within seconds I was fast asleep, far away from my damaged body.

Seven

Months went by filled with infection, fever, vomiting, and many prayers to die. I saw Honour only a few times as summer flew by and school resumed again, and Juniper not at all. My mother seemed to stay stationed outside my door along with the doctor listening for the slightest groan or movement.

But as September opened with fresh air and the smell of autumn, so did my health. The gashes lining my body finally healed, not leaving a single trace of existence. Not one scar or red patch could be found anywhere on my peach flesh. This puzzled the doctor but he blew it off, happy that I was breathing.

On September second as dawn struck the dark sky, alighting it with smears of color, I buttoned my boots. I wanted to see my sister; I wanted to know why she hadn't been around. Marriage was not an excuse for absence from your family. And I was not going entirely based on my own selfish reason but on the cries of my mother.

She was not faring well under my condition and with the removal of another family member. I pulled my favorite black dress on, laced the things that needed to be laced, adjusted my bodice, and grabbed my shawl from the peg by the door.

The air was chilly and crisp, it stung my cheeks and nose, and made my eyes water. It was bliss after the endless hours I spent in my steamy room with quilts piled upon me while my body perspired heavily.

I would not deny there was a certain spring in my step despite the lull in my heart. Unfortunately, modern medicine did not cure broken emotions. I pushed this thought away, focusing on happy thoughts, determined not to spiral myself into a bottomless depression.

I was going to see my sister, finally, after months of missing her. I made my way across town into the uppity district where my sister resided with her new husband on Manor Lane. The houses that lined the cobbled streets here were a far cry from what I was accustomed to. The people found within the walls of the perfectly painted exteriors snubbed their noses at humans like me.

I was but a stain on their linens that needed scrubbed away. But I straightened my shoulders and swept my eyes across the houses for their numbers until I found the one that belonged to Juniper and William. It was charming, I had to admit.

Red bricks layered to form the walls only punctured by the floor to ceiling windows draped with silk curtains. I tilted my head back to see up to the third floor where a woman wearing black and white passed the window unaware of her observer.

The grass outside was a rich green and the flowers lining the walls were all varieties of exotic and polished. An iron fence with an ornamental "C" stood in front of me, like a soldier ready for orders. I pushed the gate open with minimal effort and strode up the path to the white coated door.

There was a small gold bell with an embroidered string attached to it to the right of the door frame. I pulled hard clashing the metal against itself. The sound was horrendous and loud beyond explanation. It wasn't a full second before the door opened. The woman from the window above peered out at me, a false smile plastered on her face.

"Can I help you, ma'am?" she asked sweetly. Her lips were flaky and her eyes tired. I glanced down at her hands to see calluses from endless laundry and dishes. But other than these minor faults, she was well put together.

"I am here to see Juniper." I replied mildly.

She opened the door wider and stepped aside to allow me entrance. I crossed the threshold, my boots clicking on the polished floors. She led me without another word through countless doorways until finally we entered a room like no other.

Books lined every wall, starting near my feet and stopping far above my head. Leather bound, paper bound, whatever case it may be; books, books, and more books. The carpet was lavish; it muted the sounds of my shoes. Tiny flowers were intricately sewn into every square inch with care.

A window twice the height of myself was on the far wall, thick red curtains were drawn casting a soft glow on the room. And located in the center of it all, at a desk so clean I could see my reflection, sat my sister pouring over a small book.

Besides her better quality makeup and clothing, she hadn't changed much. Her hair was in a loose braid and thrown over her shoulder and her green eyes swept across the pages quickly. She was so engrossed in the tale that she didn't even hear us enter.

The servant coughed notifying Juniper of her appearance and then disappeared through the door. Juniper stuck a small square of paper between the folds of the pages she was on and closed the book, standing and looking up for the first time directly at me.

"Oh." She looked shocked to see me.

I marched across the floor and sat myself in the chair opposite her without comment. She promptly seated herself again, smoothing her skirts with her gloved hands. "You seem absolutely thrilled to see me," I commented.

"It's not that, not at all. I just did not expect you. Usually someone sends a letter before visiting" Her voice was slightly punctuated. She had adopted the lilt of a high born lady.

I folded my hands in my lap, suddenly feeling out of place. "I didn't realize I couldn't come see my sister without first notifying her."

"Of course you can! I didn't mean it like that at all." She smiled pleasantly. "How are you, dear?"

"Dear? Are you fifty? I had no idea in my absence you had aged thirty or so years." I snorted.

She looked down and coughed. "I've just adapted to this life style, I assume."

"I can tell. I'm doing better, by the way. Thanks for coming and seeing me at all. I really appreciated your company." The sarcasm in my words was thick, she flushed.

"I-I meant to..." She reached across the table and her bodice moved to reveal a dark bruise.

I leaned forward in my chair. "What is that?"

She looked down and hastily adjusted herself to cover it. "It's nothing; tell me more about what happened. Was it Ember? Did he attack you and kill Colson?"

I waved her question away. "Who did that to you?"

"It was a mistake of my own. Drop it." Her tone had become icy.

A light turned on in my head. "He's hit you."

Her sideways glance told it all before her mouth even opened. "N-no."

"Don't you dare lie to me about something as severe as this. How many times has this happened?"

"Just the once." Another sideways glance.

"Do not lie to me! I don't care how rich he is, he has no right to lay hands on you." I was furious.

She dropped her voice to a whisper. "If you love me you will keep quiet. He is home right now in his study above us and if you are too loud he will be able to hear." She paused staring directly into my eyes. "Do you want it to be worse for me?"

My mouth went dry. "No...of course not."

"Then a subject change is due." She raised her voice again. It was delightful and cheery and completely false. This was not the sister I had grown up with. "Tell me about your wounds. I want to know every last detail. Did Ember do it?"

I recounted the tale to Juniper, leaving out no detail. I told her everything from the attempted rape to seeing our father. She sat still listening attentively. It was almost as if she hadn't had a conversation in ages she was actually interested in.

"And he has not been to see you?" she asked, incredulous.

"No, I have been surviving in a haze of blankets, medicine, and the care of our mother, sister, and doctor for weeks. This is the first day I have been up and about." I replied.

"Do you think he hurt you that severe on purpose?" her nails were digging into her book in excitement.

"Truthfully?" I hesitated thinking over my answer. She waited patiently. "No, I don't think he did. It was my idea to begin with; he even told me it was possible if he wasn't careful he may kill me."

"Oh, you live such an exciting life!" she brought her hand to her chest in awe.

"I... I guess." I was hesitant. I didn't necessarily call near death experiences exciting.

The maid bounded back into the room, apparently used to visitors being around her mistress. Her cheeks were flushed and sweat gleamed on her forehead. She had obviously been disrupted while hard at work. "Ms. Cundy, ma'am." She bowed low to the floor, her skirts ruffling. "Mr. Cundy would like a word."

She stepped aside and in flaunted William Cundy. An air rose around him of aristocracy and ignorance. Juniper rose, once again smooth her skirts and straightening her bodice to hide her bruise. I rose too, although I didn't particularly want to.

He held his arms out as if to hug me then dropped them to his sides again. "Ah, Reyenne, how nice to see you up and about." His smile was as false as his gentlemen demeanor.

"You wanted to see me, darling?" questioned Juniper sweetly.

He turned to face her, his smile wavering. "Yes, yes." He pulled the chair next to mine up and seated himself, and waved a hand in the air for us to be seated. The maid sulked back out of the room and I resumed my spot. "Did you order roses for the front foyer?" He turned to me as if letting me in on their secret life. "We have many guests coming for a dinner party this weekend."

I nodded, barely listening. Juniper coughed. "No, I forgot."

He gripped the arm of the chair. "I do not ask much of you, Juniper. As my wife I expect you to do these simple tasks. In fact, I should not have to ask you at all. You should already know that if guests are to be in our home you will take every tedious labor into hand."

She glanced at me then back at him. "Dear, could we please... discuss these matters later? I do have a guest currently."

He swiped his hand through the air. "As if Reyenne doesn't know how you are, she did live with you for fifteen years."

He made to leave but I found my voice. "Excuse you?"

He turned yet again in my direction, an expression of annoyance plastered on his perfectly pampered face. "Yes?"

I stood to give myself some leverage. He stood also, towering over me. "I do not appreciate the way you speak to my sister, William."

He scoffed. "I'm sorry. I had no idea I was now to be taking advice and orders from a low born woman such as you."

"And what exactly is that supposed to mean? Because I am not as rich as you or have the male anatomy I do not have a say? I can tell by the way you talk to and hit my sister that you disrespect her every chance you get?"

He sent a striking glare at Juniper. No doubt he assumed she had shown me the marks that crossed her body on her own free will. She stammered, "R-Reyenne, it is all really fine. We have a lovely marriage, even trying for children. I do not need you to say more."

I ignored her, still glaring at the man that stood before me. "Do not test me, William. I may be as good as the dirt on your shined shoes to you but I do have friends in high places. And if need be I will take matters into my own hands. Do not dare lay another finger on her head. She is your wife, your other half, your partner." I looked over my shoulder to Juniper who was shaking and then back at him. "She is your equal, treat her as such. I will henceforth be by for weekly visits. I will not have you handling her as your brother handled me."

I grabbed my skirts and stepped around his statue frame. I reached the door and looked back. "I will see you in seven days' time, Juniper." I swept my gaze over the back of William then sneered, "And you also, Mr. Cundy."

Eight

It was October before I saw Ember. I was simply lying in the field, watching as the clouds rolled past. All Hollow's Eve was close and being from an Irish immigrated family, my mother was in full holiday swing. I loved the holiday, but could not stand to cook anymore food or help Honour with her costume anymore.

I needed my space and so I had come outside to enjoy the chilly weather. Footsteps crunched on the frozen grass. I sat up on my elbows to see who the intruder was. Ember strode towards me, his head down, his hands stuffed in his pockets.

He wore his usual black pants and boots, but with a long, black coat that reached his knees. Six gold buttons in two rows gleamed in the sunlight. I had no doubt he wore his usual white button up under the garment.

I rose to my feet, hugging my shawl around me as a gust of air whipped my hair forward and around my face. He glanced towards me, saw that I was looking at him, then stared back down at the ground. Once he was only a few feet away, he stopped.

I slowly closed the space between us; the frost coated my boots in wet streaks. "Hello." My voice was timid, steam rose into the air.

He peered up through dark curtains of hair. "Hey."

He was acting shy or wounded, not at all like himself. "I haven't seen you in a while."

He shrugged. "I've been around as usual, I saw you, but I didn't think you would want to see me."

I clutched my shawl tighter, having already assumed he had been following me. I had heard footsteps when I was the only one tending the dying gardens and smelt him while walking through the streets of town running errands. "Why wouldn't I want to see you?"

He looked up, exasperated already with the conversation. "I almost killed you, Reyenne! I got carried away. The smell of blood, the ripping of flesh... I am truly a monster. You called that one right."

I held my hand out wanting to touch him then thought better of it. "But I am fine." I made light of the subject. "I was bedridden for weeks with a fever and oozing wounds but look." He raised his head and I pushed the fabric of my dress and shawl away from my arm. Where once had been a gruesome slash was now nothing but unperturbed skin. "See? There aren't even any scars. I am fine. And I forgive you."

His eyes bore into mine with a ferocious intensity. "What if I had killed you? Reyenne, I can't die. If you had I would have been stuck once again alone, but for the rest of eternity. I would have had to live with the knowledge that I killed the one thing that meant more to me than anything else."

I put my hand out and this time did touch him, I gripped his chin and forced him to keep eye contact with me. "I am here, unhurt and uncaring. I still love you and want to be with you despite your abnormalities."

He smiled for the first time, my heart fluttered alive under his gaze. He reached his arms out and wrapped them tightly around him. I welcomed his icy touch while he no doubt rejoiced under the warmth of mine. He rested his chin on my head. "Oh, how I have missed you. You haven't any idea how torturous it was for you to be right out of reach."

I smiled, my cheek pressed into his shoulder. "I need you to promise there will be no more killings. I need to know my family will be safe if I keep you around them."

He pushed me back to arm's length and pressed his fingers firmly into my shoulders. "There will be no more incidents. I will travel far from here during feeding times, and I will spare you the horrific details. I will even thoroughly wash myself before coming anywhere near you," he frowned. "I will take every precaution to ensure that you do not deal with my... condition no more than you have to."

I beamed, grabbing his hand and beginning to drag him towards the house. "Then it is settled." I said over my shoulder. "You are moving back in."

Heat washed over us as soon as we entered the tiny home. My mother sat in her usual chair sewing a piece of Honour's costume while Honour herself sat cross legged on the floor beneath her dressing her latest doll.

"Back already, dear?" asked our mother without looking up. That was, until Honour saw Ember, squealed, and ran to hug him. She plowed into him, wrapping her arms tightly around his torso.

"Ember! When did you get back?" my mother asked astonished at the sight of him.

Ember rubbed his hand over Honour's hair and smiled across the room towards her. "Just a few hours ago. How have you been in my absence?"

She set the garment she was working on down and stood. "We have been fine, a few mishaps." She averted her gaze to me at this then back to him. "But fine indeed. I have been missing the man strength around here."

He chuckled. "Well, I am back and would like to stay if that's alright with you?"

Honour let go and turned to face our mother. "Why yes, of course! You always have an invitation to our home. I will go get the bedroom ready. Since Juniper's marriage we have a spare bed I can sleep in and you can have my room again."

She bustled out of the living space and down the hall towards the small bedrooms. We heard the door creak as she opened it and began shuffling around tidying things up. Honour skipped over to the chair and picked up the dress our mother had been working on. A needle and thread hung down as she held it up for us to see.

"I am going to be a dead rich lady for Halloween." A wide grin spread over her face. "What are you going to dress as?"

Ember laughed. "I'm afraid I haven't thought of that, you'll have to help me come up with something."

At this comment she dropped the dress and fled the room, no doubt going to grab her magazine filled with costume ideas. Ember turned to me once we were alone and without speaking pressed his lips firmly to mine.

I draped my arms around his neck and shoulders, and gave myself in to the taste of him. I had truly missed him, despite the injuries he had caused.

"Oh... excuse me." I heard my mother say from across the room. We split apart swiftly and I blushed a deep crimson.

Ember spoke before I could. "Excuse us, Susan. I have just missed your daughter terribly much. I'm afraid my affection could not be withheld any longer."

My mother also blushed. It was no secret she found Ember charming and the perfect gentlemen. She also appreciated that her social status did not deter him from treating her like a highborn lady. "It's fine, fine. I just did not expect to walk in on such a spectacle." She fidgeted with her dress and coughed. "Are you hungry?"

Ember went with me the next day to see Juniper. I had stuck to my word and visited her every Wednesday at five in the evening. So far this had not been cause for an issue. William played along, even though he acted highly annoyed, and Juniper seemed to like the attention.

We entered through the gate hand in hand and Ember pulled the bell string for me. As usual, it was mere seconds before the maid, whose name I had learned was Addie, opened the door. She had grown accustom to my visits and seemed to like me.

"Reyenne! How dear to see you, your sister is right this way." She stepped back to let us in, not questioning the strange man with me, and led the way into the parlor.

This room was the smallest of the house. The walls were covered in cream wallpaper that bore light pink flowers and the furniture was all neatly adjusted. Each piece was the color of cream and cleaned until glistening.

Juniper sat casually on the couch, her hair for once unbraided and flowing down her shoulders and breasts to slightly pool in her lap. She wore a light gown with a long sheer jacket that had long bell sleeves. The colors consisted of dull blues and gold.

She turned at our footsteps and shot up at the appearance of Ember. She quickly wrapped the jacket around herself the best she could and flushed. Addie exited the room quickly as usual. I led Ember across the room and onto the small couch that faced the one Juniper had just vacated.

She lowered herself slowly back down. "I did not expect you to bring company; I would have been more appropriately dressed." She claimed, flustered.

Ember waved his arms in dismissal. "You look absolutely stunning. Do not change on account of me; I like you to be comfortable in your own home."

She blushed deeper and let her grip on the jacket go. It fluidly drifted away from where she had been holding it and fell back in place. I could see now why she had been embarrassed. She wore no bodice or corset, nothing; it seemed under the fragile dress. Her breasts could be plainly seen.

I spoke up. "How have you been?"

She adjusted her hair to cover her chest and looked back up. Her green eyes were wide with excitement. "Well, I may have some news."

I shifted in my seat. "Yes? Do tell."

She glanced back and forth between Ember and I then confessed, "I may be pregnant."

Ember immediately congratulated her while I stayed silent with shock. I knew William had made a few comments about trying to have a baby but had never taken them seriously. In all honesty, I didn't expect the marriage to last. He was a cruel, hateful man that was rarely around due to business ventures and mistresses.

I found my voice in time to ask, "How far along?"

She delicately clutched her hands in her lap. "The doctor visited two days past and said by the look of things possibly two months. I told William last night and he seemed thrilled."

Ember grasped my hand with his; obviously knowing I was not amused. "That is delightful, Juniper. You will make a lovely mother." He added.

"Oh, I hope so. I am elated yet frightened." She responded.

"Well it is a big responsibility, but I think you are up for the challenge." Ember stated.

Her cheeks turned the color of roses. "Thank you, dear. Your flattery is refreshing." She stared at me. "Do you not have any more to say on the subject?"

I coughed; I had not expected her to call me out on my silence. "I am happy for you, truly, but as always I hesitate in my feelings. You know my opinion when it comes to William and this toxic marriage. I only worry about the safety of you and the child."

She waved my comment away. "You have been here every week for over a month, Reyenne. You know no damage has been done. Things are looking around, they are nice. Besides, I rarely see William due to business anymore. He comes to bed at all hours of the night disheveled and exhausted. Sometimes he doesn't come home at all."

"I wonder then, how you managed to become pregnant?" The question was out before I had time to think. I clapped my hand over my mouth.

She glared at me. "I will not amuse you with conversation of my private affairs with my husband. That is wildly inappropriate."

"I'm sorry." I murmured.

"It is quite alright." She grumbled. "Let us move on to something else, something more entertaining. Ember? When did you get back?"

Ember stood, removed his coat, and slung it over the back of the couch. He resumed his seat then acknowledged Juniper's question. "I just arrived today."

She nodded. "It is terribly good to see you, especially after the fiasco with Reyenne's wounds. I thought you would never show your face again."

He paused; I felt his body go stiff. "I was unaware you knew of their origin."

"Oh, yes." She chimed. "I have been informed of it all."

Ember turned to me. "I thought it was clear you were not to tell anyone of my condition."

I grimaced. "I didn't know if I was ever going to see you again."

He turned away from me and once again regarded Juniper. "That was all a mistake, I got carried away. I did not mean to destroy the life of Colson Cundy either, my deepest apologies on your brother-in-law."

She tittered then lowered her voice. "Between us, I am glad that fool is gone." Her whisper carried over the space between the couches. "My marriage is better off without him lingering around trying to grope me and then telling William otherwise. He did that often during our courting. And Reyenne is well, so I guess that means all is well! Just do not let my husband hear you talk of such things."

As if on cue William Cundy entered the parlor, a swagger in his step. I groaned inward at his appearance. I had hoped not to see him at all this visit. He glanced from us to Juniper and sat himself next to her, keeping a small space between them.

"Hello, Reyenne." He tilted his head at me, then turned his gaze to Ember. "Ember, my fellow, I must apologize for my wife's appearance. It seems modesty has evaded her this afternoon."

Juniper awkwardly gathered her garment to her chest once again; her fingers were white from the force. Ember seemed to take this comment in stride. "As I have already said to her, she is fine. I expect her to dress comfortably in her own parlor, and she did not expect my visit. It should be me apologizing for intruding."

William grinned, his teeth dazzled in the candlelight. "Quite the gentlemen you are, Mr. Sky. Quite the gentlemen, indeed. What do you say we leave the women to their petty chat and take ourselves to my study to have a cigar?"

"Thank you, but I will have to decline. I am here to see Juniper foremost and make sure her health is in order. I have heard of some inappropriate behavior taking place and as a dear friend of Juniper's, I had to come see she was well." Ember retorted.

William's face turned the shade of ripe cherries. He shot daggers at us all before standing. "I see my presence is not welcome here. I will take my leave." He strode out of the room, his back and shoulders upright despite his mouth being twisted into a frown.

Juniper giggled. "I know I should not have found that response amusing but sometimes I am just unable to help myself."

Nine

Halloween came at last. I helped Honour with her costume and made her face ashen. She giggled and fidgeted in elation. Ember had decided against dressing up as had I. I grabbed a satchel and handed it to Honour as we went to leave.

"Wait," called my mother. "Make sure you're all back before ten! You know we're having a big dinner!"

"Okay, can we go now?!" Honour jumped in excitement.

"Yes, yes." She shooed us out the door. "Don't you eat too many sweets before you get back!"

Honour waved her away and skipped off into the distance. Ember and I followed a few feet behind, strolling hand in hand. Snow had already begun to litter the ground; it swept a chill that dug into my bones through the air.

Ember didn't seem to notice, but my fingers had already begun to turn pink. I had been thinking endlessly about him for days, knowing he was only a few feet away in the room next to mine. Yet instead of the toxic thoughts one would expect from an adolescent, I was merely curious.

I had come to the conclusion I didn't know much about him. I hadn't any idea his age, his family, where he lived before he came here, or why he came here to begin with. In fact, the only things I did seem to know didn't make much sense.

I gulped in the frigid air. "How old are you?"

He swept a sideways glance over me then breathed out, a puff of white smoke escaped from his lips. "I'm a teenager, just as you."

I twisted my mouth into a straight line. "No. I mean... how old are you really?"

"What do you mean?" He was playing dumb. It slightly irritated me.

"When you came back you said if you had killed me you would have had to live an eternity without me. You said you couldn't die. So, if that's the case... then, how long have you lived already?"

He didn't seem to hear me at first. He simply kept walking, watching the children run around with bags full of sweets and coins. Finally, he sighed deeply. "I lived here once, you know. Not this town precisely but in London. I went to school, had friends, even had a best friend named Edgar." He paused staring into the distance. "I do miss him so."

I kept quiet. I was unaware of this. He had never told me he lived in the same general area as I did, but the note in his voice led me to believe many years had passed since he had lived here. I didn't want to speak, I was afraid if I did he would stop opening up.

After several agonizing minutes he continued, "I haven't been human since the early seventeenth century. I really don't know the exact year of my creation, as we call it, because we don't keep track of such miniscule details." He gripped my hand tighter. "But I haven't seen my family, my friends, my school... anything since then. I do have a sort of mother, of course. She taught me the ways of our species. She was the one who created me. Her name is Ebony Vail."

I stifled a gasp. He was several decades older than I and here I was holding hands with him. He was old enough to be my ancestor. It disturbed me deeply yet I kept a firm grip on his hand. "Where did you live before you came here?" I questioned.

He sighed yet again. "Curious today, aren't you?" he chuckled. "We have a castle, huge, white marble... beautiful. Especially at night when the torches are lit, they shimmer and the entire thing seems to sparkle. Most of us dwell within the walls. We have a queen, of course. A beautiful woman with enormous black wings and milk white skin. She proceeds over us all."

"And you lived in this castle?"

"Oh, yes. I had my own room and everything. My mother, Ebony, is what we call a Royal so her room was located a few stories above mine, but it was easier for me to keep her close. Coming into Mayhem is a hard task to accomplish."

I scrunched my nose at the word he had used. I had never heard him say it before. Mayhem. He said it with such casualty that I almost missed it. "What do you mean mayhem?"

He glanced in my direction and then down. "Mayhem, as in Mayhem Fairies. That's what we're called, that's our species. I thought I already told you this."

I searched my memory for any recollection of the official name of his people but drew up blank. "If you had I have forgotten." I smiled sheepishly.

He shrugged nonchalantly. "It is no matter now, the details are unimportant. I am never going back."

This statement shocked me. I didn't know how he could leave his family in the blink of an eye for people that did not understand him. The thought of leaving my family through marriage was hard enough. I couldn't begin to understand the torment he may be facing.

Before I could say anymore Honour ran up to us with her hair a mess and her satchel thrown over her shoulder. She had a small cake in her mouth and was chomping furiously. I looked up to find we were standing outside the small medical supplies store.

"I have so much! It's so good!" she bellowed.

The air around us was becoming chillier by the minute; the sun was completely gone, encasing us in darkness. Children all around us were running to their individual homes, no doubt excited to dig into their treasures.

I pulled my hand away from Ember's and placed it on Honour's, leading her back towards our street. Snow sloshed under our boots as we made our way through the dark roads. Honour pulled another small candy from her bag and chewed it swiftly. She went to reach for another but I stopped her.

"I thought mother told you no sweets? We're about to go home to ensue in a dinner, do not spoil your appetite." I chided her.

I watched her roll her eyes in the darkness. "A few will do no harm. Besides, she knows I hate half the foods she makes for Halloween."

Ember strode next to us in silence, his hands warmly in his pockets. "You're not very talkative." I commented.

He smirked. "I am just enjoying the night and the batter between the two of you. I have nothing to say."

Honour piped up at this. "Tell us one of your fairy stories." She snuck another candy from her bag and I shot her a glare.

"Ah, okay then." He looked through the air as if trying to grasp the words he was looking for from the chilly wind. "Have I told you the one about Ebony and Dravven?"

"No!" she beamed.

"Ebony, as you know is my mother and Dravven... Dravven is quite insane. He acts very childish although he is very old, and Ebony cannot stand it. She is a very serious woman with small moments of laughter. So, Ebony tries her best to stay away from Dravven, although it is clear to us all she actually adores him. But we play along and pretend like she despises him although we all see how she helps him with tasks and keeps him grounded. Well, one night, very similar to this one-"

I flutter and a thump landed behind us. His words were cut off and he turned. We too turned to look at what had disturbed him but were unable to see anything in the pitch black. I looked quizzically over at him. His features had seemed to freeze, his breathing had stopped completely. He clutched his hands in fists at his sides.

"Ember?" I inquired.

"Reyenne, I want you to take Honour and get home as fast as you can." He muttered. I barely heard him over the sudden gusts of wind.

"But Ember-"

"Now. Do not question me." He cut me off.

I took Honour by the hand and swiftly raced off, leaving Ember alone on the seemingly empty street. I glanced over my shoulder every few seconds to see if he had caught up but the street was deserted, spooky even.

Honour trembled next to me. Her hair had completely fallen down and her makeup had been wiped off. "What's going on?" she quaked.

I peered over my shoulder once again then led Honour up the hill to our house. "I'm not sure, but we're almost home. It's all going to be alright." I assured her although I was unsure myself.

We made it to the house without incident and stepped inside to the warmth found within. I immediately turned and bolted the door then ran to each window making sure it was locked. After ensuring no one could get in without our notice I made my way to the kitchen.

Our mother was busying herself with the last preparations of our late night dinner, a tradition in the Montgomery house. Honour sat as if nothing had happened scavenging for goods within her bag.

"Where has Ember run off to? Surely he hasn't disappeared again." My mother questioned while watching something simmer over the stove.

I sunk into a rickety chair across from Honour. "No, no. He is just... tending to some business is all. He should be here at any moment."

She shook her head in understanding then went back to tending the food. My mind was racing. I hadn't a clue what was going on, or what had scared him so badly. Needing to busy myself I set mismatched plates and dishes on the table.

Honour seemed content with shoving as many sweets in her mouth as she possibly could while our mother scolded her from across the room. Dinner went by rather smoothly without any sign of Ember returning.

At midnight I reluctantly made my way to my room. I slid out of my dress, and lazily threw my nightshirt over me. I was worrying more than I knew I should be. He was a grown man... and a Mayhem Fairy; he could take care of himself.

I plopped down on my bed and began braiding my hair so that it didn't become knotted throughout the night. Suddenly, there was a tapping on my window. I let go of my hair and turned, my heart nearly beat out of my chest.

The tapping came again. Tap, tap, tap. As if a branch was being pushed by currents of wind. I made my way across the room cautiously and threw back my curtains. Ember stood before me, his hair a mess and his cheeks windswept.

I threw open the window and helped pull him in. He was colder than usual and he laid against me for support. I helped settle him on the bed then shut the window. It wasn't until I sat next to him that I noticed the blood stain on his shirt.

I gasped and put my hand on the injury. He breathed deeply and swiped the hair from his eyes. "Please don't touch it." He rasped.

"But... w-what happened?" I stuttered.

He pulled his shirt up to expose a long gash going down his torso, but even as I stared the skin mended itself. "It'll be fine within the hour. It's just a scrape."

"A scrape? I almost died from wounds such as this!"

"Because you didn't have my healing abilities. I assure you I will be fine. I just need to lay here for a bit." He flopped his arm across his eyes and his breathing became shallow.

I folded my hands in my lap and watched him. My hair hung over my shoulder in a half braid, the ends were already matting themselves together. "Are we in danger?"

He shifted his arm to gaze at me. "Do you want the truth or a lie?" he mumbled.

"The truth, of course." I replied.

He sat up, gripping his side and grimacing. "Perhaps."

It was a single unassured word but my world seemed to melt away. I found it hard to breathe and grasped at my chest trying to open my lungs to air. I had stupidly trusted him yet again. My family was in danger again because of my actions.

I gathered my bearings before speaking again. "What do you mean? Who did you encounter?"

He drug a hand down his face leaving red marks where his hand had been then settled on his elbows. "The queen has sent a scout, that is all. That either means she is worried about me or irritated with me. I am guessing the latter."

"But... I don't understand. Why would the queen be irritated with you?" I shuddered.

"I didn't do what I set out to do, and I've broken just about every rule by staying with you and telling you who I am. She probably wants my head." He concluded.

I gazed at him in wonder. I couldn't believe how casually he spoke of death. As if it was something he encountered on a daily basis.

I stopped my thoughts. Death was something he encountered on a daily basis. But to talk so freely of his own death still concerned me. I tried to put myself in his shoes. He had immortal life, strength, healing abilities. Everything I wish I had and more.

If I had lived for several decades would I be willing to give that all away for peace? I didn't know. There was no possible way I could know. My mortal mind screamed no.

"Is my family in danger?" I feared.

He was staring into space. "No, I don't think so. It is me she wants, not any of you. She couldn't care less what becomes of you. I just don't see her wasting her strength and energy on those below her." He assured me.

I wrinkled my nose at his description of humans. Surely he didn't think this way? It was only his queen. I didn't want to ask for fear of the answer, so I lay back on the bed and put my hands behind my head.

"You will keep us safe?"

"Even if it means I die in the process." He agreed.

I turned to stare at him, resting my head on my hand. "I love you."

He smiled. "I love you, too."

It was the first time I had outright said it in months. It made my entire body tingle in satisfaction. I grabbed the blanket, forgetting my hair, and pulled it over us. He wrapped his arm around my waist and we drifted off immediately into sleep.

Ten

Strange things began to happen the following week. Every morning I would wake to take Honour to school and find my bedroom window wide open. The curtains would be fluttering about in cold gusts of wind and a small amount of snow would line the floor.

I would slam it shut and scold Honour for sneaking into my room at night. She would deny ever being in there but I knew it must have been my mother's method of checking on Ember and I. She disliked that him and I had been sleeping in the same bed.

But this wasn't the only strange occurrence I noticed. After I dropped Honour off at the schoolhouse I would begin my trek back home in feet of snow. I was used to this having lived in the area my entire life, but what I was not used to was finding dead animals every day.

Their small, frail bodies would be ripped open and discarded in my path. No blood would be scattered on the snow and no footprints would lead to the scene of the crime. I would try my best not to look at them for fear of becoming queasy.

I told Ember about these things but he brushed them off as freak accidents. Yet as the weeks progressed I became more and more frightened. I would often find my belongings buried in the snow, only exposed by my disturbance.

My brush I had found in the drift by the front door, and my childhood doll in the garden with her arm ripped off. I took to only going outside in daylight, and cautioned Honour to never go anywhere alone. I even rescheduled my weekly visits with Juniper for three instead of five so I would have ample time to get home.

It was on my way to see Juniper that the most frightening of events took place. I was still two streets away from her house and no one was out. The recent snowstorm had caused many people to stay holed up in their homes with fires raging and ample amounts of soup.

I was watching my footing, making sure not to slip on thick patches of ice when it happened. Someone whispered directly into my ear. It was a woman's voice I was sure. It was cold and intimidating. I jumped and slid, landing on my bottom with my skirts soaked in snow.

I whipped my head all around to find the person who had startled me. But there was no one about. The street looked deserted, covered in undisturbed snow and locked up houses. I shook my head and brought myself up, dusting off my dress and proceeding towards Juniper's.

My heart beat furiously the entire way there and I couldn't help but feel as if I was being watched. I made sure to check the area behind me every so often until I got to the gate and swiftly made my way to the porch.

Addie opened the door slower than usual, but I was glad to feel the warmth of the house as I walked in. All my fears vanished as feeling came back to my fingers and face. Addie directed me towards my sister's bedroom then left us alone. Juniper laid on her bed, sweat on her brow and her face ashen in the dark room.

I pulled a seat up between her and fire, rejoicing in the warmth. Juniper had not had a good pregnancy. She often experienced cold flashes and spells of dizziness. The doctors and midwives had told her to expect a deformed child.

She glanced at me and smiled then went back to staring into the fire. Her nightshirt was soaked with sweat making it completely sheer. Her body seemed weak, all her energy being drained to the small bump in her middle.

"How are you feeling?" I prompted.

"I have been better. William has told me that if our child has a defect we will be sending it away. We cannot have a... monstrosity in our household. He asked, what will the neighbors think? He

said, people would be scared to come over for fear of our child."
She whimpered. "I do not agree. Defect or not, this is my baby.
This," she placed a hand on her stomach, "is part of me. It will be
perfect no matter what abnormalities it may possess and I will not
rid myself of it."

"It is not his decision to make." I counseled her.

She turned her head to me, strains of hair stuck to her face with
sweat. "Is it not? Unfortunately, we live in a world where all
decisions are the man of the household's. My anatomy prevents me
from having a say." She argued then sighed. "He used to not be
like this. When we courted he was lovely. I trusted him with my
soul. But now? Now I dare not say something wrong in his wake
for fear of being slapped or humiliated."

Anger rose in my throat and threatened to spill out but I calmed
it down. "Has he hit you again?"

"Oh dear, yes. Several times. The servants are so accustomed to
it they just turn a cold shoulder on the scene, all except Addie. Of
course, she can't do anything while it is happening, but she rushes
to my aid as soon as he leaves. Bless her soul."

I clenched my fists in my hands. "Why haven't you told me?"

"Oh, Reyenne." She patted a fragile hand on mine. "It is no
worry. He doesn't dare do much when I am only a third of the way
through my pregnancy."

"Do not make excuses for him, Juniper." I gritted my teeth.

She winced. "Please, your voice." She tenderly put two fingers
on her temple and rubbed.

Within the hour I stayed not much else happened. Juniper talked
in circles no doubt from her fever and medications, and I tried my
best to assure her she would be fine. We talked of the upcoming
Christmas holiday and what she was going to do, and how she was
going to bring the New Year in, then I bid her farewell and left.

Addie sheepishly smiled at me from the hall where she stood
with a new nightshirt, bottles of medicine, and wet clothes and I
snaked my way through the house to the front door.

I recounted the visit to my mother once I was home. She was sick with worry, wringing her hands habitually and shedding glistening tears. I assured her she had not failed as a parent, and that she should not blame any of these events on herself.

Although I didn't think she believed a word I said, she agreed and went back to her sewing. She was constructing a maternity dress with a stretched center for Juniper. It was light green with cream ribbons, a perfect match for her hair and eyes.

I made my way to my room where Ember was already fast asleep. He had taken to disappearing for most of the day and returning at dusk completely worn out. I ran a hand through his dark hair and smiled.

Swiftly, I changed into my nightshirt, braided my hair, and crawled into bed next to his icy frame. It was mere minutes before I was dreaming.

Honour sat in her nightshirt in a pile of snow giggling and flinging it into the air around her. I chided her. Why was she out here in the middle of the night with no coat on? But when she looked up there was a vacant expression in her eyes.

I took a step back. This seemed to satisfy her. She went back to flinging snow in the air and watching it drift back to the ground in white blurs. "Honour, you really shouldn't be out here!" I called. "Please come inside, you know it is dangerous at night."

She stood and brushed her nightshirt off. I held out my hand, glad she was finally listening and waited for her to trudge over the uneven ground towards me. But she didn't. Instead she stared long and hard at me then smiled. I nervously smiled back, slightly scared of her behavior.

"The snow is lovely." She giggled.

"I... I suppose so, yes. But if you don't come in you're going to get frostbite." I answered.

"Too bad it will turn red." She laughed.

"Red? Why will it turn red, Honour?" I was beyond scared, tempted to turn and run back in the house. But I couldn't just leave her in the cold by herself. I once again put my arm out and beckoned for her to come to me.

"Death is in the air."

I gasped and woke up, my entire body was trembling. Ember still slept next to me, but the window was once again open. I groaned, banishing the dream from my mind, and got up to close it. The snow that had made its way in melted under my bare feet. I grabbed the sill and stuck my head out into the dark, relishing the cold air.

And that was when I heard it, screaming from the woods. But not just any screaming, the distinctive screaming of Juniper. I froze, my blood went cold, and I gripped the sill so hard I cut my hand.

Several seconds went by without any noise. Maybe I had imagined it. I shook my head and went to close my window but the screaming started again. I staggered backwards and fell into the bed in shock. Ember stirred.

He yawned and stretched his arms out. "W-what is it? Why are you up so late?"

The screaming echoed again and this time he heard it. He shot up in bed and pushed the covers away. Within seconds he was clothed and his wings were standing at attention. His eyes glowed in the darkness, his hair whipped in the wind from the window.

The screaming was nonstop now. Without thinking I stripped from my nightshirt and pulled my dress and boots on. He was already climbing from the window when I jumped down next to him.

I went to walk but he stopped me. "No, you go back inside. This could be dangerous."

I glared at him and shoved his arm away. "That is my sister out there!"

Without another word we were off, hand in hand, making our way through the thick piles of snow. My legs sunk in up to my knees and drenched my bare legs and dress. Ember seemed to be having an easier time maneuvering through the ice and snow.

We reached the edge of the woods, the screaming was louder here, more intelligible. She seemed to be repeating the word 'no' over and over again. And then, "Reyenne! Please! Help! NOOO!"

I jolted into action, letting go of Ember's hand I darted between the trees following the sound of her voice. Ember called after me but I barely heard him through the whipping of wind and the sound of my feet hitting ice.

"REYENNE!"

It was so loud it made me cringe. I was almost there, I was almost to her. "I'm coming! I'm coming!" I tried to shout back but it only sounded like a whisper between my panting.

I ran out from between two trees and there she was. She still wore her nightshirt and her hair hung loose down her back. She was sitting the snow bent over, holding her stomach and weeping. I sprinted the remaining steps and knelt next to her.

"You're here." She gasped and smiled at the same time.

I scanned my eyes down her body. The snow steamed, little waves of white smoke drifted into the air. Warm blood seeped from between her legs. I placed my hand on her thigh and could feel the heat drifting from it. The entire bottom of her nightshirt was coated in carmine.

I tried to conceal my terror, afraid I was going to startle her more. I brushed hair away from her forehead and caressed her cheek. "It's going to be okay, I promise. It's all going to be okay."

She relaxed at my words and fell silent. I pulled my shawl off and wrapped it around her for warmth then ripped a piece of my dress off to blot her face with. I then began cleaning her legs and lower body of blood.

Ember broke through the trees and abruptly stopped. I turned to face him, fear etched all over my face. He walked slowly a few paces then stopped, his wings fluttered behind him. "Reyenne..."

I turned, tears streaming down my face, and continued dabbing at the blood. "Ember, please, help me. Help me get her back to the house. She needs medical attention"

"Get away from her." His tone was stern and unquestionable.

I whipped around to face him. "Juniper is dying!" I cried out.

He scanned the area around us, squinting at certain places, then shook his head. "I can't believe I didn't see this coming. I can't believe I fell for it."

"What are you talking about?!" I screamed into the night. "Help me!"

"That is not your sister." He whispered.

I turned to look down at my silent sister and then back to him. "You are delusional."

I began soaking the blood up again, and rubbing her arm in comfort. If I had to do this alone, then so be it. There was suddenly a crashing from nearby; a tree fell inches away from me. I yelped and jumped in alarm.

Ember was at my side in an instant, holding me close to his body. I struggled to get out of his grip. "Let me go! Help Juniper!"

"Look! LOOK!" he yelled over at me.

I followed his gaze to my sister's body. Blood was appearing from her throat and gliding its way down her torso. Slowly, her clothing and features began to change. Her nightshirt turned into a maid's outfit, and her face became Addie's.

I screamed in alarm. Where Juniper had previously been, lay Addie with her guts spilling out. She choked and gurgled on blood, her eyes opened wide, then she flopped back on the ground. I was still screaming, a ringing was sounding in my ears.

Where was my sister? What was going on? Had Ember done this? He hugged me to his chest tightly. Another crash came from behind us and a tree fell. I turned and buried my face in his shirt. "What is happening?" I mumbled.

"She's here."

Eleven

"Who-" I was cut off by a loud cackle. I turned in Ember's arms to
see the most beautiful woman I had ever laid eyes on. Her skin was
pastel, her hair black and long. She wore a silk dress that seemed
to flow over her every curve. But the thing that grasped my
attention the most were the two enormous black wings that jutted
from her spine.

A silver rope was grasped tightly in her delicate hand. A large
animal trotted behind her, its eyes were a deep wine and its skin
black as the night around us. It had a mane of silver and a long
horn protruding from its forehead.

I suddenly couldn't breathe. Ember tensed behind me, his hands
firmly grasped my shoulders, his nails dug into my flesh. This
must be his Queen.

"Nice work, StarFyre." Her voice was a song on the wind with
an edge of power.

I glanced to where she was staring and saw that Addie was now
standing completely intact. Her hair was loose and dark red and
her skin was pale. Wings of yellow protruded from her back. She
was a fairy.

My eyes wandered back over to the magnificent woman and her
beast. The creature swung its head back and forth, and pawed at
the ground, obviously wanting to be let loose. But she kept a firm
grip on the rope, barely giving a thought to its wants.

"You have a unicorn." I blurted without thinking. Immediately I wished I could retract the statement. She smirked in all-knowing and placed a hand on her smooth hip.

"What an ignorant girl you have here, Ember." She stuck her nose up. "This is not a mere unicorn. This is a Monokeros. Deadly, like its owner." She flashed a smile at this. "It's horn, made of the purest fairy dust, will rip through you before you even register what has happened."

"Oh." I gasped.

She stroked the silver mane and the... Monokeros leaned into her touch. This animal felt safe in the presence of this woman. "This Monokeros," she continued, "is my personal beast. His name is Asphodel. My trusted steed. I brought him in case things... got out of hand."

Once again my breathing hitched. Addie, or rather StarFyre, crossed the unsteady grounds to be near her master. My thoughts wandered to Juniper. If Juniper was not here, was not dead, did that mean she was safely at home?

"Where is my sister?" I pondered aloud.

Ember hardened even more behind me. He was a statue in fear or anger, which I did not know. But if he was not going to ask questions, then I was. She twirled the rope in her hands and hummed a soft melody.

"Juniper?" she wondered. "Juniper has been dead for about... what? StarFyre?" she turned to her vicious companion. "Has it been a week already since we disposed of that filthy human?"

StarFyre tapped her chin in contemplation. "Yes, I do believe it has been. Yet I still can taste her lungs. Ah, so sweet they were!"

They both chuckled at their own comments. If Ember had not been gripping me so tightly I would have fallen. My knees buckled under the pressure of their words. Juniper had been dead for a week, and I had no idea.

I set my face into a grim expression. I would not let this woman intimidate me. She had already killed one sister; I would not let her kill the other, or my mother. "Where is her body?"

The woman snapped her fingers and suddenly a gray mass lay before me. Ember let go of my shoulders, subconsciously or consciously I did not know. I fell to my knees near the body. Juniper was but a carcass lying in the snow.

Her once vivid blonde hair and green eyes were now nothing but gray masses. Her entire frame was brittle. I did not want to touch her for fear of her skin disintegrating under the pressure. "What have you done to her?" my voice cracked from choked tears.

"We ate her."

The words were so simple. There was not a care in the world behind them. Not one bit of sympathy or pity for what they had done. These women were unlike Ember in every way. Humans were the inferior species in their eyes, there was no room for care where we were concerned.

We were simply a meal for them.

I stood and retreated to Ember's side. He still had not moved or said a word. His gaze was locked on her in shock and rage. His wings did not even flap in the small bursts of wind circling us. He looked as if he had been carved from ice.

Suddenly, the woman let go of the silver cord holding her Monokeros in place. Asphodel trotted forward in no rush. He nudged Juniper's body with his horn and back away. Before my eyes my sister turned to ash. It glittered in a puff of smoke then settled on the snow, making it glitter under the moon.

The woman snapped her fingers again and a large vial appeared. She handed it to StarFyre and pointed at Juniper's ashes. "Retrieve." StarFyre obediently took the vial and began scooping the dust into it.

"W-who are you?" I stammered unable to control myself any longer.

The woman threw a stray lock of hair over her shoulder casually and grinned ear to ear. Her teeth were perfectly straight and white. Her lips were the color of roses in full bloom. I could not deny her beauty, but I also could not deny my hatred for her.

"I am Queen Tranquility Erasmus of The Mayhem Fairies." She took a slight bow. "Daughter of Albion Aeneas, the Praised One. Wife of Athan Erasmus, the Immortal Worthy of Love. My mother was Ebony Enora, Black Wood of Light, the strongest Queen of our race to ever live." She sighed splendidly. "But you, my dear, may call me your worst nightmare."

I was supposed to be impressed by these titles, I could tell, but I had no clue what any of them meant. StarFyre clutched the now full vial to her chest in amazement and wonder, clearly under the spell of Tranquility.

Ember seemed to finally awaken next to me. His wings began to flutter in time to the swishes of air around us and his fingers twitched at his side. I grasped his cold hand in mine for comfort. "Why are you here?" he wondered.

Tranquility laughed and threw her arms in the air. "You broke some rules, my dear."

"I left our race for Reyenne. I cannot break rules if I am no longer under them." He retorted.

Her black eyes bore into him with such ferocity I had to glance away. I could not tell if she was purely angry or insane. Perhaps a little of both. "You think you can just leave our race? You think it is that easy? That you can strip off your wings and suddenly be a filthy human again?" she cackled. "You are two centuries old, Ember Sky. If you want to be human again then I can arrange for your death. Does this creature you swoon over know you could be her great-great-great grandfather?"

I looked between the two of them. I had never thought of his age like this. The thought was impure, disgusting... revolting. The truth of it was like a smack in the face. Our love should in reality be impossible.

"I see not why any of this matters. If I no longer want to live as a Mayhem Fairy then I should not have to. Nowhere in our rule books does it state that we have to abide by our race at all times. Nowhere does it say that we can't revert back to our old ways." He argued.

She once again grabbed Asphodel's rope and twirled it between her fingers. "You poor creature." She mused. "You cannot change who you are or what you are. You will never again breathe from necessity rather than habit, or feel full from human food instead of organs. You will never be human again."

Ember crushed my hand in his. I heard my bones crack and cried out in pain. He did not seem to notice. I tugged on my hand trying to loosen it from his grip but it only tightened. More cracks came from my bones and I fell on one knee, still being held up by his bone-crushing clasp.

Hot tears made their way down my face and melted in the snow beneath me. The entire bottom of my dress was soaked and my hair was matted. I struggled against him to the best of my ability; blackness was appearing on the edges of my vision.

"Let her go." Tranquility's voice was stern.

Ember let go immediately, I fell face first into the cold earth and clutched my hand to my chest. It was a mangled mess. My fingers stood at odd angles and my hand seemed folded in half with bones trying to break through the skin. I leaned to the side and puked, all the contents of my day billowed out of me like an avalanche.

When there were no more contents in my stomach to empty I stood, still grasping my hand firmly to my chest and whimpering in pain. Tranquility frowned, StarFyre casually leaned against Asphodel. Ember seemed to be staring into space, unaware of the damage he had just caused.

Tranquility glided over the ground to me and held her hands out. "Oh, darling, let me see."

I glanced from her to Ember, then held my shaky, grotesque hand out for her to view. Her touch was so soft and motherly I almost wept. I did not expect such kindness from a creature like her. She slid her slender fingers across the protruding bones so delicately I did not feel it. Then, with words spoken under her breath my hand was healed.

I swiftly pulled it away from her and examined it. Every finger and bone was back in its right place with no pain coursing through my entire limb. Ember had never told me they possessed such power as this. I bowed my head to her and she walked back to her spot next to Asphodel.

"Now, Ember, your punishment." She continued.

"My punishment for what?!" he yelled.

She sighed, seemingly exasperated. "Telling a human about us, breaking the rules of the game, hurting a human in the presence of your Queen; the list goes on and on."

He clenched his hands into fists and shook from pure hatred. "You made me hurt her."

I tensed. She had been controlling Ember, and to think I had felt affection for her while she was healing my hand. I shivered in the night air, wishing I had a coat on. I was in the presence of beings outside of my grasp.

I wanted my sisters, I wanted my mother. I wanted Juniper to be alive. I had made a grave mistake when I took Ember back, no matter his heroic actions. If it hadn't been for him none of this would have happened. I would still be in bed, knowing my family was safe. Knowing Juniper was alive.

Tranquility waved her hand in dismissal. "The details are unimportant. The Royals and I have already decided your fate. You will be slave to me henceforth until I decide to let you go."

With another wave of her hand gold chains wound themselves around Ember. He struggled against them to no avail. I wanted to help but didn't know how. I had no powers or strengths. I was an average human.

Ember fell face first to the ground. I ran over to him and helped him back up. I felt helpless. The man I loved was being attacked right in front of me and I couldn't do anything about it. It was enough to drive a person mad.

"And my mother? What does she say about this?" Ember inquired.

"I long ago dismissed the opinions of Ebony Vail. Any fairy that tries to overthrow me is no friend of mine." She replied.

StarFyre stroked Asphodel. He was growing impatient wanting to attack. I could almost see the bloodlust in his eyes; feel his anger like cool air on the back of my neck. She had brought him to attack someone.

Ember hung his head; the chains clinked softly around him. "I will do whatever it is you wish, my Queen. But please leave Reyenne unharmed."

My heart fluttered at his proposition. He was sacrificing himself for my safety. No one had ever done something like this for me. I wanted to gather him in my arms and kiss him, but refrained. Tranquility was pondering the suggestion; she tapped her slender finger against her perfectly sculpted chin.

"How adorable," she finally declared, "sacrificing yourself for true love. Very noble of you, Ember. Too bad it is not going to work."

Before anyone could reply gold chains were winding themselves around my torso and legs. I struggled against them just as Ember had, but they were too strong. Their cold metal seemed to burn my skin as they tightened. They crossed over my stomach, chest, and arms smoothly.

I wanted to cry again. I wanted to scream about the absurdity of all this. I had only known Ember roughly a year, how could we have gotten in so much trouble in that time? None of this seemed fair. I didn't know why I was being punished by a species I was not part of.

"Please, let me go!" I shouted. "Plea-" I was cut off by a cloth gagging me. It was roughly tied around my head; it bit into the flesh of my cheeks. It smelt of strong perfume and was a deep gold.

Ember stared at me then turned his head back to Tranquility. "What is the meaning of this? You have no jurisdiction over her. She is not a fairy. I am the one that broke the rules, I should be the only one punished."

"Oh, but Ember, I am punishing you." She pointed a finger at me. "She is the only thing you care about, the best weapon to use against you in any fight."

StarFyre giggled. Her wings airily bounced as her shoulders shook. I despised them all, even Ember. If not for him my sister would be alive and I would be safe. I had foolishly followed my heart instead of my head. This was all my fault. My poor judgment had put everyone in danger.

Tranquility pulled Asphodel's rope. He trotted to her side and swung his head back in forth. His horn glinted in the moonlight. "Asphodel, if you would please injure her. Nothing life threatening, of course, just something to show her who is in power. I smell arrogance coming off her."

Asphodel seemed to nod in reply. My eyes widened in shock, my breath hitched for the millionth time in an hour. He was going to stab me for her. Ember fought against the chains even harder.

He was screaming the word 'no' over and over again, but it seemed muffled.

Everything around me seemed distant. I could only focus on Asphodel stamping one hoof into the ground. His nostrils flared and his breathing deepened. I swore his eyes narrowed but my mind could have been playing tricks on me.

Flashes of my life were making their way through my mind. My father pushing me on an old swing while my mother watched, Honour coming home giggling at herself covered in mud, Juniper weeping in front of our father's grave on a daily basis. I was never going to see any of them again.

Asphodel reared back and charged me. I tensed my body and closed my eyes against the impact. I felt his horn as it sliced through my hip. Pain like I had never felt before exploded throughout my entire body.

Someone was screaming in the distance. I was falling backwards onto the ground. The entire right side of my body burned like I had been caught in a house fire, or had stood too close to the stove. Asphodel jerked the horn from my flesh and turned to go back to Tranquility.

StarFyre was laughing madly along with Tranquility. I watched with half closed eyes as my blood leaked off Asphodel's horn and sizzled on the snow strewn ground. Everything was becoming blurry. I numbly felt the chains slithering themselves away from my body, I mutely registered Ember on his knees next to me, still bound and hardly able to move.

I was dying. I could feel the life draining from me and soaking into the Earth below. I had only lived sixteen years. I hadn't lived at all! I had never travelled, never married, never bore children of my own. I couldn't believe all the things I would be missing.

But then I thought of Juniper. She would be missing almost all of it too. With this thought a certain peace descended on me. I was going to be reunited with my father and Juniper. I almost couldn't wait to see them.

I closed my eyes trying to hurry the process along. I could feel my heart slowly coming to a stop and my mind unable to comprehend my own thoughts. I kept my father and Juniper perfectly pictured and hung onto that image the best I could.

With a sudden sweep all was black.

Twelve

I awoke with a start. Everything was pitch black. My arms and legs were bound by something and my hair was hanging in my face. Where was I? Was I dead? There was no longer a pain in my side from Asphodel's horn.

I must be dead.

"Juniper? Father?" I croaked into the darkness.

An inhuman grunt sounded from across the space. I froze. Red eyes gleamed at me through the darkness. Asphodel was here with me. I bit my lip suppressing a scream. The eyes merely glared at me. Two red orbs floating in midair.

"Asphodel, please don't hurt me. I mean you no harm." I pleaded.

He didn't seem to register my words but didn't seem to advance on me either. I wished I could see more than his eyes. Someone coughed to the right of me, too close for comfort. I jumped and the chains holding me jingled in the silence. I squinted, trying to see who was hung next to me.

"Who are you?" I questioned.

They coughed again. "I am no one. Do not speak to me."

Their reply flustered me. "Why not?"

They sighed in annoyance at my questions. "She will hear." A door slammed from across the room. "Look what you have done." They said to me under their breath.

I readied myself for the worst, my heart felt as if it was going to burst from my chest. A candle was lit directly across from me. It illuminated a plain wood door and muscular man. He had brown cropped hair and dark skin, along with two red wings tipped with spikes. His attire consisted of a knight, all the way down to the jagged spear he held firmly. I found it odd that he had tan skin.

"Excuse me?" I piped up.

He turned his head to look at me. His eyes did not glow; they looked to be plain brown. Was this a hoax? Asphodel stood near the far wall grazing on something in a bucket. I did not wish to know the contents.

I directed my attention back to the knight. He finally replied, "Be quiet."

His voice was not harsh or commanding. In fact, it was almost gentle. He was only suggesting I not talk it seemed, for fear of what may happen to me. I pressed my lips firmly together. He nodded in my direction and continued to light candles around the room with the snap of his fingers.

Each light easily blared to life. They cast a yellow glow on the room. Candle by candle things came into focus. Asphodel continued to eat; his horn had been cleaned back to shiny perfection. The knight's armor seemed to glow under the lights.

I looked at my wrists. They were indeed bound by black chains. I was suspended against a wall in midair. The person to my right looked terrible. He had been beat bloody. His face was unrecognizable as human from so many bruises and welts. He hung limp against his restraints, the fight long gone from his body.

More chains hung without occupants on every wall. I was obviously in some form of a dungeon. The final candle was lit and the knight turned to leave. "Queen Tranquility will be here in a few moments."

He opened the door a crack, making me unable to see the hall outside it, and slipped out. I twisted around the best I could, looking for some way to get down. I couldn't just stay here helpless and let her do as she wished to me. I would not be her slave.

The chains dug painfully into my skin. I ignored it the best I could and continued trying to break free. The man next to me sighed deeply. "It is of no use."

I stopped and glared at him. "Because you've obviously tried."

He shot an equally terrifying glare at me. "You think I have just hung here awaiting her destruction? I am simply out of ideas. I have been beat and...bit." He paused and a shudder passed through him. "I just do not know what else to do."

Tears welled in my eyes from sympathy and frustration. "W-what is she going to do to me?" I stammered.

He shook his head. "I don't know, I truly don't. But most people that walk through that door never return. I have not left here in months."

"Months?" I almost screamed the word but contained myself. "She has kept you in this room for months?"

He grimaced. "I have never seen another part of the castle. Occasionally, Oberon, the fellow who was just in here, will give me news of the outside world, but other than that I am completely cut off. When there are no other prisoners I am let down to roam this room as I wish."

I shook my head in disbelief. She had kept this man confined to one room for months. What would she do with me? "Does your family not miss you? Do they not look for you?"

He coughed and began to sob. His shoulders convulsed and his chains jerked and jingled with his movements. "S-she killed t-them all." He cried. "R-right in f-front of me. There w-was nothing I c-could do."

He continued to wail. Asphodel momentarily left his food to peer up at the man then decided it was uninteresting, and shoved his face back into the bucket. I felt terrible. I should have known, I shouldn't have asked. "She killed my sister." I whispered.

The man raised his head once again to look at me. Tears streamed down his swollen cheeks and splattered on the dirt floor. "I am Rye Cager."

The introduction caught me off guard. I was not expecting it after his breakdown. His tears seemed to vanish almost instantly. This was a man who had been broken beyond repair. I smiled the best I could. "I am Reyenne Montgomery."

He nodded in understanding. "I would shake your hand if I could."

"As would I." I assured him.

He grinned, exposing missing and broken teeth encased in a bloody mouth. She had ruined this man. It enraged me. If not for his wounds he would have been quite handsome. His hair was black and his beard had streaks of brown. His eyes were the color of freshly made caramel and his skin was milk white.

He was underfed and had not had enough sleep. If she didn't kill him he would surely die from starvation or insomnia. I pitied him to the fullest extent, and yet worried about myself at the same time. Was this what she had planned for me? Would I be changed just as Rye for months?

He broke my useless thinking. "I am from America."

I studied his face. Where were we anyway? "England." I carelessly replied.

He nodded again. "Does this make us enemies?" he chuckled.

I grinned despite myself. "Perhaps."

He began to reply but was cut off by the hinges of the door creaking open. He immediately resumed his position of hanging his head limply and acting as if he was asleep. Tranquility slithered her way into the room, shaking her hips through the doorway.

She wore new attire. The dress she wore had long sleeves and a high collar. It billowed out at her hips and swept the floor with elegance. It was made entirely of black lace and was entirely see through. I could see the silk slip she wore under it perfectly.

This was a woman who was not accustomed to modesty, and did not find the latest trends worth her time. Her lips were dark red, from lipstick or nature I did not know. Her black hair hung in a loose braid down her back.

She turned and clapped her hands together in joy. "My humans! Oh, how lovely. Oberon, aren't they lovely?"

Oberon stepped through the door behind her, still making sure we could not see the outside world. The hand with which he grasped his spear was white from pressure. "Yes, my Queen."

She patted Asphodel on the head. "Please take him to the stables with the others."

Oberon bowed his head to her and took Asphodel's rope in his hand. "Yes, my Queen."

In record time he was out the door with the beast and gone. Tranquility smiled at us like a small girl would smile at her new doll. I tried my best not to make eye contact with her. She crossed the room and cupped Rye's face in her hand.

He flinched back as she examined the cuts and bruises she had made. It disgusted me, her look of hunger. She tilted his head this way and that, then finally let go and stood back. She acted as if she was examining a piece of art.

"This will not do." She tsked. She waved her hand in the air and his face immediately cleared of abuse. He was more handsome than I had imagined. His huge eyes scanned over her looking for signs of trickery, then settled into contentment. "There, that's better." She smiled.

Rye grimaced in return, trying his best to show delight. But we both knew she only did this so that she had a blank canvas. Tranquility turned to me next and with a whoosh of her hand my chains broke. I fell onto my hands and knees on the floor and stayed crouched there, awaiting her punishment.

"Up, darling." She cooed. I obeyed immediately, not wanting to upset this monster further. She hated me enough already for things out of my control. I glanced back at Rye who seemed casual. No doubt he was used to being left here while others were freed.

I dusted my torn dress the best I could, there was a huge gash in the fabric where Asphodel had punctured my side. Although there were was no sign of a wound. Tranquility clapped her hands together yet again. It was only then that I noticed her nails, or rather, claws. They were black and jagged, animal-like. My breathing became shallow.

"What are you going to do with me?" I questioned nervously.

Her eyes narrowed. "My dear, you do not ask questions here. This is my home, my territory. I speak, you listen." She stroked Rye's face. "Isn't that right, love?"

He nodded vigorously hoping to please her. It seemed to do the trick. She calmed down almost instantly. She was not after a play thing but submission. Her need to have power over people disgusted me. I couldn't relate to this in any shape or form. I was an advocate of equal rights.

She pulled her hands away from Rye and clasped them in front of her. In this position she almost looked innocent, young, even. Of course, she was physically young. I highly doubted she was very far out of her teens, but I had no idea what her actual age was.

"Now, Reyenne, if you would please follow me." It was not a question or a suggestion, but a command I was to obey.

She crossed the tiny room and opened the door enough for me to walk through. I followed, casting one last look at Rye who smiled sheepishly. Once I was in the hall Tranquility closed the door behind us. The scene wasn't what I expected to find at all.

I expected to walk right into a dining area where hundreds of fairies would be sitting ready to devour me piece by piece. Instead, I found myself in an ordinary hallway. The floor was still covered with dirt, the walls were white and glittering but cracked, and torches were set every few fight lighting the way.

Tranquility said nothing but started walking off into the direction of our destination. I silently followed, absorbing my surroundings, committing them to memory. I might need to escape from here.

There were wooden doors placed at odd intervals along our path, but I could hear anything from the other side. There seemed to be no one here except the two of us and Rye in a distant room.

The walk seemed to take forever. It was several minutes before we finally reached a set of stairs. Like the walls, they were white and the only light came from unwavering torches. Tranquility took each stair gracefully, her skirts sweeping behind her. I had to focus so as not to step on them.

I held back a gasp at the scene we walked in on. Fairies were everywhere, laughing, chatting, and gliding across the floor. Another large staircase stood to our far right, a black and gold carpet running up it. The only other piece of furniture in the enormous room was a chess table with two chairs.

Two fairies sat pondering over the glass pieces in front of them while their wings flapped soundlessly behind them. Tranquility entered the crowd and I followed close behind. I was frightened by my surroundings. I was in a den of animals, and I was the food.

The fairies closest to me seemed to sniff the air as I passed; their eyes would glow for a mere second before they would return to whatever they were doing. I stuck like glue to Tranquility's side until we reached the second staircase. I looked up to find a banister above us with even more fairies. As we ascended, rooms came into view and the fairies turned to stare at us.

They all bowed and did a strange hand gesture at Tranquility, she nodded her head in acknowledgment at each of them but no smile cracked her stoic face. I had never seen creatures of such beauty. It was hard not to admit this.

None of them seemed to have a flaw. Their faces were sculpted to perfection, their hair glistened, their pale skin seemed to glow. A few women had swept rouge across their cheeks which only enhanced their natural allure. If not for their wings, which were of all shapes, sizes and colors, I would think I was simply surrounded by models.

We reached the end of the long hall and Tranquility knocked on the last door. Only a few seconds passed before a petite woman opened it. She wore a brown plaid shirt that was buttoned all the way up, men's black trousers that stopped at her knee, white stockings that covered the rest of her legs, and small black buckled shoes.

Her hair was long, a dull brown, and fantastically wavy. She held a small snake in her left hand and the door frame in her right. "My Queen." She bowed low and almost dropped the snake which seemed to be slithering wildly trying to free itself from her grasp.

Tranquility did not bow in return or even nod her head. Instead, she shoved her way through the door and into the room. I followed unsure of what else to do. The woman shut the door behind us and placed the snake on the floor. It quickly slithered away to find a hiding place.

The entire room was gray and rather drab. A large circular window showed miles of forest outside, and small tornadoes of air whipped around flinging objects. My hair flew back from my face and I stepped aside when a shoe went sailing across the room.

Tranquility sat in one of the gray chairs next to a small table and gestured for me to sit in the other. I did so without a word. The woman stared at Tranquility obviously awaiting her orders. I was having a hard time trying to figure out if this woman was human or fairy.

She had no wings, and other than the small swirling bits of air, the entire room seemed normal. I folded my hand in my lap and awaited my next instructions.

Tranquility coughed and finally spoke, "Ebony Vail."

Ebony bowed, "Tranquility."

There was friction between them; it passed like a current between their bodies. I shivered, hoping that this would be over soon. Ebony shoved her hands into her pockets and stood with a small lean. Her body language matched that of a man's.

"I have a task for you." Tranquility continued.

Ebony seemed to ignore her statement and instead countered with her own question. "Where is my son?"

My heart beat rapidly; I finally understood who this woman was. This must be Ember's mother. She fit the description he had given me, and her hatred of Tranquility was obvious. I wanted nothing more than to hug her tightly and weep into her shoulder, but kept my composure. Just because she was sweet with Ember did not mean she would be with me.

Tranquility sighed and gripped her hands on the table. Her nails left small indents on the wood surface. "I told you, you will never see him again."

Ebony pulled her hands out of her pockets and set them on her hips. "You are keeping him in the same castle as me, and yet I cannot see him? What blasphemy is this? Do not punish me for his crimes! I want to see my son. I demand it, Tranquility Erasmus."

Tranquility stood, almost tipping her chair backwards. She pointed a finger at Ebony. "You dare command things from your ruler? How dare you! I should have you locked away in one of the dungeons. Perhaps the room where we keep our food." She tilted her nose down in disgust.

Ebony rolled her eyes, not at all phased by this threat. I silently commended her for her bravery. I could never do such a thing. "Do whatever it is you wish. As long as I see my son before you do so."

"What makes you think I will comply?" Tranquility inquired.

Ebony looked down, for the first time she seemed to be struggling with words. "H-he's my son. And I was your best friend."

Tranquility softened at this and sighed. "Fine." She gestured towards me. "Watch over her. I will be back momentarily."

We both watched as she left the room, chatter from the hall seeped in for a moment before the door was closed once again. Ebony had a wide grin plastered on her face at getting what she wanted. I stayed silent, not yet knowing how to act around this creature.

She bent over and picked her snake up once again, it slid across her fingers with ease. She whispered softly to it, words I could not hear or distinguish. They sounded a bit like Latin.

Finally, she glanced up at me. Her expression was one of shock. Had she already forgotten I was here? She hurried over to Tranquility's vacant seat and sat down. She rested an elbow on the table and the snake on her shoulder. She was grinning at me like a madwoman.

"So it is you. You are the woman my son has chosen." She acted delighted at this prospect.

I turned to face her and cautiously rested my hands on the cool table. "Your son is Ember?"

Her smile grew wider. "Ember Sky, yes, that's him. That's my love. Of course, I am not his biological mother, but I am his Mayhem Fairy mother."

I crinkled my nose at this. Of course she wasn't his biological mother. She actually looked to be younger than him. "So, you are on our side?"

"Your side?" she repeated the question in confusion. "Why, of course, my dear. I simply want my son to be happy, and if he has found happiness with you, so be it. You seem lovely."

I blushed at her compliments. I felt a strange trust for her. "That's nice to hear. Thank you."

The smile disappeared from her face. "But, you are human. That presents a problem."

"So you are a fairy too?" The question seemed ridiculous once it was out. It hadn't sounded nearly as stupid in my head.

Without a moment's hesitation two purple wings shot out of her back and a ring around her pupil radiated violet. I did not gasp or reel back like I had countless times before at this. I was growing accustomed to watching seemingly normal people slide multicolored steel from their spines.

She tapped her nails on the table and retracted her wings. Her eyes went back to their dull brown and she sighed in frustration. "We need to get you out of here."

Before I could register what she had said she jumped up and scurried to the far wall. A small shelf held many vials of strangely colored liquids. She shuffled through them, looking for whatever she suddenly needed.

Glass clinked against glass and the contents of each vial swished as she moved them aside. A small vial filled with yellow liquid toppled over and Ebony cursed under her breath. Smoke erupted from the fluid and filled the room with an obnoxious gas.

Ebony flapped it away as she continued to look. "Ah!" she cried in delight. "Yes, here it is." She pulled a slender vial from the very back of the shelf. The liquid inside seemed to bubble and churn on its own. She made her way back over to me and placed it in my hand.

I kept it a good distance from my body, afraid of what it might do if I somehow spilled it on my clothing. "What is this?" I questioned.

"This will make your eyes like ours. It will make a ring around the pupil glow whatever color it chooses for you." She fiddled with her hands as she spoke. "I need you to drink it so that we can walk through the castle to safety. The others will think nothing of it if they can see your eyes. No need for wings. Although..." she trailed off.

Before I could protest she was back at the shelf shifting through the vials. She found the one she wanted this time much more quickly and brought it over. This vial was rather large and the contents were milky white. It almost looked as if she had somehow stuck a cloud in a glass jar.

She too handed me this. I twirled both vials in my palms, staring at the contents. "And this?"

"Will give you wings." She finished.

My mouth hung open in surprise. "W-wings?"

She nodded vigorously. "Yes! Now, drink up. We haven't much time."

She took a step back and waited for me to spill the foreign contents into my mouth. I carefully set the wing potion down and stared at the other. The fluid continued to bubble and burst at the surface. I closed my eyes and downed the contents in a single gulp.

It tasted bitter and foul. I squinted and shook my head, trying to expel the taste from my mouth. Ebony didn't say a word, she only stared and waited. I reached my hand out to grasp the second vial but before I could pain shot through my eyes.

It was as if daggers were being stabbed repeatedly straight into the windows of my soul. I pressed my palms into them and allowed them to water. My teeth ground together in agony. I caught myself wondering if I had gotten the right impression from Ebony. For all I knew she had just poisoned me.

I banished the thought from my mind. This woman was the mother of my beloved. If he trusted her, then so could I. The scorching in my eyes dulled down enough for me to quickly consume the second vial.

I awaited sharp pains in my back, or a throbbing sensation, but nothing came. I sat perfectly still, wondering if the effects of this potion took longer than the last. But suddenly, with an unbearable pule, wings erupted from my back.

I felt my skin tear and blood leak down the back of my now even further destroyed dress. A weight like I had never carried before bore down on me, and the world spun. Ebony stepped back in shock, horror, or delight.

I stood to the best of my abilities and peered into her looking glass. My eyes were fully dilated with a single red line that seemed to radiate from the abyss. And standing on either side of me were enormous black wings. They towered above my small frame and made me seem even frailer than I had.

It was grotesque yet alluring. Ebony scurried to the side of the room where her bed lay. She dug through a chest and brought out a small pail of paint and a brush. I furrowed my brow at her. Surely there was nothing else that needed to be done. Was there?

She pushed me back into the seat without comment and began to swiftly glide the brush now coated in blue paint across my new wings. She whispered under her breath again, her mouth was set in a grim line. It quite frankly concerned me.

"Why are you painting them?" I inquired.

She was nearly done with one wing. Her speeds were obviously very inhuman. She paused for a moment to glance at me then went back to swiping the brush across the hard feathers. The paint dried instantly. "This is very peculiar. Very peculiar, indeed. It will raise more questions than we are ready for."

I shifted in my chair uncomfortably at her comment. "What do you mean? I look like one of you now. Surely there are no other problems."

She made her way to the other wing and began painting. Her entire arm looked like a blur from her swift movements. She mumbled a bit more before replying, "I have never seen black wings on anyone except Tranquility."

"But... these are fake. It does not matter." I airily replied.

She shook her head. "But it does. Those potions are especially designed to show you, if you were created, what you would look like. If she suddenly decided to turn you, your wings would be black and your eyes would be red." She hesitated then spoke again. "That is most curious... most curious, indeed."

She finished with her painting and returned the bucket to its original place. I once again looked at my reflection but no longer liked what I saw. It seemed wrong to me somehow. Not the idea that I suddenly had wings but that they were a light blue instead of a coal.

Ebony gently set a cloak on my shoulders and clasped it at my throat. There were already slits cut into the back to accommodate my newest additions. She let her arms fall limply to her side and strode across the room. Her face still gave away that she was still pondering over the wing color.

I followed close behind; not wanting to get lost in the throng of people I knew was right outside the door. She sighed and swung the door open as wide as she could. The fairies lingering in the hall did not seem to notice the newest people.

She ambled through the people, careful not to hit any of them with her girlish wings. I, on the other hand, was not having an easy time. While no one was staring rudely at me this time, they were complaining when my wing accidentally touched their flesh and blood began leaking from their bodies.

I apologized shyly several times before we descended the stairs and exited into a great hall. Gruesome works of art lined the walls and chandeliers hung above us. Solid wax hung suspended from them, giving an eerie cast. Ebony beckoned me forward and we rushed away from the noise of chatter.

Our feet clomped softly on the marble floor and went completely silent when we padded across carpet. Two large doors came into view. I was sweating under the weight of my wings and the paint was beginning to chip off. I hoped these doors led to a great beyond.

Ebony's pace quickened and I followed suit. We were so close, just a few feet away. I would be back to my mother and sister in no time. I could sleep in my own bed, watch snow fall from my own window, and eat at my own table. My heart was elated in joy.

Ebony reached out to grasp the enormous gold handle. Her fingers slid with ease around the intricately carved "M." I wanted to shout in bliss. I was finally going home! I could forget any of this ever happened, move on with my life, start a family. This would all be but a distant memory, a dream.

"HALT!"

The shout sent chills down my spine. My happiness deflated like a balloon that had been popped. Ebony reared back, I almost slammed into her. She pulled her hand from the glittering handle and turned. "Damn." She whispered.

I closed my eyes, willing myself not to cry, then rotated to see my tormentor. Tranquility treaded down the hall towards us. Her hair glinted under the dull light of the candles; every crinkle of her frown was shadowed. She had changed into a gold and black silk dress that covered her like fluid.

Her shoes clinked against the floor with purpose. A shiver disgorged throughout me. Goose bumps lined my exposed flesh and I felt my hair stand on end. This was it. She was going to kill me... and Ebony for helping me. How many more people was I going to hurt before I ended this all?

Tranquility stopped a few paces away and gingerly set her hands on her hips. This seemed to be her signature stature. Ebony stared straight at her from my side. She didn't seem in the least frightened of her.

I tried to mimic her bravery but ended up with a coward's hunch. Tranquility's frown deepened at my appearance. She had just noticed the wings and eyes that masked my human looks. Her eyes darted between Ebony and I, and it finally registered what had happened.

Her smirk was tantalizing. I wanted to rip it off her face. "What do you think you are doing?" she bellowed.

I flinched at her words. Ebony did not seem in the least affected. "We are leaving."

Tranquility's demeanor briefly changed from anger to shock before she gained her composure. She was obviously not expecting such a straightforward answer to her question. I wanted to giggle at Ebony's attitude, but refrained for fear of being slaughtered.

"Did I not ask you to stay in your room with our... guest?" she quizzed.

"Did I not ask to see my son?" Ebony countered.

Tranquility nodded her head at this. "Touché. But I still see that as no excuse to defy your queen. Especially when it requires meddling in affairs you are not part of."

Her hand shot from her side faster than I could blink. My feet were sliding across the slick floor without my consent. I struggled to fight against it; I looked back at Ebony as if willing her to help me. But she was frozen in place, quite literally, her eyes locked straightforward.

"P-please!" I begged as I got closer to the monster.

She sneered and faced her palm out. I stopped moving completely. My limbs were locked in their place and my eyes would not move for me to see where Tranquility was going as she strode around me. She tsked every now and then resumed her place in front of me.

"What possessed you to become a fictional character?" It was a rhetorical question, I couldn't answer. My lips were glued together. "How dare you, a pathetic human, pretend to be one of us."

Her arms flung out and my makeshift wings were savagely ripped from my flesh. My knees protested the restraint; they wanted to buckle under my weight. My eyes burned from unshed tears. The pain was excruciating. I hadn't a clue how I was still conscious. Blackness lingered at the edges of my vision but did not consume.

She moved her arm in a casual gesture and my mind jumped wondering if she would tear my eyes from their sockets next. But she did no such thing. Instead, she leaned over and picked one of the severed wings from the ground.

Her hands were cut open as she examined it but she paid no mind. Before anything but a trickle of gold could escape, the wounds would heal themselves to perfection. She peeled the blue paint back from the black wing and her brow furrowed in anger or curiosity.

"Ebony." She called in a smaller voice, and almost frightened one. Ebony came to life behind me. She gasped for air and her knees hit the floor with a thud. I wanted to turn to check on her, to see if she was okay, but I was still frozen.

I listened as Ebony stood back up. "Yes?"

Tranquility ignored that she had failed to add "my queen" at the end of her response. All of her attention was consumed by peeling paint off the wing. Flakes of pale blue littered the white floor. "What is this?"

Ebony didn't miss a beat. "A wing."

I found myself again wanting to giggle at Ebony's blunt sarcasm. Ember had failed to mention she was like this. He claimed she was serious.

Tranquility ignored this comment, too. She ran her hand over the feathers, leaving a gold trail behind. "It's black."

"Yes." Ebony simply replied.

It was obvious she knew what Tranquility was getting at but did not want to play into her game. She was making herself the one in charge of the conversation. I respected her wit. Tranquility was, again, too engrossed to notice this.

She finally looked up. "Why is it black?"

"Well..." I heard Ebony teeter back and forth on her feet. "I guess that's her color."

"But how?" she questioned but did not wait for a response. The wing fell from her grasp with a loud clatter. "OBERON!" she screamed.

It was a few heartbeats before he appeared from down the hall. A black chain was held in his grasp; at the end of it was Ember. His head was hung low, his hair stringy, and his clothes dirtier than I had ever seen them.

I wished I could move. I wished I could embrace him and tell him how sorry I was for getting him into this mess. But instead I stayed still under Tranquility's powers. And Oberon slowly made his way down the long hall with Ember at his side.

Ages passed before they finally made it to Tranquility. Ember did not move from his hunched position. He had the aura of a defeated man. My heart bled.

Tranquility shoved Oberon aside and stood in front of Ember. She grabbed his chin roughly and made him look at her. I had never seen his eyes so dead to his surroundings. He still had not caught a glimpse of me. "Where did you get it?"

A puzzled look crossed his face then disappeared. He had decided to no longer care. "Get what?" His voice was raspy and dull. Nothing like the enchanting melody I was used to.

"The poison! Where did you get it? Did you steal it? Have you betrayed me for a final time?" He flinched from her yelling in his face.

"I don't have any poison." He responded.

She let go of his chin and reared back. I heard Ebony run forward but it was too late. Tranquility had slapped Ember across the face as hard as she could. Four jagged cuts lined his cheek in her wake. They oozed golden blood down his face and stained his already ragged shirt.

Tears welled in his eyes but he banished them quickly. He sniffed then defiantly plastered his uncaring face back on. "You have it. You've taken it."

He sighed and almost rolled his eyes but caught himself. "I don't even know what you're talking about."

She screeched at this but made no move to strike him again. "Oberon!"

Oberon who had been lazily laying against the wall, no doubt accustomed to her outbursts, snapped to attention. "Yes, my queen?"

"Go check the Throne Room."

"Yes, my Queen." He made haste in leaving the scene. His shiny boots clanked against the floor until he disappeared from sight.

Tranquility wheeled on Ebony. Her anger was obviously shifting. I was almost relieved to be frozen and apparently thrown from her thoughts. "You said the Kingdom Poison was safe in your possession. You lied. Again, you lied. You have betrayed me!"

Ebony, who was now in my vision, shifted her demeanor. Her hair had come loose and her clothing was much baggier than I had originally noticed. She was a very modest woman. "Will you stop?! Not everyone is out to get you! The Kingdom Poison is safely put away, as you will know when Oberon returns. No one wants your damn position!"

If I could have gasped I would have. Ebony's bravery seemed to dissolve into stupidity. Tranquility was going to lash out at her for these remarks, and I didn't want to be forced to witness it.

But Tranquility did no such thing. Her face contorted into a rage but her body did not follow suit. "You know nothing of ruling a race, Ebony Vail."

"I know enough!" she retorted. "I have watched as you dealt with problem after problem. And you handled them all horribly! You killed your own people, you made them hate you, you spit on the title of Queen. And yet I stood next to you through it all and you threw me away, too."

I suddenly felt as if I was in the middle of something I should not be. This was beginning to run deeper than it was originally intended. I felt like an intruder on an intimate conversation. I wished I could at least cast down my eyes as Ember had.

Before Tranquility could respond, Oberon thankfully clanked his way back down the hall. Tranquility swiveled on her heel, disregarding Ebony, and awaited him. He stopped in front of her, his armor clanking to a halt. "My queen."

"Yes?" she urged him on.

"It is safe."

She sighed in contentment, not at all embarrassed or ashamed by her ridiculous outburst. "Thank you."

He nodded and returned to his position near the wall. Tranquility finally faced me. Her eyes glimmered and I was set free from my invisible bonds. I fell to the ground gasping. It felt as if I had been underwater for ages.

I wasn't allowed to get my bearings though. I was thrown into the air by an invisible force. I looked up through my mess of hair to see Tranquility with her hand pointed towards me. "I haven't any idea what game you are playing, human, but I will find out."

I didn't know what she was talking about. She was threatening me over something I had no knowledge of. I glanced at Ember who was painfully staring at me. He wanted to help, I could tell by his expression. I silently willed him to stay out of the way. It seemed to work.

Ebony was not the same though. She stubbornly stood up to the queen. "Put her down, Tranquility."

I lingered in the air, my breath held, as Tranquility shifted her gaze to her long time best friend. "Stay out of it."

"I cannot stay out of it when you harm my family." She retorted.

Tranquility seemed taken aback by this statement. She unintentionally loosened her grip on me and I fell. Ember came out of his trance long enough to leap to my rescue. Instead of landing on the fatal marble, I landed on him. Out of breath I reached up and kissed him without thinking.

His lips were as always cold under mine. I smiled and he smiled too. Our surroundings seemed to vanish, but then I heard Tranquility in the distance. "Your family? You have no family, Ebony."

I stood, still in Ember's arms, and watched as another argument ensued. "If Ember loves her, she is now my family."

Tranquility scoffed. "Ember is not your real son! Do you forget? You have no connection to either of them!"

Ebony folded her arms, not at all phased by this comment. Ember tensed behind me. I swiveled around on my heel, looking for a path of escape. If we could leave while they were arguing, we would have a head start.

There was a door just a few feet behind us. I began shoving Ember back. A look of confusion shot across his face, then he too saw the door. We slowly edged our way backwards.

"I created him, Tranquility! It is in your rules that the creator should treat their creation as their offspring! " Ebony shouted.

We were in reaching distance of the door now. Ember slowly turned the handle. It opened with a faint click. "There is a difference between creating a fairy and having legitimate blood."

Ember pulled the door open slowly and shoved me inside. Immediately all conversation was muffled. He shut the door behind us and we were encased in darkness. I reached my hand out for him and he grabbed it.

"What now?" I whispered.

He paused before speaking. "I... I don't know." He stroked my cheek with his icy hand. "I don't want her to hurt you."

"Should we run?" I looked around, trying to see anything in the pitch black.

He muffled a laugh with his hand. "It seems we are in a storage closet, my dear."

"Oh." My newfound hope seeped out of me. We had just trapped ourselves. I let go of his hand and made my way across the room. My legs bumped into common cleaning supplies. Brooms, buckets, and piles of rags. I hadn't expected a superior race to own such things.

I made my way back to Ember and wrapped my arms tightly around him. His arms gently laced their way around my torso. "What are we going to do? We've trapped ourselves."

He sighed in my ear; cool breath tickled the hairs on my neck. "No. We're safe for now. She'll think we somehow made our way to the gate. I know her."

I pulled back. "How do you know her so well?"

He hesitated before speaking; I could almost feel the shame emanating from him. "The Kingdom Poison she was speaking of, I have it."

I gasped. "Y-you stole it?"

"No!" he almost shouted in response. "It is in my tears, in my blood. I was created with it. It means... it means I am to be King next to Tranquility."

I furrowed my brow at this news. "Then that means... you are destined to be with her."

He let go of me and stepped back. I wrapped my arms around myself, I was suddenly shivering. This had all been for naught.

Juniper dying, my being ripped from my family... everything. I could not be with him.

"I do not want to be with her." He replied, moving closer to me. I took a step back. "I love you, only you. I would rather die than become her mate."

I nodded my head. I believed him. "But how will this work? She will kill me and marry you. That will be the end of this all."

He placed his hands on my shoulders, this time I didn't back away. I wanted nothing more than to lean into his touch. I wished we were back in my room, cuddled together under the covers. "I don't know, but we will figure it out. I won't let her win, Reyenne. I promise."

Thirteen

I yawned and stretched my limbs. I had just had the most terrifying dream. I was trapped in a castle with a blood thirsty woman, and she was after me. I had been hiding in a storage closet with Ember. I turned and put my arm on his chest.

But no. We were in bed. I smiled to myself. Ember shifted under my touch and turned into me. I outlined his lips with my finger in the darkness. It must still be early morning. A crash from upstairs brought me out of my thoughts. I cursed Honour under my breath... then realized, we didn't have an upstairs.

I shot up and took in my surroundings, which weren't much. The only light came from a small crack under the door. It lit up the bristles of a broom, the wood of a bucket, and our feet covered in several dirty rags.

I wanted to weep. It wasn't a nightmare after all, this was all really happening. I tried my best to brush through my hair with my fingers. I probably looked frightful. I was still wearing the same clothing, rips and all, and I knew I must have dirt covering my flesh.

Ember rolled away from me. I could see the outline of his back. His shirt was stained with gold blood and his hair was a matted mess like mine. I couldn't help but think this was all my fault. I should have sent him away for good when he told me what he was.

Tranquility would have never found out I knew, and I would still be safely with my family. Ember could have married the queen like he was destined to, and I would have married some man my mother gave me to.

Everything would have been as it should have been. Tears trailed down my grimy cheeks. I tried to banish them but the more I tried to stop, the harder I cried. I covered my face with my hands and let everything out. I heard Ember between my sobs as he rose, then felt his hand on my back.

He started to speak but I suddenly felt sick. I quickly scurried over to the wooden bucket and emptied the remaining contents of my stomach. Ember stood next to me and pulled my hair away from my face. I blindly tried to push him away, knowing he could see better than I in the dark. I did not want him to see me like this.

"It's alright." He cooed behind me.

Sobs and dry heaves racked my entire body. My stomach clenched in pain as it tried to dispel whatever it could. My body finally seemed to realize there was nothing left to rid itself of and I stopped. I turned and leaned against the wall, I clutched my stomach with my hand.

Rivulets of sweat dripped down my face. I caressed my belly with my hand, sharp pains emanated from it. That was when I realized my abdomen was protruding a bit. I looked down although I could not see anything. I pressed my dress tightly to me and felt my swollen belly.

It could not be. My eyes widened in horror and shock. Ember and I had, of course, embraced as lovers often do, but I had always used medicine. I had used every remedy Juniper had told me of to ensure this did not happen.

Ember laid his arm across my shoulder. I had almost forgotten he was sitting next to me. I let go of my dress and let it hide the bump. He must not know. I could be mistaken. I placed my head on his shoulder and sighed deeply. Things had just grown much more complicated.

"I have an idea." He whispered into my ear.

I sat up and tried to look at him. I could see the outline of his pupil as always, but nothing more. "What?" I questioned.

"The gate, I want you to go through it. There is a small building that used to be used for guards about a mile into the woods. You just have to follow the path leading from the castle and keep walking straight. At this time of morning there should be no one out there, and the building has been long deserted. I want you to stay there while I try to talk to Tranquility." He explained.

I shook my head vigorously. "I am not going without you!"

He smoothed my hair from my face. I was growing nauseous again. The smell of my own vomit permeated the air. "This is our only chance. If I go with you she will just come after us over and over. Her anger will grow with each obstacle we face her with. I must speak to her. If she will not let me go, she may let you."

Tears welled in my eyes once again. I was growing tired of crying. "What will she do to you?"

He leaned in closer to me, our noses were almost touching. "She will do nothing to me. She wouldn't dare. Especially if she believes I will take the throne next to her."

The front gate opened without a sound or problem. I kept my eyes on Ember until it closed then turned to face the outdoors. I almost expected to be ambushed on the spot, but no such thing happened. I placed both hands on my belly in protection then dropped them. I would not do this. I would get rid of it somehow.

I straightened my shoulders and made my way down the marble stairs and onto the wooden path. My shoes clacked softly on the surface, but other than that, there was no sound. A deep worry had settled in my heart for Ember. I was afraid of what Tranquility might do once she realized he had let me out of the castle.

I shook the thoughts from my head. No. Ember was right. She would not harm him as long as she thought he wanted to be her mate. Hopefully, he presented a convincing enough case to her.

Snow littered the ground in small patches and the wind was not on my side. I shivered under my scraps of clothing and once again placed a hand on my abdomen. I jerked it away almost immediately. "Stop it, Reyenne." I furiously whispered to myself. I had more important things to worry about.

The wooden walk went on forever. I crossed plank after plank and made it nowhere. I turned to look at the castle behind me and saw that it was indeed growing smaller. I just wished this journey went a bit faster. I did not want to be stuck with my own thoughts for too long.

The woods came into view after several more minutes of walking. My legs were cramping up and my fingers were turning blue. I hurried into the trees and began searching for the building. Ember had said it was only a mile or so into the trees.

I stumbled over roots and branches until I finally came upon it. I groaned in despair. I had been hoping that the building, like the castle, would be extravagant and warm. But what greeted me was a rundown wooden shack with a door falling off its hinges.

I sighed and made my way to it. Luckily the inside was not entirely bad. Wind whistled through cracks in the wood and everything was covered in a film of dust, but other than that it seemed quite alright. I pulled the door closed to the best of my ability and secured it with a piece of rope I found on the floor.

It somewhat protected me from the harsh conditions outside. I scavenged through the small, broken cupboards for food and blankets. There was one can of mush and a single, moth eaten blanket. I tossed the food aside for when I was really hungry and hunched in the corner under the blanket.

I closed my eyes and tried to sleep. I had no clue when Ember would come for me, or if he ever would. I just hoped he was okay. I hoped that Tranquility hadn't hurt him over me. I couldn't live with myself if she did.

I was stuck somewhere between being asleep and awake. My body felt at rest but my mind was racing over a million possibilities. What if Ember never came to get me? I would die in this little building with no one around. They would find my skeleton years from now.

I shoved these thoughts from my head and rubbed my stomach once again. I had given up telling myself not to. There was no other explanation, I was pregnant. I tried to think back to when it could have happened.

It had been months since I was last intimate with him. That meant I could be halfway through my pregnancy by now! The idea frightened me. Not only was I going to die, but this child inside me was too. I really was bringing everyone down with me.

I traced my fingers over the small bump, which I realized in the light wasn't that small at all. In fact, it protruded a nice distance from where my stomach usually was. I laid my head back against the rough wood and once again tried to fall asleep.

I had just begun to doze off when I heard a sharp cackle. My eyes shot open in terror and I clambered to my feet, ready to die fighting. But instead of Tranquility standing before me, it was a small boy. He could be no older than Honour and had brown hair that hung in his eyes.

He wore a vest that was too large for him with tight black pants and buckled shoes. His face was twisted into a sardonic smile and he was staring at my stomach. I grabbed the blanket and covered myself. He laughed again, the noise pierced the silence.

"Who are you?" I trembled.

He pointed at my stomach. "Pregnant, are you?"

I clutched the blanket tighter. "H-how did you know?"

He rolled his eyes, his eyelashes catching on his hair and flipping it out of the way the slightest bit. They gleamed orange and yellow, he was one of them. I should have guessed.

"Well, it's rather obvious, isn't it, love? Most women don't go around sporting protruded stomachs without a cause... and you don't look like the liquor type to me." He giggled.

I pressed my back against the wall and kept my eyes glued to him. He paced back and forth across the small shack and fidgeted with his hands like he couldn't stay focused. "W-what do y-you want with me?"

He snapped his fingers and turned to face me once again. "Ah, now that is the question. Ha-ha!"

I crinkled my nose at this. "You're insane."

In the blink of an eye he was across the room with his hands pressed into my shoulders. I stopped breathing. His eyes peered deeply into mine and I realized no breath escaped from his lips or nose. "No human calls me insane, love." He pulled a hand back and placed it on my stomach. "Wouldn't want anything to happen to the child now, would you? Ha-ha!"

He stepped back and I exhaled. "I'm sorry." I sincerely apologized.

He waved it away like he had not just threatened my child's life over my statement. "I am not here to harm you, rest assured. I am here on Ember's orders."

My heart fluttered alive in my chest at his words. Ember had sent this lunatic to save me. That meant he must have won Tranquility over. It had taken him no time at all! I should have not doubted him as I had.

"Then I am free? We are out of harm's way?" I inquired hopefully.

He gazed at me. "Free? Ha-ha! You will never be free, especially now that you have that... creation in your stomach. Ember has simply told me to take you to Ebony Vail's room so that she may watch over you. He no longer thinks it wise for you to be out here alone while he is in the dungeon."

"The dungeon?!" I gasped.

He laughed at my reaction, it angered me deeply. "Did you really expect Tranquility to listen, love?"

I hung my head low. "No... I suppose I didn't."

He held his hand out and giggled at himself. "Then shall we go?"

I strode across the room in confidence. If Ember trusted this man then I should too. I placed my hand delicately in his and he pulled me towards him with a roughness I did not expect. In a flash we were standing in Ebony's room.

It was just as I had left it. Everything was gray, her snake was slithering across the floor, and chatter could be heard from the other side of the door. The boy let go of my hand and turned to leave. "Wait!" I called.

He turned on his heel and stared at me. "Yes, love?"

"What is your name?"

"Oh! Ha-ha! It seems I have forgotten it myself in all the chaos... Dravven Chaos." He cackled and disappeared through the door.

Dravven Chaos. Ember had told me about him. He had said he was the opposite of Ebony, yet they got along. He was a man I could trust. I exhaled, not having realized I was holding my breath in anticipation of a disaster. Ebony did not seem to be in the room yet. I sat down in the chair I had occupied before and awaited her.

Hours went by; I dozed off in the chair, and would wake at every sound outside the door. Ebony was clearly not coming to my rescue. I worried that she had perhaps been taken by Tranquility as Ember had.

I didn't know what to do. I couldn't leave the room without risk of being spotted by one of the fairies standing outside. They would rip me to shreds and feast on me. I decided to wait; someone would eventually come, even if that someone wasn't Ebony Vail.

The door opened moments later. I jumped to my feet expecting Tranquility instead of Ebony, but got someone entirely different. It was Dravven. I bit my lip hoping I had not trusted him too soon. He carried with him an abundance of fabrics and other sewing materials. I furrowed my brow.

"Where is Ebony?" I asked as he set his supplies on her bed.

He dragged a hand down his face, he seemed weary. "Taken, love. But I am not here to discuss such things. I am here to construct a Creation Gown."

He began pulling fabrics out of his pile and lay them aside. The most predominant color was light pink. I crossed the room to stand near him, making sure there was enough distance between us to run. "A what?"

He stayed focused on removing the light pink fabric from his pile then turned to open a trunk. Inside were hundreds of different shaped diamonds. He began pulling different pieces out. "A Creation Gown, love. She is going to turn you."

I shook my head in confusion and backed away a step. "She... what? Who's going to do what, Dravven?"

He set the diamonds on his fabric, and pulled string and a needle from his vest. He thread it in record time and produced a stool for me to stand on from nowhere. He took my hand and ushered me onto it, I obeyed, my mind still spinning.

"Tranquility has decided it would be best if you were brought into Mayhem, love." He giggled although it seemed rather somber. "I am here to make your Creation Gown, which is what the women of our race wear when they are created."

"S-she's going to turn me into... one of y-you?" I stuttered.

He scoffed at this. "Well, don't seem too excited about it, love! I am not a monster! Just a victim of my nature."

A thought occurred to me. "Will I be able to be with Ember if this happens?"

He stopped gathering fabric and faced me. It was as serious as I had seen him so far. "That, I do not know." He whispered. "Now!" he dropped the fabric on the floor near me along with the diamonds. "I am afraid I must ask you to take those rags off, love."

I paused. I was to undress in front of this man? What an absurd idea. I crossed my arms over my chest. I may be a lot of things but a harlot was not one. "I cannot," I stated.

He giggled. "You are telling me, love, you can become pregnant before marriage but cannot undress for a tailor who can no longer feel desire?"

I paused to think this over. He was right. My mistakes were beyond fantasy creatures and deaths. I had messed up my life long ago. I quickly pulled my dress off and stood in my undergarments. I felt extremely uncomfortable on a pedestal while a man stared at me.

He didn't say word, but pulled a string from his vest and began measuring different parts of my body. He started at my neck; he wrapped the string around my skin and hummed to himself. Every now and then he would randomly laugh at this own thoughts but I was growing accustomed to it.

Next, my arms. He placed the string against my armpit and pulled it down the length of my arm, the string elongated to get my full measurement. I stared at it in wonder. When he measured my stomach I cringed. There was no way I could wear a corset with my protruding abdomen.

He finished with my legs then began sewing furiously. His hand moved as a blur. I tried to keep up but it was impossible. He continued to hum and cackle at random intervals; his eyes would even glow at unexpected times. Perhaps he truly was insane.

After no more than ten minutes a beautiful light pink dress was presented to me. The top was tight while the bottom flowed with sheer fabric. It was absolutely lovely. I would have died for this dress at one point, and now I may die in it. It was strange how fast things could change.

He slipped it over my head and produced a three sided full length mirror in front of me. I gasped at my reflection. I looked like a horror in an expensive dress. My hair was tangled and sticking up at odd angles, and my skin was covered in dirt and blood.

"Oh, Dravven!" I cried. "I cannot wear this while I look like this! I am going to ruin your dress."

"Nonsense, love." With a snap of his fingers all the grime was off my skin and my brown hair was in soft curls down my back. I let out a cry of shock. I was not yet used to these powers. "I have just a few last minute touches."

He pulled his thread and needle back out and gathered the diamonds he had pulled out before. Yet again with an inhuman speed he sewed them onto my hip in the shape of a glittering flower. For a moment I forgot this dress sealed my doom. I was too swept up in the richness of it all.

I had not grown up in a wealthy household; I was used to my mother sewing my clothing for me. This was a completely new concept to me. I wanted to relish it but for a moment. "Dravven, this is gorgeous. You do lovely work." I commented once he had stepped back. I turned this way and that, admiring myself in the mirror.

He laughed. "Your belly can still be seen. I am afraid there is nothing I can do about that, love." He seemed to apologize.

"It is no matter." I responded. "There is not much that can be done about that.

"Oh, but there is." A voice replied from across the room.

I swiveled on my heel to see who had spoken. I almost fell off the stool when I saw who the voice belonged to. Tranquility leaned against the bed-frame, her hand gracefully on her hip. I silently cursed her. I did not want anyone to know of the creature growing inside me.

Damn this woman for being able to appear anywhere she wanted, when she wanted to. Now what was I to do? Dravven had backed away bowing to his Queen. He would be no help to me. They were all under her rule, under her spell, but I was not.

I stepped down from the stool, careful not to step on my newly made dress. Tranquility crossed the room to meet me. She towered over me in height, but I was not letting her scare me once again.

"What do you want from me?" I asked fearlessly.

"Oh." She cocked her head. "Brave now, are we?"

I glanced down, ready to bolt at any second, but kept my façade. "I have just decided I no longer should be frightened of you."

"Dravven, leave us." She commanded over my shoulder. Dravven disappeared from the room in a flash, leaving all his belongings behind. I felt completely alone, my bravery wavered.

My body urged me to take a step back but instead I took one forward. "You cannot hurt me."

"I can't?" she feigned innocence.

"No. You wouldn't dare harm the offspring of Ember, even if it means letting me go." I countered.

She reached a hand out and placed it on my stomach. I cringed inwardly. I didn't want her touching me. She didn't seem to notice the look of disgust that crossed my face; if she did she gave no acknowledgement.

"Girl, six months along." She stated then removed her hand.

My eyes welled with water at her words. I was going to have a daughter. And in three months! How could I have been so naïve to my own body? But then I considered all that had been going on. It was no wonder I had not realized.

"So, that is it." I replied. "You cannot create me or harm me now that I am pregnant with Ember's child."

"Oh?" she tsked. "Don't be so sure, dear."

Before I could reply with a snippy comment, she had reached her hand out and plunged it into my stomach. My eyes widened and I screamed in pain. My knees buckled and I fell. I could clearly feel her hand churning my guts. Her icy fingers grasped in my womb.

She retracted her hand and I slid onto my side, holding my organs in. She held a red mass in her hand that resembled a small human. But it had two spindly wings attached to its back. She gazed down at it in wonder then it disappeared.

My vision was growing hazy. I watched as my blood pooled around me. A ferocious banging was coming from the door, along with cries of blood and human. The other fairies had smelt me. I watched through a glaze as Tranquility crossed the room and opened the door. "There is nothing here for you, mongrels. Leave us!" she shouted.

They backed away from their queen, bowing all the way, and she closed the door on them. I reached a shaky hand out towards her, trying to yank her down to my level. She easily side stepped me and pulled one of the chairs toward my body. My arm splashed in my own blood.

"Do not fret. I will heal you soon enough. I just want you to suffer a bit for your arrogance." She smiled. She shaped her hands into a steeple in front of her and watched me with excited eyes.

"M-my b-baby." I croaked.

"Oh, do not worry over that monster. She is perfectly safe. I will simply implant her in one of my loyal subjects so that she may grow in our world. You should be happy for her. I am giving her a life you never could." She smiled.

I tried to rise in anger but feebly fell back down; my blood splashed into my face and coated the dress Dravven had carefully put together. Everything was going terribly wrong. This was not how it was supposed to happen.

My vision blackened. I was dying. Was she truly going to save me? Or was that just another lie from her lips? My body went limp; I decided to succumb to the darkness. It was better than having to live in a world where she existed.

I struggled to take my last breath, but right as I exhaled a gust of wind was forced down my throat. I choked and coughed on it, I even tried to dispel it from my body. It spread through every nook and cranny of my flesh and breathed life back into me.

I sat up, no longer in any pain. I felt my stomach for signs of damage but there were none. Then, with a sound like a drink being sucked through a straw, all my blood disappeared from the floor. My dress was still torn and I was a complete mess again, but I was alive.

I didn't know whether to cry in despair or joy. Did I want to be alive? I caught a glimpse of my scars that littered my wrist.

No, I wanted to live. I needed to live. Ember, and now my child, needed me. If I couldn't help them now, then I would help them eventually.

Fourteen

"There, love. Back to perfection." Dravven giggled and smiled.

I tried to smile back but it just didn't quite make it. There was no way out of this. Tranquility was going to make me into one of them. I was going to be a monster, and my daughter wouldn't even know who I was. Nor her father.

I began to weep uncontrollably. I sat down on the pedestal and wiped my eyes with the back of my hand. "I-I'm sorry, Dravven. The dress is b-beautiful. This is just so h-hard." I cried.

He knelt next to me and placed a hand on my leg. "Now, now, love. Everything will work out for the best, I assure you." He cackled but quickly suppressed it.

I sniffled and stared at him. "How do you know?"

He glanced away for a moment then back to me. "I have been around a very long time. If there is one thing I have learned, it is that Tranquility rarely ever gets everything she wants. Someone always comes along and ruins it for her and she has to start all over again." He patted my leg. "It will work out, love."

He stood and gathered his things with a twist of his wrist. I stayed on the stool which he so generously did not take and watched him as he walked from the room. Before he closed the door he turned to look at me one more time. "And I am accidentally leaving this door unlocked. Oops!" He cackled and vanished.

I jumped into action. I had to leave; I had to get out of here. I would disappear off the map. I could go to Paris, or Holland, or even America! The possibilities ran through my head rapidly. I did not have to stay enslaved here; I did not have to have my vengeance. I could leave now and never look back.

I gathered the skirts of the dress around me and ran towards the door. I opened it; first glancing out to make sure no fairies lingered in the hall. The hall was deserted. I smiled inwardly and took off in a run down the hall and stairs.

Tranquility would not get the best of me. I was only sixteen! I had an entire life ahead of me. My mistakes did not define me as a person. I had had poor judgment, and for that I was sorry. I had put lives in danger and had even caused deaths, but I was not the only one to blame.

The corridors were deserted; luck was on my side for the first time since... since forever! Excitement was growing in me like a bomb about to go off. I was being given a second chance, and I was taking it. Forget Tranquility, Ebony, Dravven, and Ember.

Ember.

I shoved the thought aside to make way for my new ones. If he truly loved me he would find me, no matter the circumstances. I could not put him before me. I had before and where did it get me? Here. With a dead sister, aborted child, and a delusional queen after me.

It was high time I put myself before anyone else. And I deserved to live. I wanted to live. I was over the affairs of others. I turned a corner sharply, and found another set of stairs. I descended them rapidly and continued on my journey through hall after hall.

One way or another I was leaving this castle, never to return. I was going to be normal for once. Not poor, not rich, normal. I would not have to worry about stares and whispers of how my father had died, or made fun of for the clothing I wore. I would blend in; I would live as every other person.

Finally, I turned a corner and there before me stood the front gate. I wanted to weep in joy, but not yet. Almost there did not mean anything. I ran faster, exerting all my energy to make it to the door before I was caught.

My boots clapped on the marble floor and echoed throughout the hall. I ignored the paintings on the walls and paid no mind to the wax dripping on the floor from the chandeliers. I was about to be rid of this species forever.

I let go of my skirts with my right hand and reached out for the gold handle. The same handle Ebony had tried to open, this magnificent door, with what seemed like ages ago. I yanked as hard as I could and the door swung open with ease.

There before me was the marble staircase and wooden path. I smiled despite trying to contain myself. This was it! I hurried down the stairs and shot down the path with a speed I did not know I possessed.

My feet seemed to fly over the panels, my hair ripped away from me in the wind. Freedom had never tasted so good. The torches lining the path in the darkness flickered as I moved past them. Their temporary heat felt good.

I hadn't noticed the snow falling rapidly around me until I lost feeling in my face. I was shivering uncontrollably in the light fabric. I paid it no mind. It didn't matter. I would find a nearby village and stay the night then take off tomorrow morning.

Visions of strange towns, new people, and beautiful hotel rooms filled my mind. I could live a life of luxury. How I would get the money, I did not know. That was another matter entirely. Perhaps I could marry a rich man and live comfortably for the rest of my days with our children.

The idea seemed ludicrous even to me. I did not want to be the typical housewife. I did not want to lower myself to my sex's status. I would rise above. I would make something of myself, be a successful woman. My name would go down in history!

I could see the trees now. I was almost off the path. I was really going to escape. I couldn't believe my luck. I ran even faster, my feet hit earth and I cried in bliss. I slowed down a bit, but not much. Just enough to catch my breath so I could continue running.

Sweat dripped down my chest and back, but froze as a gust of air swept over me. I carelessly swiped my tears away. This was not the time for crying. It was the time for action. I was almost in the trees now. I glanced behind me to make sure I was not being followed. No one was in sight. They didn't know I was gone.

I giggled and turned around; I began to run then skidded to a halt. A black figure had emerged from behind one of the trees and was making its way towards me. "No." I whispered to myself. The word carried over the wind, the figure nodded.

I backed away and stumbled, landing on my behind. I scrambled back as the figure approached. Once in the light of the torches it removed its hood. But instead of Tranquility, it was Ebony. My brow furrowed in confusion. She had been taken!

She held a small hand out for me; I took it and got to my feet. "How?"

She placed a finger to her lips and took the cloak off. She handed it to me and I draped it over myself, grateful for the immediate warmth it gave. She took my hand and led me into the trees. She did not speak until the castle could no longer be seen.

"I ran." She whispered. "I had a feeling she would do something like this, but I knew Ember would never fall in love with a woman that just bowed down. I knew you would somehow escape."

"She has done something terrible, Ebony. She took my-"

She cut me off with a shake of her head. "We haven't the time." She murmured. "I have no doubt she has done some wicked things to you, but you can tell me later on. We have a full night's journey before we make it to the first village, but I do not wish to go there with you. We need to go to the second."

"The second?" I questioned. "Why?"

"The first is small, a feeding grounds. We will be seen by a fairy and they will report right back to Tranquility." She mumbled, I strained to hear her over the wind. "But the second is completely populated with humans. Tranquility rarely goes there. It is a rather large village and they would know if something was amiss. You could blend in."

My heart soared at this prospect. I could stay there for days while I gathered my bearings and then set out on my journey. "Thank you, Ebony. Thank you so much."

She smiled in the dim light. "I will not accept any thanks until you are safely away."

"But what of Ember?" I asked.

"Do not worry about him, my dear. I will protect him with my life. Tranquility will not lay another finger on him without feeling my wrath. I know her ways; I know her strengths and weaknesses. I have known that woman a long time." She responded.

We carried on silently for a while longer. Snow pelted my face and the wind continually blew my hood off. I gave up, instead deciding to let the elements do as they wished. Ebony began to speak but a twig snapped behind us.

We were being followed. Of course. Ebony cast a glance at me then placed her fingers to her lips yet again. We continued to walk, acting as if we heard nothing. Then another twig snapped and someone yelled, "HALT!"

"RUN!" Ebony screamed at me.

I took off through the trees, my legs screaming in protest, already sore from all the running I had done earlier. I felt faint. I had not eaten in days. I urged myself forward. I could eat and sleep once I was safely inside the second village. I just had to wait a few more hours.

Ebony disappeared from sight, but I could hear a battle raging in the distance. The sound of metal was clashing and I could see sparks between the trees. A scream echoed and I sprinted away. I had not gotten this far just to be dragged back.

My legs moved me faster than I had ever moved before. The trees blurred past and I paid no mind when I stumbled, instead I brushed it off and kept going. My skirts caught on low branches and the fabric ripped. I silently apologized to Dravven.

"Stop!" someone yelled from behind me, the voice was tiresome.

This time I did stop. I knew that voice, I knew it well. I turned, a piece of pink fabric from my dress drifted away as I moved. Ember stood a foot away, leaning against a tree, clearly out of breath. I smiled, ignoring everything around me.

I strode towards him. "You found me."

"Of course." He replied, panting. "But if I were you," he paused. "I would be wishing on raining stars."

I followed his gaze skyward. The snow falling now did look as if stars were falling to meet the earth. I sent a puzzled gaze in his direction. "Why?"

He grabbed my hand quite roughly and pulled me along with him in the direction I was headed. My legs silently thanked me for slowing down and giving them a break. For once, Ember's touch did not feel like ice. My skin was already numb.

"Tranquility obviously knows you've escaped, and she's angry. In fact, I have never seen her this angry in all my years of living in the same castle as her." A saddened expression crossed his face. "I don't want her hurting you. I shouldn't have brought you into this."

I shook my head in refusal. "I don't care what she does to me. As long as she doesn't hurt you."

"But that isn't how it works. I am the man in the relationship, I should be protecting you. And I have failed, miserably. I'm so sorry, Reyenne." He grimaced.

I gripped his hand tighter. I didn't want him to feel this way. I wanted to respond, but I didn't know how. How do you address a broken man? No words would console him. His dignity and pride had been smashed into pieces.

We reached the top of a rather large hill and stopped. The first village sat below us. Lights flickered through the snow in the distance. The houses littered the ground like ants on a hill. Ember smiled over at me, but I did not share his hope.

"Ebony said we should continue on to the next village." I told him over the roar of sudden wind.

He shook his head. "We won't make it. It's no use. This will have to do."

He wrapped his arm around my shoulders and we descended the hill to whatever awaited us.

Fifteen

The savagery of the castle had nothing on the village. Everywhere I looked was poverty and dirty people. Sewage lined the streets, but people did not seem to notice. The smell was horrid. It took all my strength to keep my hand away from my nose. I did not want to offend anyone.

Ember didn't act like he noticed anything amiss. His nose stayed in the air and he didn't flinch once. Even when a scraggly man bumped into his shoulder, leaving a fresh stain. But the smells and appearance of people were not the biggest problem.

In every nook and cranny there was a body. They were stuffed into alleys, hidden behind trash bins, and some were merely strewn across the road. Blood coated most of the buildings and windows, and remnants of organs could be found among the fifth.

Ebony had not been kidding when she said this was not the village to stay. I wanted to flee for the second village. It had to be better than this one. But instead I let Ember drag me along as I looked at the scene in horror.

Just like the sewage, the people did not seem to notice the bodies. And if they did they did not care, or were too frightened to show concern. I began questioning every person we passed. Was that man near the General Store really a peasant in rags, or a fairy in hiding? Or that woman carrying a small child close to her breast. Was she really a concerned mother, or a beast with an unnatural bloodlust?

I could not be certain of any one. So I trusted Ember and Ember alone. Even when he pulled me into a grimy hotel to procure a room for the night. He did not bother with a key or addressing the homely woman at the desk. Instead, he took me straight up the stairs and into the room with no number.

He shut the door quietly behind us and locked several deadbolts. The room, like the rest of the town, was not very welcoming. Everything was covered in a film of dust, and blood stains had been halfheartedly scrubbed out of the carpet.

I turned on him. "Have you killed in this room?"

The question seemed to take him off guard; he shoved a hand into his torn pocket and looked down. "Yes."

I had not expected this answer. I had expected him to reprimand me and ask if I really thought he was that low. "Oh." Was all I could reply. It stung deeper than it should have. I knew what kind of animal he was; I knew what his diet consisted of.

I sat on the bed; a puff of dust clouded my vision. "I have to survive, Reyenne."

I barely heard him over the dull ringing in my ears. My eyes stayed focused on the faded stains of the floor. Were they from one of his victims? Had he murdered a woman like me on this very bed? The questions would not subside.

I wiped a stray tear from my eye and pulled the cloak off. "I know, I know. I am being foolish. I am unfortunately being very emotional. It must be from my lack of sleep and food over the past few days."

He rubbed my back gently. "I would get you food if I knew where to find it. All the humans here keep it hidden away for fear of us stealing it from them."

I turned to face him. His face was covered in dirt and scratches that were already mending. I had no doubt I looked the same way. "You steal their food?"

"I don't, I have no need for it. But crueler beings than I make a game of it." He admitted. "But do not worry yourself with such things, you look weary enough. It is time for some rest."

He helped me under the covers and draped my cloak over the back of the desk chair. Despite everything going on around me, I had to admit it felt good to be back in a bed. Even if that bed was filthy and probably contained insects of all sorts.

"Are you not going to sleep?" I asked, already yawning.

He stroked my hair away from his face and grinned down at me. "No, I don't necessarily need sleep. It is nice, I admit, but not something I need. I will keep watch to make sure no one intrudes."

I nodded, beginning to doze off. His face became a blur of colors and then I was out.

I woke to the sound of crackling flames. I sat up to see a chair that had been pulled up to the small fireplace. Flames licked the blackened bricks and the blissful heat encased me in cozy feelings. It made me miss home even more.

I could not see Ember over the high back of the chair but could sense his presence. A shift of fabric every few seconds let me know I was indeed not alone. I pulled the covers back and placed my bare feet on the warm floor. I padded over to the chair and rested my arms on the back.

"How long did I sleep?" I groggily I asked. He shifted and stood. My heart stopped and I backed away. "What have you done with him?" I whispered.

"Oh, he is far away." Tranquility responded, her evil smile painted on her face.

"What do you want from me?!" I was frantic. I could not escape her no matter what I did. Every sliver of hope I had somehow mustered melted away in a few seconds time.

She leaned against the mantel. "You know what I want." She responded in a bored tone.

I wanted to weep but tears would not come. "You have killed my sister, taken me from my family, taken the love of my life from me several times, and ripped my child from my womb. I have nothing else I can give you."

She laughed; it was a soft melody that caused the flames to flicker and dance. "I want your life."

"M-my life?" I stuttered in shock.

"Not in that way, darling. You would be no use to me dead in a putrid alleyway." She explained. "I want you to become one of us. I want you to let me create you."

I glanced down at the tattered dress I wore. A few diamonds were missing and the entire bottom had been ripped away. "The dress. That is why you had it created for me."

She rolled her eyes. "That much was obvious. This is nothing new to you." She explained. "You knew when you decided to run that I wanted to create you into Mayhem." She leaned forward, her long hair swung carelessly. "I could give you eternal life. You could be in the presence of Ember as much as you wish. I could even put your child back inside you."

"But you hate me."

She chuckled. "I do not hate you, silly child. But you are a threat to me. Especially in your current state. If you would only let me create you! You would be idolized! You would have everything you have ever wished for and more. Riches beyond your comprehension, the ability to be across the world in minutes, and most importantly, power."

I considered this. I had not seen this side of Tranquility before. She was acting civil, explaining her motives. But should I trust this woman? After all she had done? "If you just wanted to create me, why didn't you simply ask? Why did you have to kill Juniper and tear my child from me? Why did you have to lock me up and torture Ember? Why all the fuss?"

She paused. Her eyes glistened in the firelight and her hands were gripped tightly in front of her. "Juniper was a casualty I am truly sorry for. I did not intend for her to be murdered, but I had waited long enough and StarFyre, or Addie as you knew her, got carried away." She glanced at the floor then back into my eyes. "After that, things spun out of control. I knew you would never willingly come with me and that Ember would not agree to let you be alone with me. But I also did not expect you to run, and that complicated matters further. I could not let my people see me outwitted by a human."

"So, it was all a mistake." I pondered.

"Yes, several mistakes I hope you can forgive me for. You are a powerful woman, and I need a powerful woman to join my race."

She straightened herself to her normal towering stance. "So, will you join my race?" she inquired then added, "Please."

I waited before answering; I wanted to think this over before I signed my life away. She seemed sincere in her apologies. Her empathy towards me over the harm that had come was great. Perhaps I had misjudged her before. It was true I had been the one constantly running from her.

I had formed my opinion of her based on the feelings of others. I had never once tried to talk to her or explain my side of things. This woman could be quite pleasant, if I gave her the chance.

But what of turning into a fairy? I would never see Honour or my mother again, this was obvious. But I could gain so much more. I could have a family of my own, and live among a species that accepted me no matter my past.

I had made up my mind before I turned to Tranquility. I nodded in approval. She smiled, this time I noticed a tinge of kindness illuminating her face. I smiled back, suddenly comfortable in her presence.

In a matter of seconds we were in a dark room.

Sixteen

"Now," Tranquility held up a small vial filled with gold liquid, "these are fairy tears. Once I open the flesh of your arm and pour them in your creation will begin. I cannot promise it will be pleasant but I also cannot promise it will be painful. Every fairy experiences it differently. Some will stay asleep for weeks, and some will pop up a minute after ready for their first kill."

I nodded in understanding. The room we were standing in was quite dark, illuminated only by the few candles Tranquility had lit with her hand. Like everything else surrounding this species, they were a deep gold color.

Not a single sound could be heard. I assumed we were somewhere in the dungeons considering the dampness of the room and the cold that sweltered in from all sides. I knelt before my soon-to-be Queen and awaited her next direction.

"There would usually be quite a few fairies here to witness this. Then we would have a marvelous banquet afterwards. But the conditions with you have been rough and things have changed. That is why I am allowing you to wear those rags during this special event." She continued.

"I understand." I replied sheepishly.

"I understand, what?" she countered.

I bowed my head in respect. "I understand, my Queen."

"That's better! You need to get used to saying that. Always address me in such fashion. The other rules will be explained to you once the process is over. They are quite simple, I have no doubt you will catch on quickly."

"Yes, my Queen." I responded almost robotically. I just wanted this to be over with. I was having second thoughts at a most inconvenient time.

"Your arm, please." She held her hand out.

I raised my arm and set it in her hand. I did not bother to look up. I did not want to see what was about to take place. She was going to slice her claws into my arm deep enough for me to bleed out before emptying the vial into my system.

It would be painful, I knew.

She traced her nail playfully across my skin, causing goose pricks to erupt on my skin before she dug the sharp tip in painfully. I bit my lip and allowed tears to cascade from my eyes. I was silently weeping in torment.

I could feel warm blood gushing down my arm and coating my elbow. It splattered on the floor like heavy rainfall. She wasted no time dumping the tears into the wound. It burned badly. My flesh healed itself but the poison was deep in my veins.

It coursed through my body with the ferocity of fire. I knelt forward on hands and knees, and screamed until I thought my lungs would burst. Everything was becoming clearer. I could hear my blood rushing, sense the tears zipping through my every vein.

But this was not the most interesting part. My surroundings came into focus almost instantly. Instead of staring at a darkened floor, I was staring at a dirty floor. Every piece of dirt and grime was clear as my pain.

Then, as if a switch had been turned off, it was over. I struggled to my feet and stared at my Queen. She thrust her hands together in delight and squealed. "You are beautiful!" she exclaimed.

"I... what?" I asked confused. Other than my heightened senses, I felt no different. I had not grown taller or gained strength or became extremely intelligent. I was just me.

"One moment." She held her hand up then turned to a writing table behind her. Wax melted off the candle and hit the surface of the table in clarity. I could smell the wax as it softened. "Ah, here!"

She turned back around and handed me a gold ornamental looking glass. Roses were intricately carved into the handle and the initials "T.E." decorated the back. I flipped it over and viewed myself.

I was shocked by the person who stared back at me. She was not plain but gorgeous. Her eyes were black and her lashes were thick without the help of cosmetics. Her skin was white as snow along with her hair which spilled over her shoulders and settled near her breasts. It was completely straight, unlike my usual waviness.

"I'm... I'm beautiful." I exhaled handing the looking glass back to Tranquility.

She giggled like a small girl and placed it back on the writing desk. "Of course you are. There are no ugly fairies. We must appeal to people to gain their trust, so that we may get them alone. It really is quite simple. But now is not the time for such things, you will learn that all later. There are some changes."

"Some changes? You mean quite a few." I grinned.

"Not the physical type, darling." She smiled. "You are to go by a new name. Each fairy is assigned one after creation as a way of... welcoming the rebirth. Instead of Reyenne, you are now Victoria Renae. A bit common, I must apologize, but I did not have much time to ponder it."

I stared at her in wonder. I was becoming a completely different person. Reyenne was gone, Victoria was taking her place. I admired my nails and pale skin while Tranquility cleared her throat and continued to speak.

"You will gain the use of your wings and nails, and of course eyes, as time moves on. For the next several days you will experience changes you won't quite understand, but have no fear, it is all natural. We all went through it, I assure you."

"Is that all, my Queen?" I questioned, wanting to leave to see Ember.

"One more thing." She assured me. She pulled another vial from a hidden pocket in her dress. This one's contents were filled with a gray dust that shimmered in the candlelight. I could see each individual fleck. "Hold still."

I stayed as still as I possibly could and watched as she uncorked the bottle. She poured a small fraction of the dust into her hand then before I could speak, blew it into my face.

"Wha-" I was unable to finish. I grew dizzy quickly and fell to the floor in a heap. My head smacked against the ground and my thoughts were into a frenzy. She had drugged me!

I raised my head as much as I could and gazed at her. Her evil smile was back, the sweet innocent one gone. "You stupid, stupid girl."

It was the last thing I heard before everything went out of focus and my new body went limp.

1907

Seventeen

I picked the stack of leather bound books up from the floor of the Guard's Quarters, Ember stood by watching in amusement. I scowled at him. "You could help me!"

He folded his arms across his chest. "And you could tell me exactly what you meant down in the dungeons."

The top book fell off the stack and I tried to pick it up while still holding the rest, Ember swayed over and casually threw it back onto the pile. "I meant exactly what I said. I know how to kill her."

"Yes, I know, but you have failed to mention how." He replied once again crossing his arms in defiance.

I glanced around the empty space. Weapons lined the right wall and books the left. A few fairies fluttered in and out of rooms further down the hall, but other than that not a noise could be heard. "Do you want someone to overhear us? We would surely be killed." I whispered furiously.

"As if Tranquility isn't already out for you." He scoffed.

"I would rather not have the rest of the castle after my blood, too. Now where is Ebony?" I asked frustrated.

"Where do you think Ebony is?" he rolled his eyes.

I glared at him then walked away. I did not want to speak of what I knew just yet. There were fairies we had to find, and with both Tranquility and Dravven missing we were shorthanded. Ember followed behind me as I exited the Guard's Quarters and made my way through the castle.

The trek up the stairs to the Royal Hall was not something I wanted to do with such heavy books, so I extended my large black wings and flew to the balcony. I landed with grace. Ember took the stairs, but I had no time to wait for him.

I pushed open the door to Ebony's room and dropped the books in a messy pile on the floor. Ebony was sitting among her small tornadoes of air chanting an incantation over a glass of boiling liquid.

"Surge, surge. Et coques, et contremiscunt." she recited rather loudly.

"Ebony." I called over her chants. She looked up and the wind immediately stopped swirling. The liquid in the container fizzed and sparked out.

"Victoria!" she jumped up and ran across the room. Her arms wrapped tightly around my torso and she breathed deeply so as not to cry. "I thought she had killed you!"

I returned her embrace then pulled back. "No, thankfully, I know how to kill her now."

She gasped and threw her hand over her mouth. "Y-you do?"

I gestured to the pile of books that had fallen over and open across her floor. "Yes, but I need some help. Do you know where Dravven has gone?"

"I thought he was with Ember." She pulled her hand away from her face and began piling the books neatly on her small table.

I walked over and helped her with the mess I had created. "Ember said he flew through a window and disappeared. I had hoped you knew where he was going."

She sat in one of her tall-backed chairs and ran a hand over the surface of the wood. "I'm afraid not, but who knows with that lunatic? He could be anywhere."

I sat across from her and pulled a book down from the pile. The cover read, "Creation Dates of Royals." I flipped it open to the table of contents and slid my finger over the cryptic letters. "I need to know something." I started.

"Yes? Anything, my dear!" she exclaimed.

"Did you know two fairies by the names of Keelan and Ceintra? They were twins that could see into the future." I explained.

She froze, the finger she had been tapping on the table stopped and remained halfway through the air. "We all know of Keelan and Ceintra. They caused the Queen much grief. Are you sure these are the fairies you need?"

The door opened and we both turned to look. My mouth was hanging open in fright of who had possibly heard us. Ember sauntered in and shut the door quietly behind him. "Did I miss anything?"

I rolled my eyes. "Forever late, you are."

He shrugged his shoulders and flopped onto Ebony's bed. "What can I say? Always fashionably late!"

I turned back to Ebony. "As I was saying, I'm fairly certain. Something... happened when Tranquility cut me with her wing. I thought for sure I was dead but I ended up somewhere called The Mayhem Realm."

Both Ebony and Ember turned their heads in sudden alertness. "You were in The Mayhem Realm?" gasped Ebony.

"Y-yes." I stuttered, not expecting their sudden reaction. They acted as if someone had just told them their dear mother had died. I slammed the book shut and placed it back on the pile. "What is it?"

They were both looking at each other in awe. Ebony turned away from Ember and placed her hand on top of mine in a motherly fashion. "It's just... no fairy ever comes back from The Mayhem Realm. This is a huge show of your power. I had no idea you would be able to do something as drastic as that."

I pulled my hand away. "I am the rightful Queen! Of course I can do things as powerful as that. It's normal... isn't it?"

Ebony tapped her nails on the polished table then stood and began to pace. She lifted her trusty snake onto her shoulder and concentrated on the floor. If I hadn't known better I would think the answer was plainly written on the carpet. "Perhaps. I know Tranquility has been there before, I just had no idea you would possess all the powers she does." She shook her head of the thoughts. "Anyway, do tell what happened."

"I was addressed by four fairies... although now I can't remember their names." I racked my brain for their names and faces but couldn't recall them no matter how hard I tried. How peculiar. "They told me of Tranquility's past, that much I do know.

When they came to the part of Keelan and Ceintra, something clicked. Keelan and Ceintra can help us, although I'm not sure how."

Ebony resumed her spot and stroked the yellow snake with her hand. "No one knows where they are though."

"What?!" I almost shouted the word. How could two especially important fairies go missing? Surely this was a joke.

She nodded her head in utter seriousness. "I'm assuming these... fairies you spoke with told you this. Keelan and Ceintra disappeared not long after their creation. They couldn't stand being in this castle with all the thoughts and fairy's futures to be heard. They ran."

"Oh." It was all I could say. Now that Ebony had explained this I did remember being told about their departure. I stood without a word and left the room. I counted the Royals Rooms as I passed until I reached rooms two and three.

With a rough shove I had opened the door to room two. The door creaked from not being used and dust flew into my face from the frame. I sneezed and brushed it away. The room itself, despite the thick layer of dust, was very neat. Everything was white and blue, and exactly in order.

Elixirs and potions lined a tall, white bookshelf. Despite the age of them they still fizzed, bubbled, and popped. Books with white spines lined another bookshelf across the room, I ran my hands over them and came back with gray dust covered fingers.

The titles could barely be seen under their films. The few I could read said things such as, "Looking through Eyes of a Seer" and "How to Keep Premonitions a Secret." A painting over the bed told me this was Ceintra's room. She had clearly been devoted to her powers.

I left the room, not finding anything that would tell me of their whereabouts and slid into Keelan's room. His room, unlike Ceintra's, was a mess. Books scattered the floor covered in grime and old clothing chewed by mice were piled on the bed. He had obviously fled in a rush.

I bent over to examine one of his books. Unlike his sister's, they were ordinary brown leather. The entire room smelt of moth balls, I crinkled my nose. The title of the book I was looking at was,

"Destroying the Gift of Seeing." I pulled back in shock. He was definitely a contrast to his sibling.

I left the room, careful to close it completely and made my way back to Ebony's. She was once again sitting over her elixir chanting. Ember sat on her bed carefully watching her, he was absorbing every word she spoke.

"Swirl vestrum iter incipiunt." Ebony spoke softly to the liquid. It turned blue then green, then fizzed some more.

"I found nothing." I piped up. Ebony's head snapped back in terror. She threw a hand over her heart and stood.

"I did not hear you come in." she admitted while taking the elixir over to her shelf and corking it. "You frightened me. For a moment I thought you were Tranquility."

Ember stood and ambled over to me. He rubbed my arms with his hands and looked at me in concern. "So, what now?"

I shook my head. I had thought Keelan and Ceintra would have left something behind besides old books and clothing, but the rooms had been bare. I didn't know what I had expected to find. A map, perhaps? But that would have been too obvious. They didn't want anyone following them.

"I'm not sure. Honestly, I don't have that many ideas. I thought it would be an easy path, especially after everything we have been through in the past few days with Tranquility trying to kill us and the battle. But like I said, I found nothing." I admitted already defeated.

Ebony cleared her throat and Ember let go to look at her. "I think I may know of someone who could be of some assistance."

My heart elated once again I asked, "Who?"

Ebony dawdled across the room, her eyes suddenly aglow. "There is another seer in our species that goes by the name of Mystic. She does not live here, but instead with a coven of fairies in Moscow. She may be able to help you."

I regarded Ember. "Up for a trip?"

"A trip?" he complained. "It's not nearly as fun now that we don't ride in automobiles or take trains. Just flictate and go!"

I laughed at his comment. "But it means we're that much closer to overthrowing Tranquility.

Eighteen

We left Ebony with quick goodbyes and flictated to Moscow in record time. We landed gracefully hand in hand and stopped. My hair was windblown as was his, we quickly fixed it and trudged up the hill to whatever it was we were looking for.

"Surely our kind is not residing in one of these shacks?" commented Ember.

I shrugged in response; I had no idea about any of this. I really didn't know much about the man whose hand I was holding. Yet it all seemed natural. I sniffed at the air, something peculiar was wafting into my space. I cocked my head and turned to gaze at the small building to my right. "They're in there."

He said nothing but led the way to the dingy structure. The wooden panels were deteriorating and the mat that had been placed outside as a way of welcome was worn and torn. Ember knocked and stepped back.

It was a few minutes before anyone answered. The woman was middle aged which took me by surprise. I hadn't seen such an old fairy. Her hair was dark brown and in a loose bun while her eyes were chestnut with a gray circle glowing around her pupil.

Ember cleared his throat. "Mystic?"

She tightened her flowing robe around her and stared at him in wonder. "That is me. Who are you?"

Ember gestured between us nervously. "I am Ember Sky and this is Victoria Renae, we were told you could help us."

She opened the door further and beckoned us inside. I exhaled deeply, glad that she had not questioned us further. The home was... in the least unsatisfactory. A fire raged in the hearth and a few mismatched pieces of furniture were placed around it for warmth.

Doors lined the wall leading to bedrooms where I could clearly hear fairies moving about, but not one came to greet us. Mystic pulled out three teacups and a kettle. "Tea alright?" she quizzed.

We both shook our heads in response and she went about boiling the water with her hand and pouring it into the cups. In the matter of minutes we were sitting on the couch nearest the fire and holding steaming cups of brown tea.

Mystic sat across from us in a rather large arm chair. She sunk into it and sipped from her own cup. "Now, how may I assist you?"

I spoke before Ember had the chance. "You are a seer, correct?"

Her eyes lit up in excitement and she leaned forward. I had obviously struck a chord deep inside her. "I have not been asked that question in years," she admitted.

"So it is true?" Ember inquired.

She took another drink from her cup before responding. "Oh yes, I can see into the future with the use of fire." She nodded at the raging flames. "A peculiar talent, even in our race."

Ember acknowledged this statement with the shake of his head. "So, you are aware that you are one of three ever in our species to... uh... acquire this gift."

"Yes, of course. I came centuries after Keelan and Ceintra." She paused. "That is who you are after."

We nodded our heads in unison and I sipped the tea from my cup. "Can you help us?"

"Yes, yes. Wait just one moment." She stood and left the room. We waited what seemed like centuries before she reappeared holding a tray of herbs and potions. She set it on her lap as she sunk back into the chair. "Now, I will need you to answer a few questions so that I may see clearly. Is that alright?"

"Of course." I agreed.

She shuffled through the herbs looking for specific ones and began asking what she needed to know. "You have not been in Mayhem long, how old are you in fairy years?"

I glanced at Ember then back at Mystic. "I... I don't know. I was created sometime in the nineteenth century but the queen put me under a sleeping spell. I just awoke not too long ago."

"And you are to overthrow Tranquility and take her throne?"

I paused at the question. "How did you know that?"

She stopped moving the leaves she was counting and looked up. "I'm a seer, dear. I already saw this coming," she smiled.

I nervously looked at Ember who was staring intently at Mystic. I continued, "Yes, I learned shortly after I was woken that I was to be the next queen, and that I could only accomplish that if I killed our current one."

She nodded and started counting the leaves again. "And Keelan and Ceintra? They will help you on this journey?"

"Yes, I believe so." I answered.

"Alright then!" She clutched the leaves in her hand and pulled a pink potion from the tray. She moved it aside and knelt next to the fire. The flames crackled and spit as the logs burnt under their intensity. "I ask that you please stay silent, and whatever you see in the flames, do tell me of afterwards."

She tossed the leaves into the flames, they immediately curled and disintegrated. Then, she uncorked the pink potion and tossed it on top of them. The fire turned green and smoke began to billow thicker than before.

She started her chant, "Videamus flammis, ut, quae dici possunt."

Ember and I shifted from our seats to better to see the green flames. Almost immediately I saw a figure dancing. It swirled around the flames, genderless and nameless, and pranced over the logs. Then, came another figure. This time is was clear it was a woman.

Her skirts swished over the open flame and her hair trailed behind her. The other figure, a man now, took her hand and they danced together. They were happy being together. Not in a romantic or intimate way... but a sibling way. They got along, they understood each other in a world that didn't.

But everything suddenly changed. They cowered in fear as another woman came into the flames. Her entire demeanor depicted dictation. She wanted them to see for her, she was going to use them as pawns. They ran out of the fire and disappeared. The third woman went up in smoke.

The flames went back to their normal orange and red. I shook my head and looked away. My eyes were watering from the intensity. Mystic resumed her place in her chair. "What did you see?"

I explained the people to her, how they were frightened of the third figure. She merely nodded her head in agreement until I was finished. Ember had seen the same thing as I, he simply agreed with everything I said.

"You saw Keelan and Ceintra run from our queen. They were not happy in her presence and so they left to seek a quiet place for them to learn their abilities and grow," she explained.

I furrowed my brow. "But this does not tell us where they are."

"That is the tricky part, I am afraid. Since they are seers they can block others out." She paused and knotted her hands in her lap. "I am unable to see an exact location. I know they are deep within a forest in... Canada. It is cold and dreary but they have grown accustomed to it."

My eyes widened. "Canada?! We've never been to Canada! Isn't it huge? It will take us years to search the entire thing and by the time we have they will probably be long gone!"

"Ah, but there is one more thing." She continued, "Another of our kind is already with them, a dear friend of yours. Someone that perhaps disappeared and you are unable to find? Track them and you will find what you are looking for."

Ember and I glanced at one another. She had to be speaking of Dravven; there was no one else it could be. We stood and thanked her for her time then left the small shack. Ember took my hand and we trudged back over the hill and out of sight.

He turned to me once we were away from mortals seeing us. "It's Dravven, isn't it? The friend that has disappeared? It wouldn't be Tranquility; their entire reason for leaving was to flee from her."

"It has to be." I agreed. "But how do we track him down? That seems no easier than finding Keelan and Ceintra."

He pondered this a moment before speaking. "We need Ebony. She somehow always finds Dravven, no matter where he has wondered off to. She'll be able to help us."

Nineteen

"Dravven is with them?!" shouted Ebony.

"We believe so." I responded, afraid of her next outburst. She had not been happy about Dravven disappearing in the first place.

She sighed. "Of course he is. That fool!"

"Ebony, we need your help finding him so that we can find them. Mystic told us they were somewhere in Canada, in a deep forest with no one around. Do you think if we took you there with us you could locate him?" Ember spoke.

She tossed her hands in the air. "I have no idea, but it's worth a shot, isn't it?"

She set about throwing clothing, all the same outfit, into a large bag she produced from nowhere. Ember slid out of the room in search of his own quarters to get his things, and I stood still, unsure of what to do. I had nothing but the maid's outfit I still wore which was torn beyond repair.

Ebony hummed to herself while she threw her items into the bag then turned and looked at me startled. Then realization seemed to dawn. "I forgot to tell you where your room is. I put it all together after you got here." She snapped her fingers and beckoned me to follow her. "Come with me, dear."

We descended three flights of stairs and ended in a corner of the castle I had never been before. Did this building ever end? Fairies ambled up and down the corridor, walking into rooms and leaving them. It was an entire section dedicated to living spaces.

Ebony counted the doors to our right as we passed them and finally stopped at one located in the center of the hall. She produced a key from her pocket and unlocked the gold door. We stepped inside. I gasped.

The entire room was white and gray. It was rather small, smaller than Ebony's room for sure, but comfortable. A bed with a striped duvet sat in the middle of the far wall and two shelves stood to the sides of it. Books and small whirling trinkets lined the shelves.

Ebony strode to the door located on the right and opened the closet door wide. Gray and white outfits stood ready to be worn at her intrusion. Scarves, hats, coats, shirts, pants, and other clothing stood at the wait.

Ebony turned to me. "Tranquility specifically ordered these colors, perhaps because of your lovely white hair. I am unsure, so I am sorry if it does not meet your standards." She apologized.

"Oh no!" I brushed her apology away. "White is a truly lovely color."

She smiled and produced a gray bag from thin air. She handed it to me then turned to leave. "Pack swiftly then meet back in my room. Oh, and take those rags off. You have a new wardrobe to try out." She winked then left.

I ran my hands over the fabrics. Although I could not remember my past life, I knew I had never owned anything such as this. Something deep in the pit of me screaming my fortune. Even with everything bad happening around me.

I pulled down a simple white dress and tore the ugly maid's one off. The white lace was soft and felt good against my skin. I pulled on gray tights and slipped on white flats then began packing my bag. I shoved just about everything I could put my hands on into it, not knowing when I would be back.

After ten minutes of this I buttoned the bag closed and pulled on a long, gray coat I had found deep in my closet and buttoned it to my neck. The journey back to Ebony's room was tedious with the heavy bag but I managed.

I entered and threw it on the floor. Both Ebony and Ember turned to look at me. Ember's eyes drifted up and down my frame, taking in my new clothing. Finally, he smiled. "Ready then?"

"I believe so." I replied.

"Now," Ebony continued. I saw now they had been pondering over a rather large map. I sauntered over and studied it with them. "I believe we should flictate to this spot. It is in the heart of these woods. It is as good a place as any since we really don't know where we are going."

Ember piped up. "But how will we know what to chant? We can't just say Canada and end up in that exact spot."

Ebony thought this over, still staring intently at the colorful map. "Say... say Regina. We will go there first then start our trek. We can also load up on food while we are there."

I caught what she had said almost instantly. "You don't mean we're going to kill in such a populated area? Won't others see us?"

Ember and Ebony looked at each other and laughed, apparently in on a secret I was not part of. "We'll be fine. I forgot you haven't had a proper hunt." Ebony responded.

Not another word was said. I grabbed my belongings while Ember and Ebony fetched theirs and we left the room to find the front gate. Each time I saw a corner or new wall I would have a sort of flash. It would be me running through this exact hall, extremely frightened, and having no idea where I was going.

I ignored these flashes, knowing they must have been my memories as a human coming back to me. I hoped they would be restored soon; I was growing tired of not knowing anything except what was happening now.

We reached the front gate and Ebony swung it open. The world outside was chilly, but not bitingly cold. We descended the stairs and stopped on the wooden walk. I had a flash of a figure wearing all black in my mind, but shoved it aside to listen to Ebony.

"Let us hold hands so we do not end up in separate places." Ebony suggested.

I shuffled my bag to my other shoulder and clenched Ember's hand in mine. In return, he did the same with Ebony. I closed my eyes and it began, our voices joined in unison over the dreadful silence.

Our wings snapped in the air. "Flictate."

"Flictate." I could clearly hear Ember's deep voice over mine and Ebony's.

"Flictate." The familiar feel of my wings flapping.

"Flictate." My feet left the ground so that I was hovering in midair.

"Flictate." All three of us zoomed into the sky and out of view of the castle. The world became small under me. I clutched my bag tightly so it did not fall. A fiasco like that was not ideal.

We left the atmosphere without stopping, I was no longer afraid of doing this. Once we saw the stars Ebony reared back and pulled us with her. "Remember what we are to say?"

Ember and I nodded in agreement and Ebony started our next chant. Once again, our voices blended in perfect harmony. We could form a band! I chuckled silently to myself.

"Regina, Canada."

"Regina, Canada."

"Regina, Canada."

"Regina, Canada."

"Regina, Canada."

The stars began aligning themselves in rapid speed. They swished through the air and a few burnt my wings in their descent. It was clear this time the path was much longer. Ebony let go of Ember's hand and zoomed ahead. She obviously wanted to get there before us.

Ember and I took our time adjusted the strap of our luggage so they did not come undone or fall, then flew after Ebony. It was silent for a while, blissfully silent. It gave me time to properly think which I hadn't done since I awoke.

I wondered where Tranquility had run off to. I wondered if Keelan and Ceintra could even help us. What if they had somehow lost their ability to see? What would we do then?

Ember interrupted my thinking to ask, "Do you think Mystic was right? Do you think the twins can help us?"

I glanced at him. "I was just thinking over the same thing. It was a bit unusual, wasn't it?" I pondered allowed.

Our wings flapped in the air for a few seconds, I hit a star and it scolded my arm, which of course healed right back. "What's unusual?"

"Mystic. She was... older. I thought fairies were intentionally created young." I replied.

He chuckled. "Oh, that. I thought you were commenting on the abilities of the twins. No, not unusual. Rare, maybe, but not unheard of." He paused to gaze at me with his macabre eyes. "She was a hybrid."

I shoved myself forward with a rather strong flap of my wings. I had to circle around in order to get back to his side. Once I was back in position I shifted my body towards him. "A what?"

He rolled his eyes at me as if the answer was obvious. "A hybrid. She was born from a human that had reproduced with a fairy. It's very rare, Tranquility usually kills them. I'm assuming she only kept Mystic because of her abilities."

"But I thought..." I searched my mind for the words I was looking for. "I thought fairies were... sterile." The word made me uncomfortable for reasons unknown to me.

"We are." He agreed. "But most humans aren't. I'm really not sure about the entire process, but I know if a male fairy reproduces with a female human, a child can be born."

I nodded my head at this. How unusual of a thing. I was definitely part of a complicated race. That much was obvious from the start. Every time I thought I had everything figured out, another fact was thrown my way that tipped my world upside down.

"So Mystic, was she actually a fairy? Or just a sort of super human?" I quizzed.

"Oh, she was a fairy, but she has human qualities. Growing old, for example. She won't age like normal humans, mind you. It will take her a few centuries, but it will happen." He paused and looked away. "And she will die."

I gasped in horror although subconsciously I had been expecting him to say it. How awful of a thing to go through. She possessed powers most people only dreamed of, and would only get to use them a few short centuries. I immediately felt bad for her. My fear of death overwhelmed all other senses.

Although I was not a particularly religious person, I prayed for her.

Twenty

We landed in Regina in the early hours of the day. I assumed by the faint light in the sky that it was nearly dawn. Ember threw his bag onto the ground and rubbed his shoulder. I sympathized with him, my entire body hummed with a deep soreness.

We had hit the ground on a deserted patch of land. The city was already lighting up a few miles away and the occasional vehicle strolled past. The early workers were obviously already at it. I unlatched my bag and let it drop to the muddy ground, not caring about the stains it would leave behind.

"Where do you think Ebony is?" Ember questioned, still massaging his sore muscles.

I glanced around at the trees and road near us. Not a person was in sight. "How should I know? I've been with you, or have you already forgotten?" I teased.

He rolled his eyes then grabbed his bag from the ground. "I guess we better go get a hotel room for the night. I'm exhausted."

I followed suit and retrieved my suitcase. As we walked I began talking again. "That's another unusual thing."

"What is?" he asked, looking ahead to scope out the town we were walking into.

"If we have control over all these powers, why do we need sleep? Shouldn't we just regenerate on our own will?" My mind soared over the possibilities.

He chuckled. "You're just full of wonder today, aren't you?"

I blushed a deep crimson. "It's just... I don't really know that much about our species. I can't remember anything previous to when you found me, and I haven't exactly learned much in the process of fighting Tranquility."

He exhaled deeply at my comment. "I know, I wish there was more I could do. I wish I could remember so I could make you remember." He played with the strap of his bag. "We consume human organs, yes? So they regenerate our organs to make us stay alive. But here's the thing, human organs expect time to rest to gain energy. So in the process of us devouring their organs, our organs gain the characteristics." He ran his hand through his hair, he was quite fidgety. "That's the best way I can explain it. It's a rather complicated process."

I nodded in understanding and idly scratched my nose. I didn't know what else to say, I couldn't possibly pluck another thought from the disaster I called my brain. Truthfully, I was worn out too. I had not gotten a moment's rest since entering the castle. I was looking forward to a warm comfy bed.

"Why are we always cold?" I blurted. The thought of a fireplace and piles of blankets drove me to ask the question.

"We have no internal body temperature. We're corpses, Victoria." He grimaced at the word, but I realized how true it was. I was decades old and still had the appearance of a teenager. I should have been in a grave somewhere.

We were reaching the city line now, houses were scattered here and there, and farm animals made strange noises in the distance while in slumber. "So then... why is blood and tears gold?"

He ran a hand down his face. "That," he stopped walking and faced me, "I do not know."

The hotel we ended up in wasn't spectacular. The room was small and boxy with an average sized hearth and bed big enough to comfortably hold two people, minus wings. Ember set to starting a fire while I sheepishly changed into a nightshirt, making sure every few seconds he was not looking.

I pulled the covers of the bed back and slid into it. Thankfully, the mattress was soft and did not have a lingering smell of unbathed humans. It was delightfully warm under the stacked blankets and my skin, for once, did not feel like an ice block.

Ember left the room without comment once the fire was satisfactorily raging. He wasn't gone long before he came back wearing his own nightshirt. He climbed into the bed next to me and pulled a book from his bag which was on the floor next to him.

The title read, "The Heroic Adventures of Zad, Mayhem Fairy." He flipped it open to the page he had obviously been reading from earlier and dove in head first. He seemed engrossed by the tale, I did not want to disturb him, but I was curious.

"Who is Zad?" I whispered.

I thought at first he was not going to answer, but he put his bookmark, which was a tattered piece of parchment, into the book and rolled his head over to see me. "A fictional fairy that goes on conquests."

"Conquests?" I crinkled my nose.

"Like, saving damsels in distress using his powers and helping entire towns after a disaster." His eyes lit up as he spoke. "And unlike the real world, humans are glad he's around. They appreciate his help. So much they give him sacrifices to feed off so he doesn't have to kill innocent people."

His expressions gave away his excitement on the subject. I smiled at him and let him go back to reading. I could, on the very edges of my mind, remember having a fondness of books. I thought anyone could gain any knowledge they wanted just by reading the right things. I was upset that I had not brought one of my own from my new room.

I contented myself with watching the fire crackle and spit with dreary eyes. The only sound came from Ember flipping pages next to me. I remembered my vision of the figures dancing among the flames.

What had Tranquility done to Keelan and Ceintra to make them flee her? In The Mayhem Realm I was told they were treated perfectly by her. They had been given everything they could wish for and she even supplied them with fresh humans. She had loved them.

Despite my hatred for our ruler I could not deny that she held a special place in her heart for the twins. It was not her fault they were gifted with such abilities. They only had to speak to her, tell her they were suffering, and she would have let them go. Running was useless. It had only added to her broken heart and made her a colder woman.

What if they refused to help us? They had worked so hard to separate themselves from our race. Why would they want anything to do with us? I was almost asleep, my eyes were drooping. I could barely see the fire raging in the hearth.

Ember's book snapped shut and my tired eyes popped open. He sat up in bed and threw the book to the floor. "There's someone outside our door," he commented.

I sat up, clutching the blanket to my chest and watched as he crossed the room and placed his ear on the wooden door. "Is it a someone or a fairy?" I whispered anxiously.

He held a hand up for me to be quiet. I grasped the soft blanket tighter. Were we already under attack? My eyes burned in protest at being open. I was exhausted. I whimpered quietly, wanting nothing more than a few hours of sleep and some food.

Ember pulled the door open an inch and suddenly a figure had burst through it. I screamed before thinking and jumped up. I was not standing on the bed, my feet sunk into the mattress. Ember slammed the door shut and whipped around; his wings had been extended along with his claws.

But I did not see a raging human or ravenous fairy. Instead I laid my eyes on a blurry Dravven. He was zipping around the room giggling and throwing things. I held my hand up to the angry Ember and pointed. He seemed to recognize the fast moving image.

He reached his hand out and grabbed Dravven by the collar. Dravven peered around the room with wide eyes still laughing. Ember held him out in front of him like a disease.

"Dravven, what the hell are you doing?!" demanded Ember.

Dravven scanned the room once again then calmed down. His entire demeanor changed from that of a lunatic to a civil fairy. Ember let him go and he adjusted his vest. "It's Ebony."

I crawled off the bed and stood before them. The fire warmed my legs and feet, I relished in the feel. "What about Ebony?"

He ran a hand through his already messy hair, making it stick up on end in bulbous waves. "They've taken her. Ha-ha!"

Ember side stepped the mad fairy and came to stand next to me. "Who has taken her?" Dravven began humming under his breath. "Dravven! Get ahold of yourself!" shouted Ember.

Dravven quit moving immediately and merely gazed at Ember. He was absorbing his surroundings with precision. He did this for several minutes while Ember tapped his foot in annoyance. "The coven here."

"There's a coven here?" I asked astonished. I had not expected our kind to be so widespread across the map. I thought the majority of them lived in the castle. Obviously, I was wrong.

Dravven nodded his head a little too excitedly. His hair flopped around and he staggered having made himself dizzy. "I tried to warn her!" he exclaimed loudly. "Ha-ha! I did, I did! But she said no, she ignored Dravven!" he pointed at the ceiling. "They took her! Thinking she was Tranquility's scout, can you imagine? Ha-ha! Ebony being Tranquility's scout?! As if! Ha-ha!"

Ember reared back and slapped Dravven across the face before I could blink. Dravven's head whipped back and when he came to there was a large red mark across his left cheek. I gasped and covered my mouth in horror. Dravven licked his lips where gold blood was now seeping and an ashamed expression crossed his face.

Ember looked at his hand as if he could not believe what he had just done. I could see that his entire body was trembling and tears were welled in his eyes. He dropped his arm to his side and looked with concerned eyes at Dravven. "D-Dravven, I'm so sorry. It's just... That's my mother that they have taken... I need you to be serious for once in your life."

Dravven waved his hand in dismissal at the apology. "That would not be the first time someone has struck me!" he mildly giggled, obviously trying to suppress it.

I grabbed Ember's hand and squeezed, letting him know everything was going to be okay. "Where is she, Dravven?" I questioned.

Dravven crossed the room and sat in the only chair. It groaned under his weight and he rocked back and forth on its unsteady legs. He squirmed restlessly, trying his best to keep his energy at bay. I felt sorry for the mad fairy.

"She is with the Regina Coven. He-he! They are a bloodthirsty coven with a surprise twist!" The more he talked the more his eyes shone crazily. We were going to lose his attention soon. "They enjoy feasting on fairies."

"They... what?!" Ember yelled stepping forward. For a moment I thought he was going to strike Dravven again. Dravven obviously thought this too because he tipped his chair over and cowered in the corner.

I let go of Ember's hand to comfort Dravven. I pulled the blanket from the bed and wrapped it around him then ushered him to sit next to me in front of the fire. Ember's eyes swam once again and he too sat with us on the floor.

"Where did they take her, Dravven?" I soothed his hair from his face.

"The house they reside in... it is located on the outskirts of town, deep into the woods. She is there." He responded quite calmly.

Ember jumped up. "We should leave now."

Dravven shook his head. "They won't do anything tonight, their leader is gone. We have a couple days before anything bad happens. We need a plan."

I nodded in agreement and pulled Ember back to the floor. "Dravven is right. None of us will help her at all if we don't have a plan and some sleep."

Ember's brow furrowed. "I don't understand. How could they take her so quickly? She was right in front of us during our journey. She could have only been here a couple hours before we landed."

Dravven shook and jerked his head. His energy would burst out at any moment. "She found me as soon as she landed. I was talking with them about a poison Keelan and Ceintra demanded from me. The coven thought I had brought Ebony on purpose to take them to the queen."

He shot up suddenly, no longer able to keep himself under control, and hovered in the air. His wings had expanded and flapped noisily in the small room. Ember and I stood up to stare at him. He cackled and gestured with his hands at invisible objects.

"Where are you sleeping, Dravven?" Ember called over the noise of air being pushed around by steel wings.

Dravven folded his wings but did not snap them into place in his back. They hung limp behind his shoulders. "I have a room downstairs! Ha-ha!"

Ember nodded at this and opened the door. "I want you back here early tomorrow morning." Dravven went to leave. "And Dravven! Put your wings away!"

His wings sliced into his back and he was gone. Ember closed the door and shook his head. He drug a hand over his face. I could see now just how tired he was. His eyes were rimmed with pink and were bloodshot, and his entire body sagged under the weight of being awake so long.

I climbed back into the bed without another word and patted the spot next to me. He walked over and got in. He left his book on the floor this time. "I don't know what to do." He confessed. "This was supposed to be a simple trip to see the twins and then go home, and now we might be stuck here for days."

I sighed deeply and set my hand on his. He rubbed his thumb across mine. "It will all work out. We'll go explain our situation to the coven and they'll surely want to help in our war against Tranquility. Then we'll go see Keelan and Ceintra, and see what they can do."

He smiled but it did not reach his eyes. He pulled his hand away and jabbed it into the air. The fire became enraged and the room warmed a few degrees. He slunk down into the bed and pulled the covers to his chin. I did the same. "We'll discuss it more in the morning." He yawned.

Twenty-One

I woke up before Ember. The fire had burned down to warm embers and my entire body was once again a block of ice. I sighed in frustration. I did not want to go the rest of my eternal life freezing cold. I got out of bed, my body shivering, and tried to start the fire with unseen powers.

I waved my hand at it but only a puff of smoke erupted from the coals. I tried with all my might to will it into flames but nothing happened. I finally gave up and got a box of matches. If I couldn't do it the fairy way, I would do it the human way. It took me exactly a minute to have it raging again.

Ember shifted in the bed and rolled away from me. He mumbled something under his breath that I could not discern. I opened the curtain a crack to check outside. The sky was a light blue and pink, it was just becoming dawn.

I took advantage of Ember's slumber and filled the small bath in the washing room. The water steamed and rippled under the gushing faucet. I shuffled a few bottles of perfumes and bathing salts around until I found one that didn't attack my senses. It was a light purple and smelled of freshly cut flowers.

I dumped the contents of the small bottle into the bath and threw my nightshirt off. I climbed carefully into the tub and submerged myself into the feeling of warm water and bubbles. I hadn't taken a bath since I first met Ember, almost a week ago.

I drowned my body up to my neck and lightly splashed the water under the surface. My white hair plastered to my shoulders and collar bone, and sweat formed on my brow from the steam. My skin had turned a light pink from the heat. I examined my hand which looked almost human and caught a glimpse of my past.

I was staring at a headstone with the name Riah Montgomery carved into it. I was upset and crying, the ground underneath me was freshly turned. Three women stood near me, tears staining their faces and a priest read over burial scripture.

"That's a lovely sight to wake up to." Ember commented from the doorway of the washing room.

I quickly covered myself with my hands, although I knew my body could not be seen under the suds, and flushed a deep crimson. "I didn't expect you to be awake so soon."

He shrugged nonchalantly and gazed at himself in the mirror. "Not like I haven't seen a female body before, dear."

His response angered me deeply. I did not want to hear about his scandals with other women. How dare he talk of such things with me? But then I realized he probably meant human victims and my anger ebbed away.

He brushed his hair this way and that in the mirror until it laid flat on his head. "Could you... uh... leave so I can get out?" I hesitantly asked.

"Oh yes, of course. I am going to go fetch some food. What do you feel up to? Man? Woman? Young? Old?"

I searched his face for signs of humor but did not find any. He was being completely serious. He truly wanted to know what I craved. "It does not matter." I urged him to leave.

"I'll be back." He called while leaving. I heard the door to our room click shut and got out of the tub which was now turning cold. I began shivering almost immediately. This was going to be a miserable existence until I got used to my body temperature.

I rifled through my bag, pulling out the warmest clothes I could find. This consisted of a gray wool dress that buttoned up the back and had a slight train to it, and a pair of white stockings. For extra measure I pulled on gray boots that laced to my knee and a long white coat that had silver buttons lining up the front.

I brushed my hair in the mirror once I was done and dried the excess water from it by sitting in front of the fire. This is where I was when Ember returned carrying a body. I stood to get a better look at it; my mouth had started watering already.

Ember dropped the petite woman on the floor at my feet. Her chest was still moving with the beats of her heart and no color had left her face. "You didn't kill her."

"Of course not, have you ever had to eat cold food? Disgusting." He shivered.

We knelt down on either side of the woman and Ember's claws extended. I noticed with a start that mine had also. Ember dug his index finger into the woman's chest and sliced down to her navel. He stuck both hands into the bloody mess and pulled her chest apart. Organs were suddenly at our feet, ready to be devoured.

The woman had not moved, the color of her skin started rapidly ebbing away as her blood pooled on the ground beneath us. "Heart or lungs?" Ember questioned.

"Why do we only eat the heart and lungs?" I asked, plucking one of the lungs and in the process breaking ribs apart.

Ember pulled the heart out, it oozed under his grasp. He took a rather large bite; blood coated his lips and chin. "We don't, I know quite a few fairies that prefer kidneys or even the stomach." He explained while chewing. "We just get the most energy from hearts and lungs."

I chewed the lung slowly, soaking in the taste. Blood dripped from my bottom lip to my chin and splattered on the floor. My white and gray outfit was stained and ruined. The tissue squished under my teeth and slid down my throat easily.

I quickly finished the first and started on the second. Ember was already digging into the appendix. The carcass was swiftly emptying of contents, bones hung limply and veins were ripped apart.

The door was shoved open to our room and we both froze, thinking we had been caught in the act by a mortal. But Dravven skipped in and slammed the door behind him. "Oh, breakfast!" he cheered and pulled the liver from the body.

He ingested the organ rather quickly and slurped the intestines out. I dropped the remainder of the second lung back into the body of the woman and stood. I was more than full. My heart beat rapidly and everything was suddenly clearer.

I felt like I was invincible. Dravven licked the bones of their blood and gnawed on veins while Ember also stood, apparently finished. "My outfit is ruined." I stated, staring down at the gory mess covering my front.

Ember waved a hand in the air and the blood vanished from my garments. "All better." He replied, doing the same to his clothing.

"You must really teach me how to do that." I smiled.

Ember folded his arms across his chest and turned to watch Dravven as he finished off the woman. "You will learn in time." He assured me. "Now what to do with the body?"

"The fire?" I suggested hesitantly.

Dravven giggled and stood. "Wonderful idea, love!" Without another comment he ripped the woman's limbs off one by one. I watched in a mixture of fascination and horror.

He threw her arms, then her legs, and finally her torso into the raging hearth. We all watched as her flesh melted and only bones were left atop the logs. "But what of the bones?" I questioned.

Ember put his arm around me. "Easy enough," he exclaimed snapping his fingers. The bones turned to dust and withered away into the flames. It was done. The woman was dead and we were regenerated.

"Do you have a plan?" Dravven inquired.

"A plan?" Ember hesitated. "Oh! No, not yet."

"I think we should just go talk to them. If they're a coven that attacked Ebony over the thought that she was a spy from Tranquility, then they obviously don't like the queen. If we explain to them what we are trying to do they're bound to listen." I commented.

Ember nodded his approval. "Yes, I think you're right." He turned to Dravven. "Show us the way."

Dravven cackled and bounced out of the room. Dried blood still caked his arms and clothing. Ember sighed and waved his arm through the air, the blood vanished. "I have no idea how he hasn't been burned at the stake yet." He mumbled.

I suppressed a laugh and followed the two men out of the hotel and into the street. Humans bustled about making their way to work for an early shift or back home after a late one. A man bumped into me and almost knocked me into a pile of filth. Ember caught me and glared at the man.

I brushed myself off and thanked Ember. "Manners are nonexistent, I guess." I said.

Ember took my hand in his. "Foul creatures, and they think we're the bad ones."

Dravven had already scurried between the throngs of mortals and was making his way up a side street. Ember and I ran to catch up. This street was much calmer. The occasional person made their way down the sidewalk and a few people could be seen through windows of homes, but there was no shouting and shoving.

"Where exactly is this place, Dravven?" Ember asked.

Dravven threw a hand into the air and pointed. "Up there."

I followed his finger to a hill in the distance. A single, old mansion stood on the hilltop surrounded by trees. Not a single soul could be seen wandering the grounds. A shiver passed through me. It was spooky.

We were approaching the mansion in no time. I could feel the presence of fairies within the home but could not see any. We ascended the stairs which were old and decayed. They creaked under our weight and the front door groaned when Dravven tapped on it.

A man immediately answered the door. I sniffed the air, he was human. "Who calls?"

Dravven turned to look at us with a face of amusement. He turned back to the scrawny man. His hair was graying and his skin was droopy. He wore the attire of a servant but possessed the demeanor of a landlord. "Dravven Chaos, Ember Sky, and Victoria Renae," replied Dravven.

The man bowed and opened the door further for us to step in. We crossed the threshold which squeaked under the pressure. Everything was covered in cobwebs. The immaculate staircase, the lone table, the candelabras. I sneezed on impulse.

"Please, wait here." The man instructed us and disappeared through a door to our right. Ember grasped my hand and Dravven fluttered about. He sniffed at cobwebs and chewed on the dead flowers. Shiver after shiver passed through my body as the unsettling feeling in the house crept into my bones.

The man returned followed by a woman wearing a startling red dress. Blood coated her hands and chin, and her blonde hair was pinned to the back of her head. She reminded me a lot of Tranquility. An air of unease drifted with her.

I could not take my eyes off the blood coating her skin. Was it Ebony's? Were we too late? Ember squeezed my hand, obviously thinking the same thing, but then I realized the blood was red. Dravven stopped moving about and stood stark still.

"Oh, Dravven!" she proclaimed and wrapped her arms around him. Dravven stiffened even further. "How nice of you to come see me again."

Dravven politely pulled away. "Hello, Juniper."

Twenty-Two

Juniper. I knew the name from somewhere but could not place it. I had seen this woman before. Her blonde hair and green eyes, her flushed cheeks and dark makeup. It was all oddly familiar. I racked my brain but brought up nothing.

Ember leaned down to whisper in my ear. "How do we know her?"

"I don't know, she's familiar though." I mumbled back.

Juniper swept across the room, flinging her hair away from her face at the same time. I caught a glimpse of another fairy in my peripheral vision. He was leaning from behind a door to my left. I turned and he vanished.

I wanted out of this house as soon as possible.

"What brings you here? Surely not your dear spy. I thought I made myself perfectly clear about that one." Juniper exclaimed.

I let go of Ember's hand and strode forward to stand next to Dravven. He sighed in relief at being helped. "She was not a spy. We are all working against the queen." I said rather loudly.

Juniper stopped and turned to face me. Her electric green eyes bore into me and seemed to expose my soul. She studied me for a moment before speaking. "How do I know you?"

"I-I don't know." I stammered caught off guard by her direct question.

She swept towards me and grabbed my chin in her blood stained hand. She turned my face this way and that before letting go. "I have seen you before."

I put a hand on my hip. "I don't see how. I'm from the castle."

She went to say something but was cut off by Ember joining us on my other side. "She's to be the next queen."

Juniper stared at him then broke into fits of laughter. "The next queen?!" she gasped through her cackling. "Well isn't that fortunate! The next queen has come to visit me!" She wiped her eyes and some charcoal came off onto her hand. Her laughter subsided and she became very serious. "Seize them."

Fairies poured out of the doorways and overran us. I screamed out for Ember who was trying his best not to extend his wings. By law, we weren't supposed to harm another of our kind.

A man grabbed me from behind and locked my arms at my sides. He sneered and giggled in my ear. I could smell fresh blood on him. I pulled and fought against him to no avail, he was much stronger and much more aware of his powers.

He hit me on the back of my head and I blacked out.

"I am growing tired of being chained up like this." I informed Ember and Dravven as we hung limply against a wall in what I assumed to be the dungeon. Gold blood scattered the floor beneath us and our wings were staked to the stone walls by onyx.

Dravven giggled and his wing tore. The sound burst through the silence of the room and made me flinch. "I have been in this situation far more times than you, love."

Ember exhaled, his head was hung low and his hair blocked my view of his face. He seemed to have been hurt the worst. His clothes were torn to pieces, and bruises that were already healing lined his chin and collar bone. "Both of you be quiet. I'm trying to think."

"Excuse you?" I asked, shocked. "You're not the only one hanging here like some bag of meat. Whatever you're thinking of doing, it would be nice if you would inform us too."

He raised his head to stare at me. "Fine." His jaw was set. "Dravven, do you have your needle and string?" Dravven pulled a spool of string from his pocket and a rather large needle. He giggled but clamped a hand over his mouth to stop himself. "Good, now make as much noise as possible."

I didn't question his motives. I started screaming and yelling, and Dravven slammed his fists into the stone wall while he sang some absurd song about eating rabbits. Ember flew forward several times, his wings cracked with each movement. He grimaced in pain but kept going until one wing popped off the stake and the next followed.

He raised his hand in silence and we stopped. Ember limped across the room, gold blood and broken pieces of wings followed in his wake. He pulled the stakes from Dravven's wings with strong tugs and dropped to the floor.

Dravven dropped next to him and began sewing with a speed I had no idea he possessed. His entire demeanor was the most serious I had ever seen it and his hands flashed as the needle went in and out of Ember's wings.

Within seconds he was finished, Ember's wings were together and healing quickly. He immediately began on his own. Ember rolled his shoulders and sighed in content. "Uh, a little help here?" I struggled against my own restraints.

Ember grimaced. "Perhaps it would be better if you stayed to make some noise while Dravven and I seek out Ebony."

I glared at him with a hatred I did not truly feel. "They will kill me if you leave me here. The next time you see me my organs will be splayed across a table and I will be screaming for help."

He looked to Dravven who was still sewing his wings together then back at me. "Fine." He pulled the stakes and I bit my lip to suppress a scream. I fell forward but he caught me. I could feel the blood leak down each individual feather and felt as if at any moment I would faint.

Ember brushed my hair away from my face and hummed a strange tune in my ear. It calmed me down almost immediately. Dravven ambled towards us and pulled my wing back to begin sewing. I inhaled sharply as the needle somehow pierced the steel.

I must have lost my conscious because the next thing I knew Ember was standing me up and my wings were whole again. I slipped them into my back carefully. "What now?" I questioned.

Dravven spoke before Ember could. "There will be guards lining this entire hall. We are not the only fairies they have hidden away. Ebony will more than likely be in one of these rooms but we have to eliminate the guards before we can search for her."

"And that means being as silent as possible so Juniper or any of her other cronies don't hear the commotion." Ember added.

"Exactly. Ha-ha!" Dravven agreed. "I suggest temporary mind control."

Ember set his mouth into a grim line. "They surely have protective charms down here, and we don't have a potion to make it strong enough to break through."

Dravven flipped his hand into the air and snapped his fingers in my direction. My mind went blank. What was happening? Where was I? Who was I? I was so confused. I teetered back and forth on the balls of my feet. Dravven snapped his fingers again and I came out of it. I shook my head.

"Obviously they don't have any charms down here, love. Ha-ha! That was easy enough. This is not the smartest coven around, I tell you. Ha-ha!" he exclaimed.

Ember considered this a moment before speaking. "Do you think you can knock them all into a state of confusion with one swipe? I'm afraid that's all we'll have the time for. Surely if you knock one out the rest will notice."

Dravven nodded vigorously. "Yes, yes. We just need to open that door and I need to be able to see them all. The spell will only work if I have eyes on every single one of them." He giggled.

I finally spoke up. "And what will Ember and I do?"

"Well, you'll start looking for Ebony, love! She has to be in one of these chambers. Ha-ha! The faster we get her, the faster we can be gone and to the twins." Dravven replied.

I nodded in agreement and shoved my sleeves up to my elbows. If things didn't go according to plan, things might get messy fast. Dravven strode across the room to the door and we followed.

It was made of simple wood with black hinges that groaned when we opened it. The guard outside immediately turned around and raised his hand to bash Dravven in the face. Dravven ducked under the hit and stood in the hall.

We watched from the doorway while he waved his hand in the air towards the now alert guards and snapped his fingers. They all fell in unison. They bodies crumpled and thudded on the bare floor and some began talking to themselves. Dravven waved us out.

We stepped into the hall, which was much longer than I had expected it to be, and decided to split up. Dravven flew to the end of the hall and began barging into rooms, and Ember flew to the other end and did the same.

I turned and opened the door nearest. I expected to see the worst but found nothing behind door number one. I slammed it shut and went to the next. Inside this one a dead fairy laid sprawled across the floor. His right leg was missing and his body was covered in a coat of gold. I shook my head and moved on.

The slamming of doors and aggravated sighs went on for quite some time before Ember yelled out and ran into a room to my left. Dravven and I glanced at each other then followed. The room was darker than the rest and contained large puddles of blood.

Ember knelt in the corner holding onto the body of Ebony Vail. He shook with silent sobs and quietly begged her to wake. Dravven placed a hand on Ember's shoulder and pulled him away. It was the first glimpse I had had of Ebony.

Her hair had been torn away leaving bald patches and her face was almost unrecognizable. Both eyes were swollen and purple with blood leaking from them and a chunk of her left cheek was missing. Her plaid shirt was hanging open along with her stomach.

Her organs were everywhere.

They hung limply in her body having been pulled from their spots then carelessly placed back and her intestines were wrapped around her own legs, binding her together. I shook with unshed tears and slapped my hand across my mouth in horror. I had to look away before the contents of my breakfast came spilling out in a violent mess.

Dravven examined her body while Ember sobbed on the floor. He was covered in the blood of his mother and his own tears. I knelt next to him in a puddle and rubbed his shoulder. He did not acknowledge my existence.

Dravven stood. "They took her heart." His hands were shoved into his pockets and his hair hung limply in his face. A single tear ripped down his pale cheek.

I stood next to him, looking down at the crumpled mess that was Ebony Vail. "Why would they do such a thing? To their own kind! We are supposed to work together!"

I wanted to be upset but I was just angry. This woman had acted as if I was her own child, and had accepted me when I was confused and dazed after awakening. I had known her such a short time and yet felt so connected to her.

I wanted blood for this. I wanted to see Juniper squirm under me while I ripped her savage heart from her chest and devoured it right before her eyes. Dravven pulled his hand from his pocket and wiped his face. It left a gold streak across his nose and brow.

"There's only one person who can fix this." He said glumly.

I caught his hidden meaning and shivered. "Tranquility."

He nodded and rubbed his hand across his face again. "Only the Queen has this type of power. To bring her kind back from the dead. But she's missing and I don't know where to begin looking for her."

"But I'm a queen. I'm supposed to be the current queen. Couldn't I help her?" I suggested desperately.

Dravven glanced at me then directed his attention back to the body of Ebony. "You're not technically the queen yet, love. You don't possess all the powers Tranquility still keeps to herself. You'll only unlock them all when she dies."

I hung my head in defeat. There was nothing I could do. Ember wept in the corner and shook violently. There was nothing I could do to help him either. Dravven knelt down and untied her intestines. He coiled them carefully and set them into her stomach.

I watched as he put all of her organs in their rightful places then waved his hand to attach them again. I noticed for the first time that her blood was turning silver and her skin was turning pink. It seemed she was reverting back to her mortal self.

A thought occurred to me. It was a long shot but it might work. "What about the twins? Could they help her?"

Ember shot up at my comment. His wings were spread to their full capacity and his eyes were ablaze with anger. "Yes, that may work! We need to get her to the twins!"

Dravven sighed in utter sadness. "The only problem with that is, if you ask the twins to heal Ebony then they will not help you with Tranquility. They will only help with one task, that is how they are."

"To hell with Tranquility!" shouted Ember. "Ebony would not be laying here if it wasn't for that evil witch! We'll figure out another way to kill her once Ebony is okay."

Dravven looked to me for assurance and I nodded in agreement. My rise to power could be put on hold. Ebony needed our attention and care more than Tranquility did. Dravven knelt down and swiftly sewed Ebony's skin back together. He wrapped her clothes around her the best he could then picked her up.

Ember took her body from him and cradled her in his arms like an oversized infant. "How will we get out of here?" I asked.

Dravven ushered us towards the door and opened it. The guards outside were still dazed and confused. Some cried and others thrashed about angrily, unable to get up from their spots on the floor. We followed Dravven silently through the hall and up the creaky staircase.

Dravven snapped his fingers at every fairy we encountered without giving them the chance to say a word. Before we knew it we were outside, walking away from the house of horror.

"Ember, flictate. The last thing we need is you being seen carrying a dead body. Victoria and I will get food. Meet us at the edge of the woods to the north of town in an hour's time." Dravven demanded. Ember took off with a nod of his head and Dravven turned to me. "Let's go harvest some organs."

Twenty-Three

"You don't have to be scared of me." I cooed. I was in a flat, walking across old floorboards towards a middle aged man. His belly pushed the buttons of his shirt slightly and his brown hair was graying towards the top.

"I-I know what you are!" he stuttered and shouted in fear.

"I am just hungry, that's all." I replied slyly. This caused him to cower more. I lifted my skirts to step over a footstool and made my way closer to him.

I knew my eyes were alight with the taste of human blood and excitement. I could hear Dravven upstairs moving about. He had the man's wife cornered in their bedroom, playing the same game I was.

"P-please, what d-do you want? I have no m-money." The man begged.

I threw my head back in laughter, now a foot away from him. I could smell his stench wafting towards me, it made me salivate. "I do not want your money; I have no use for it."

There was a scream and thud from above. Dravven's job was over. The man and I both listened as her body was drug across the floor and then thrown down the stairs. She landed in a mangled heap at the bottom, blood pooled under her.

Dravven appeared a few seconds later, licking the blood from his fingers and laughing hysterically. The man in front of me whimpered pathetically at the sight of his wife. I took my chance and shoved my hand deep into his abdomen.

His scream was cut off and the light from his eyes went out as I pulled his lung out, leaving a wide gap in his chest. Dravven clapped behind me and giggled. "Well done, love. A natural, if I do say so myself."

I bowed sarcastically. "Thank you, thank you."

He pulled a black bag rimmed with a gold string from his vest and flopped it open. "Stuff the organs in here, love. We have no time to drag these worthless humans through the streets and attract stares."

I dug my hand back into the corpse and pulled his organs out carefully. I didn't want them to rip and lose their juice in my haste. Dravven did the same and in no time we had a bag full of dinner, and two empty corpses at our feet.

He pulled the bag shut while giggling then left without telling me to follow. We flictated to the edge of the woods and sat, waiting for Ember to show up. An hour went by, then two, and still nothing. The world around us had grown dark and cold before he landed quietly in front of us.

I shot up, glad to see him. A million terrible scenarios had been running through my head. What if Juniper had found him? What if humans had rioted? What if, what if, what if!? But here he was, whole and unharmed before me.

He carried Ebony wrapped snugly in a sheet in his arms and threw mine and Dravven's things to the ground. I picked my bag up and slung it over my shoulder. Dravven did the same.

"You're late." Commented Dravven.

Ember shrugged. "I'm aware. I just wanted some time with my mother before we started this trek."

Dravven shook his head and turned to walk. "Well, we better get going. It's already dark and Keelan and Ceintra only come out after midnight, strange little creatures." He giggled to himself.

Ember didn't say a word to me. Only pulled the strap of his bag tighter and adjusted his grip on Dravven then followed silently. I walked after him, wanting nothing more than to speak with him but not knowing what to say.

Our trek was long and tedious. I tripped over branches more than once, unable to see them through the darkness despite my better vision. We munched on organs every couple hours, making sure we had ample energy. Dravven had somehow kept them warm in his little bag.

We walked in silence, Dravven only breaking it to tell us to watch an especially large tree root or to scare off animals that could not sense our dead bodies wandering about. Ember kept Ebony cradled against him and once when he fell, he took the brunt of the force instead of her.

That is true love, I thought silently.

Snow began to descend on us halfway through our journey. Dravven kept saying just a little longer, but that little longer stretched into hours and hours of walking. I wondered why we couldn't flictate there and be done with this all.

I shivered despite my many layers of clothing and watched as Ember struggled to throw his cloak on without letting go of Ebony. He hugged her to his chest and attempted to throw the cloak over his shoulder with one hand.

I sighed deeply and took it from him. He dropped his arm back to Ebony and let me wrap the black fabric around his shoulders and clasp it under his chin. He nodded to me in thanks but still did not say a word. I set my mouth into a grim line.

I stood for a moment pondering over my newfound jealousy. Ebony was his mother, of course he loved her. Why was I acting like this? But I already knew the reason. The question that had been haunting me since I saw him collapse on the floor of her dungeon room.

Would he act like this over me?

"We're here." Dravven whispered back to us.

I quickly walked forward to see around the tree he was at. A fire was lit and two people were laughing and dancing around it. My first thought was that we had just entered a den of lunatics. But then I realized they were dumping potions and elixirs into the flames. They were doing a seeing.

Their home was not much. It was quite literally a shack set between two trees with a makeshift awning created from a black blanket. The fire pit sat in the middle of the clearing with tall flames rising from it.

Snow had littered their shack and hair, yet they kept dancing and shouting undistinguishable words. Dravven coughed and entered the clearing, they both stopped immediately and the flames turned blue.

"You." Ceintra spat at him. She was quite beautiful despite her tone. Her hair was sandy blonde and hung in waves to her breasts, her wings were blue, and her eyes were solid white. I thought at first she was blind but she followed Dravven's every move, and shifted her attention to Ember and I when we emerged.

"Who are they?" demanded Keelan, he was the exact copy of his sister in male form, blue wings and all.

Dravven put his hands in the air in front of him and did not bother expanding his wings, afraid that they might take it as a threat. They shifted from side to side as we drew nearer and the flames dulled and turned green.

Ember set Ebony carefully on the snow spattered ground near the fire. He unwrapped her body from the sheet and I saw exactly what was becoming of her. She was aging. Her hair had turned from brown to gray and her face was wrinkly and old.

Ember stood and stepped back from her body, tears threatening to spill over. "We need your help." He croaked.

Ceintra carefully stepped around the fire and knelt near Ebony's body. She placed a hand to her forehead and stared upwards into nothingness. We waited for her verdict which did not come for several minutes.

I held my breath until she removed her hand and ambled away from the body. She turned to her brother, a silent conversation ensuing between them before turning back to us. "And what will we get in return?"

"We can-" Dravven started but Ember cut him off with a shake of his head.

"Anything." Ember confidently replied.

"Anything?" Ceintra smiled and placed her hand on the arm of her brother.

"Yes." Ember assured her. "What do you want?"

She once again drifted her ghostly eyes to her brother and they both stood like statues for several minutes. The only movement from them came from the raise of an eyebrow or the twitch of a finger.

Dravven interrupted their silent conversation. "Will you stop that? Not in the presence of others."

Keelan turned on him. "You have no right to demand things from us, Dravven Chaos. If you want help then you will act civil and abide by our rules. You are in our territory."

Dravven slunk back into the shadows of a nearby tree and did not say another word. If I hadn't known better, I would have said he was frightened of these psychic twins.

Ceintra folded her hands in front of her, which were almost translucent and spoke. "We want the head of Tranquility, and our Royal Rooms back."

Ember didn't hesitate, "Done."

She nodded at Keelan who disappeared into their small home and returned a few minutes later with a box full of rattling jars. He opened it to expose many glasses full of potions and herbs. Ceintra looked over them and pulled a green tinted jar from the box.

She sprinkled the contents of it into the fire and the flames raged to life. They shot into the sky, double the height of me, and danced awaiting their next instruction. Ceintra once again knelt next to Ebony.

"We saw this." She spoke to her brother who had sat himself next to her. "We didn't believe it would happen. She has such a powerful soul."

Ember knelt in the grass and snow across from them, and placed his hand on Ebony's leg. "What has happened to her?"

Ceintra smoothed the brittle hair away from Ebony's face and looked up at Ember. Her white eyes made it hard to see what she was staring at. She seemed to look right through his face. "They took her heart, one of our vital organs to regenerate us. In doing so, they took her immortal life. She is still alive, but she is dying quickly. Her body is catching up to her true age, and as we all know, humans cannot live centuries."

He shivered and held back a sob at her words. "So what can you do? Can you stop it?"

Ceintra nodded. "We need to create a new heart."

Twenty-Four

Ceintra threw potion after potion into the fire. The flames went multicolored. Keelan held Ebony up by her arms into a sitting position. Her head lolled to the side, her face growing ever more saggy and wrinkled.

I sat next to Dravven against their house. The boards protested under our combined weight but we paid no mind, too enthralled by the magic happening in front of us.

I leaned over to Dravven, making sure no one could hear us. Ember was standing close to the fire, watching intently everything they did. "Is this considered witchcraft?"

Dravven giggled between mouthfuls of kidney. He swallowed. "Yes, I suppose so. Very illegal what they are doing. If townspeople find out we would have a riot on our hands. Bring out the pitchforks and torches!" he laughed again. "Ebony was always very fond of magic and its properties. She would be very pleased that they are using a method such as this."

I considered this a moment then something dawned on me. "You knew they needed a human heart. That's why you brought the organs with us."

He smirked. "I know their ways very well. I lived with them for a time, as you already know from your time in The Mayhem Realm. I assumed they would do something like this."

I laid my head against the cold wood and sighed. "Do you think it will work?"

He stayed silent, not answering right away. He watched as Ceintra and Keelan hauled Ebony's body into the fire. Flames lapped over her and crackled. Ember looked away, unable to watch as her body burned in the mixture of potions.

"Yes, yes I think it will." He stood and left me to stand next to Ember. Ebony's body had to "cook" as Ceintra had so eloquently put it for a few hours before they could do anything. It left me time to think, which was never a good thing.

I couldn't figure out how this all had happened. It wasn't supposed to be like this. In fact, I shouldn't have even been alive. I was supposed to be in a grave somewhere, in silent rest for eternity. But instead I was simultaneously trying to win a throne, keep the love of my life close, and save Ebony from a fate she probably wanted.

I fell asleep like this but quickly awoke to Dravven kicking my leg rather brutally. I yawned and sat up, my neck stiff from having been angled awkwardly in my position. "It's time," was all he said before resuming his spot next to Ember.

Keelan was shouting something to the heavens in another language and Ceintra was dancing awkwardly around the fire. I had never seen such a thing. I stood and made my way over to Dravven who wrapped his arm around me in anticipation.

Ceintra pulled the heart from the bag and held it up for the stars to see. "Educite eam!" she yelled and convulsed under the weight of her own words. Keelan had stopped moving completely and stood perfectly still, awaiting his sister's next move.

She walked slowly to the fire, saying things with each step under her breath. I could not hear her. She stepped into the flames and they crackled and spit around her. Her hair ignited and her flesh melted under the heat. I wanted to look away but was too engrossed in the horror of it all.

"MAY MAYHEM BE WITH YOU." She shouted and shoved the heart into the carcass of Ebony Vail. She jumped from the fire and danced back over to her brother who wrapped his arms around her. Her skin was back to normal along with her hair. The fire had barely touched her.

A piercing scream ripped from the flames and Ember launched forward. Dravven caught him about the waist and pulled him backwards. "No, Ember. Stop!" he yelled. Ember dropped to his knees and watched as Ebony's body quaked on her makeshift funeral pyre.

"She's dying!" Ember shouted, once again struggling against Dravven.

"She's already dead, love!" Dravven shouted back, not letting up.

I wanted to help but once again did not know how. I stood silently with my hands folded behind me and waited for whatever miracle was about to happen. Keelan and Ceintra stood side by side, mirrors of each other and watched.

Another scream ripped from the flames. It shattered the night around us and echoed through the hills. I wanted desperately to cover my ears and cower in the shack but forced myself to watch.

Ebony's body lifted from the burning logs then slammed back down. Her chest rose in deep breaths then stopped completely. Something was definitely happening. Ember shoved against Dravven, trying now to crawl towards the fire. Dravven held him back with superior strength.

"If you go in there, not only will you die from your stupidity, but she will also! Get ahold of yourself, Ember Sky!" Dravven yelled over the screaming Ebony.

Ember didn't seem to register a word he was saying. He wept and clawed at the ground, covering his hands in dirt and kicking at Dravven. I did not blame him for his actions. His mind was telling him he was watching his mother burn to death and he was not doing anything.

Ember was in shock from what he was seeing.

Ebony's body lifted completely off the ground and stood straight up. Her eyes shot open, they were red and bleeding. Not gold blood, but deep crimson. I backed away in fright. Ember had not noticed, he was turned around punching at Dravven's arms.

Ceintra squealed in delight. Apparently, she had been expecting something along the lines of this monstrosity. Ebony's body fell back down into the flames and her eyes closed again. It was like watching a bad game of chase. Every time there was hope, she disappeared again.

Dravven and Ember were now in a full on fight on the ground. They scratched and clawed at each other, and had extended their wings. Ember had gotten one of his stuck into the ground and was trying to pull it out while Dravven sat on top of him, still trying to keep him under control.

I decided not to get in between them. My eyes were glued to the flames where Ebony's hair had begun to change back to its normal brown. My fists were clenched at my sides, my claws digging into the flesh. Gold blood spattered on the ground. This was actually going to work!

Ember had seemed to notice the change of appearance because he stopped fighting Dravven and instead, let him hold him down while he watched in anticipation.

"Is it almost done?" screamed Dravven over the sudden whipping of wind and spitting of flames.

"Yes! Yes, it is!" Ceintra yelled back. I noticed with a start that Keelan was almost touching the flames. He was mesmerized by the power that had come forth from him. Ceintra pulled him back, still cheering in excitement.

She was a far cry from what she had been while living in the castle. She was active and happy; I could see it by her expression. She had been so withdrawn and sad while living with Tranquility, I don't know why I expected to see her the same.

The flames suddenly vanished and the wind stopped. We were encased in utter darkness. I drifted towards Dravven and Ember who both stood at the sudden change and Ember grabbed my hand. My heart leapt at the contact, although my mind did not follow suit.

"Something is wrong." Ceintra's whisper to her brother carried over the wind.

I clung to Ember tightly, watching in the flames for some sign of movement. Nothing happened, all was still. Then suddenly, a swish of wings could be heard above us and a thud as someone landed.

"Damn," Dravven mumbled, "She's found us."

Twenty-Five

The fire was lit again without help and Ebony's hair had turned back to gray. I shook nervously, afraid that we had lost her for good this time. We had been so close. Ember let go of my hand and dropped once again to his knees.

Someone was walking behind us. I could feel their presence like a storm coming. Dravven stood still, keeping his eyes focused on the ground. Keelan and Ceintra were silently speaking again, and by the movements of their hands it was rather urgent.

Finally, Ceintra turned. "You are not welcome here."

At first I thought she was talking to me. I was appalled and hurt. Then, Tranquility spoke from behind me. "I am welcome wherever rules are being broken, dear."

"We have broken no rules!" insisted Keelan.

Tranquility came into view. She was wearing one of her usual black dresses that flowed like water down her figure and trailed behind her collecting dirt and leaves. The bottom was stained white from snow.

She had a red cloak wrapped about her tightly clasped with a gold wing pendant at her throat. Keelan and Ceintra hugged one another and backed away. I stood by myself, inches away from her. Dravven and Ember were silent, merely staring into the flames as Ebony disintegrated.

"You haven't?" she brought her hand to her bosom and acted shocked. "But my dear, you have! Only the queen can bring fairies back to life. Your magic is not wanted here!"

A burst of courage came from nowhere. "But I am the rightful queen, and I allowed them to."

Tranquility turned and gasped as if seeing me for the first time. She had not even noticed me standing there! "You." She spat with such venom I almost backed away.

Instead, I strode forward, now face to face with her, although she was a bit taller than I. "Yes, me. The queen. I suggest you leave unless you want a repeat of the castle."

Keelan and Ceintra stood tall behind her, having gained courage from mine. "Yes." Ceintra shouted clear, it rang through the silence. "We have already told her your weakness."

It was a lie, but Tranquility believed it. She spun on her heel and faced the twins. They shrunk back a little but stood their ground rather well. "You haven't," she sneered.

Ceintra took a step away from Keelan and squared her shoulders. "Oh, but we have, and unless you leave and allow us to help Ebony you will be nothing but a figment of our imaginations."

The threat was carried with such authority that even I believed it. Tranquility took a step back and clutched her cloak around her. She pierced each one of us with her gaze, realizing she was greatly outnumbered.

Her wings flew from her back and almost sliced me in half. I jumped out of the way just in time. Dravven easily caught me before I fell and straightened me back up. I didn't turn to thank him; I didn't want to risk taking my eyes off Tranquility.

"I will see you again, Victoria." She sneered, "And when I do, you will be very sorry."

I waved my hand at her in dismissal and she disappeared into the night. Keelan and Ceintra were on the move before she left the ground. They smothered the flames and dragged the deteriorating body of Ebony out of the pit.

Ember hopped up and carefully picked her body off the ground. "What now?" he was shaking as he asked the question.

Keelan and Ceintra looked at each other briefly. "We need another heart." Keelan answered.

"I have another heart! We took it from a man!" I pronounced gleefully.

Ceintra shook her head. "No. We need one from a woman. If we give her a man's heart it is possible she will just become a human. The genders must match for this to work."

Ebony's finger fell to the ground with a dull thud. Keelan backed away and Ceintra gasped in horror. Ember picked it up and tried desperately to reattach it with just his powers. It stuck for a moment then fell again.

"I'll go." Dravven said and flew off before anyone could protest.

Ember held the finger tightly in his grip while trying to delicately balance Ebony against his frame. Ceintra quickly gestured for us to enter their home, we followed without question.

The house's interior did not match its exterior. While the outside was rundown and shabby, the inside was beautifully decorated and very accommodating. There were four rather small rooms. A kitchen, bedroom, bathroom, and living area. The living room also doubled as a library, each wall was filled with white bound books.

It reminded me much of their rooms in the castle. Everything was white or light blue. The occasional black ornament was set somewhere, and multiple vials of tears lined their hearth, but other than that the color pallet was constricted.

Ember set Ebony on the blue couch and dropped into the white chair. He was still holding her finger in his hand. I rested on the arm of the chair and watched as he realized with a start that he held a piece of his mother. He dropped the old finger to the floor and cringed.

"Oh my." Ceintra stated. She picked the finger up from the floor and placed it on the small table between us. "I do not think that can be fixed."

"So she will be damaged?" Ember asked.

"I'm afraid so. She will only have four fingers on her left hand. Of course, this shouldn't do much harm. It is just unfortunate."

We sat silently watching as Ebony grew older by the minute before our eyes. Her skin sagged once again and her hair was falling out in gray clumps. "Will her hair grow back?" I questioned.

"Oh, yes. That will be fine. The spell reverses aging, so her hair will be back to its normal shine. Of course, that does not count for limbs. Growing younger does not mean you suddenly sprout fingers." She chuckled lightly. "But I am sure our Ebony can make do with nine fingers in total, rather than ten. She is strong."

"Will she... will she continue to fall apart like this?" Ember inquired, I could tell he did not want to hear the answer.

Ceintra nodded numbly. "As I said before, her body is catching up to her actual age. And if I am not mistaken that is a few centuries. By this point in the human deterioration process, she would be nothing but bones. But let us not dwell on such things. Dravven is a rather quick hunter."

Keelan brought in two cups of tea from the kitchen and handed them to Ember and I. I grasped the cup tightly, enjoying the warmth in my hands. The snow was coming down thickly outside. He disappeared and returned with two more cups and handed one to Ceintra.

They both sat on a second couch and laid back, seemingly exhausted. "How did she find you?" Keelan pondered aloud.

Ember took a sip of tea. "She's probably been watching us. I think we all know how she is."

We all nodded in unison and drank quietly. Ebony's body continued to go downhill. For the first time, I prayed. I prayed for Dravven to be swift and for Ebony to be reanimated. I prayed that all would go well and Tranquility would be defeated. I simply prayed.

A knock sounded on the door. We all jumped then settled down, thinking it was Dravven back so soon. Keelan set his cup carefully on the table, making sure not to hit the finger, and then answered it.

I leaned over to peer around him, but instead of seeing Dravven I saw a young fairy. Her hair was brown and her eyes were deep gold. She held a small letter firmly in her grasp. It was an antiqued gold color with a black ribbon tied snuggly around it.

"By decree from Queen Tranquility Erasmus," began the fairy, "Ember Sky, Victoria Renae, Ebony Vail, Dravven Chaos, and Ceintra and Keelan Sarpin are required to attend the annual Mayhem Fairy Masquerade held at The Mayhem Castle." She shoved her hand out and placed the letter in the shaking hand of Keelan.

I was holding my breath in anticipation of a rude remark or some form of trickery. But the fairy merely nodded and vanished on the spot. Keelan turned still gripping the letter and slammed the door shut.

Ceintra stood and made her way over to him. She ripped the letter from his hand and tore it open, her eyes moved eerily across the page. "I can't believe this! How outrageous!"

Ember shot up and took the letter from Ceintra's grasp. He too read it with inhuman speed. "How could she?"

Keelan shrugged. "It is a tradition in the castle. She isn't just going to postpone it over a little fight and the death of a fairy."

I finally stood, tired of being left in the dark and confusion. "What's going on?"

Ember turned to me, his face was somber. "Every year Tranquility holds a masquerade at the castle. It's meant to celebrate our existence, and symbolize how we hide among humans. It's usually huge and rather exciting. I just can't believe she's still having it after everything that has happened in the last few days." He ran a hand through his hair which stuck up on end at the contact. "I had completely forgotten about it."

"But..." my mind rushed to keep up with this information. "She was in hiding!"

Ember grimaced and threw the letter onto the table. "How much you bet she was in the castle the entire time?"

Silence fell over us like never before. It was uncomfortable and so thick you could almost touch it. Keelan and Ceintra both fell back onto the couch in exasperation. I set myself slowly back down on the chair's arm and directed my attention to Ebony. Her condition had thankfully not worsened.

Ember paced back and forth, his hands clenched at his sides. I didn't bother to try to ease his mind; I knew there was no point. Several minutes went by without comment. Keelan and Ceintra stared into space and I kept my eyes locked on Ebony.

A thought occurred to me. "We could kill her there." The comment came out in almost a whisper but due to the silence they all heard it clearly. Ceintra sat forward and rested her elbows on her knees.

"We could." She agreed in an equal whisper.

Ember finally sat, his chin rested on his hands. "How?"

Ceintra seemed to roll her eyes although it was hard to tell. "We are seers, Ember. We know how to defeat her. I believe that is why Victoria decided to come to us."

I nodded but didn't reply. My mind was racing. "These are the perfect conditions." I finally stated. "There will be hundreds of fairies in one place. The castle will be in chaos. Tranquility won't expect us to do anything there."

"What of Ebony?" Ember asked.

Ceintra stood, a new air of power about her. "We heal Ebony and then we plan. We have a few days yet before we need to make the journey. Keelan and I will tell you what we know and perhaps with our combined force we can make this happen."

Twenty-Six

"We have a problem! Ha-ha!" screeched Dravven from the sky. He flew down in rapid speed and dug his heels into the ground. Dirt and grass came up in chunks and coated his pants in mud.

We all followed him with our eyes. It had been hours since he had left and we grew bored of sitting in the house. We moved ourselves outdoors and were watching as Keelan and Ceintra drew patterns in the fire and chanted strange things.

Dravven dropped a human heart on the ground and backed away. His entire arm was coated in dark red, sticky blood. He giggled like the maniac he was and pranced around. Ember stood with a glare on his face.

"What took you so long, you fool?!" he demanded. He had grown very impatient.

Dravven danced around while trying to remove the dirt from his trousers. His hair swung around frantically with his movements and his wings flopped back and forth. "Did you not hear me!? We have a problem!"

It was Keelan's turn to be impatient. "Well, spit it out!"

Dravven stood straight and pointed into the air. "Are you blind, love? There are fairies up there!"

"There are... what?" Ember demanded looking into the night sky.

"Juniper's coven!" he shouted then threw his head back. "Show yourselves, loves!"

A collective hum sounded through the air then all around us savage fairies landed gracefully. They wore the present fashions but added their own tools and weapons. Some carried hatchets in their belt loops while others had bows swung across their backs. They were obviously a group used to brutal killings.

Juniper landed directly in front of me. She wore men's black trousers with a crisp white button down. Her blonde hair was clipped back and her green eyes were rimmed darkly with a charcoal pencil.

I took a step back and she smiled. Her teeth were stained gold from a fresh feast. "You aren't the smartest bunch, are you?"

"How long have you been watching us?" Ceintra demanded.

Juniper turned to her, her blonde hair catching the light and briefly turning the color of straw. "Only a few minutes. Would have been longer if this imbecile hadn't come flying in."

I caught Ember's eye. He was looking between the heart on the ground and Ebony's body near the fire. He winked at me and I understood completely what was about to happen.

Dravven apparently had too because his wings sprung at attention the same time mine did. Juniper snapped her head back to me, she bared her teeth. Ceintra and Keelan were staring at each other, engrossed in a conversation.

Ember's wings slowly extended. The tension in the air was thick and weighed down upon as all. We were all in fighting stances without the act of fighting. I readied myself. I knew that when someone made a move it would be on and I wouldn't have time to think.

Juniper's wings were by far smaller than mine and a dark green. I had to admit they matched her eyes perfectly. If not for her bad attitude she would be a marvelous fairy.

Ember roared and lunged for the heart. He threw it to Ceintra who caught it with ease and dumped a pocketful of potions and herbs into the fire. Keelan shoved Ebony's body into the flames and they began their chants.

Juniper turned to go after Ember but I caught her arm and spun her around. She screeched and extended her rather short claws. They scraped across my face before I pinned them against her and began my tornado of steel.

My wings brushed into her and she screamed out in pain. In seconds she was spinning too. We were a moving mass of torture. It reminded me a lot of my fight with Tranquility, although for whatever reason I was more concerned with keeping this woman away from Ebony than myself.

I could hear yells and obscene words being shouted around us mixed with spitting flames, and the chants of Ceintra and Keelan. I was beyond exhausted but didn't let up. My wings bashed against Juniper's with sparks and the smell of fire.

Dravven cackled to my right. I caught a glimpse of him mid-spin pulling another fairy's head off and throwing it into the trees. The body grasped about then fell. Dravven tore his heart out and smashed it under his foot. I had to stop myself from cringing.

"MAY MAYHEM BE WITH YOU!" I heard screamed from Ceintra to my left. I slacked off a bit, knowing we wouldn't have to put up with this much longer.

This was my fatal mistake. An arrow hit my wing and I fell to the ground. Juniper kept spinning and clipped my side. I groaned in pain and turned to look at the arrow. They were soaring past me at rapid speeds. I ducked down to avoid being hit again.

I saw Juniper lying across from me; apparently she had been hit too. I wanted to laugh at the insanity of her being wounded by her own people but kept myself under control. I could see Ember clashing with another man not far off.

"The arrows are tipped with onyx!" I yelled, pulling with all my might at the arrow to remove it from my wing.

Ember heard this because he began ducking and maneuvering around the flying sticks. The arrow broke in my hand, leaving the tip embedded in my feathers. I had no time to claw it out; Juniper was getting up in front of me.

I leaped up and descended on her, shoving my body weight on top of her and my arms into her shoulders. She landed back against the ground with a loud thud. I shoved my claws into her neck without thinking. I could see Ebony rising in the flames out of my peripheral vision.

Juniper gasped and choked, gold blood seeped around my hand and dripped from her mouth. The chaos around me became numbed and distant. All that mattered was killing the woman under me.

She shoved her claws into my ribs but barely broke the surface. I winced at the pain but kept stretching my fingers deep into her throat. Suddenly, she changed.

I was looking down at my sister. She wore a light grey dress and her eyes were cheerful and filled with laughter. My hand froze but I did not remove myself from her. "J-Juniper?" I stammered.

I was killing my sister! How could I do such a thing?! What had happened to her? A million questions flooded into my mind with a sense of dread at the amount of blood coming from her neck. It dawned on me that I was queen and had the ability to mortally wound another fairy.

I tried to staunch the blood as she choked and spit. I covered the wound with my hands but the blood erupted between my fingers. Tears skid down my face and dripped onto hers. "No, no! Juniper, no! I'm so sorry!"

She couldn't reply, it was impossible. She was bleeding out all over the ground. Her blood seeped into the earth below us and stained my clothing. The fighting around me evaporated, all I could hear were her strangled breaths.

I pressed my hands harder into the wound but this only made her bleed more. I ripped a chunk of fabric from my jacket and placed it against the open flesh. The blood soaked through the rag and continued to poor.

How much could there be?!

Her eyes rolled into her head and she quit struggling. I could barely see through the gold film covering my eyes. My wings snapped into my back despite the arrowhead. I paid no attention to such trivial things.

I kept blotting at the gash on Juniper's throat, trying my best to make it stop. "Juniper, no. Please, no. I'm so sorry. Juniper! Come back to me!"

I gave up on trying to stop the blood flow and instead shook her shoulders. I removed myself from her and knelt next to her body. I pulled her into me and smoothed her hair back. It left a gold streak down her forehead and through her hair.

She lay limp in my arms as I clutched her tightly against my chest. "Juniper! JUNIPER!" I screamed, my shoulders heaving with sobs.

She did not move. Her head lolled to the side and her eyes stayed open and afraid. The blood from her throat had dulled to a trickle. I stayed knelt in the puddle weeping and shaking uncontrollably.

Someone grasped my shoulder. I cringed away, keeping Juniper tightly wrapped in my arms. The hand rubbed some of the tension from my back and knelt next to me. I turned, still seeing through a golden haze.

Ebony knelt next to me, her hand placed gently on my back. She was back to perfection, her hair brown and shiny and her skin perfectly pale. Her look was one of sadness. I scanned the area around me. Dead fairies lay sprawled all over the ground and the fire had died down to burning embers.

I turned back to Ebony, tears pouring down my face. "It's all over, dear." She whispered sweetly. She held her hand out for me. "Come. There is nothing more you can do."

Twenty-Seven

"You're sure about this?" Ceintra asked nervously.

I sat on the couch while Ebony and Ember talked in the corner. Dravven had just taken the arrowhead from my wing and was now working on Keelan's. He had been shot several times in the right wing while trying to chant.

Ceintra stared at me and her hands shook. She had never done something like this before. She had told me this several times. "Yes, I want you to give me my memories back."

"Okay..." she elongated the word, her entire body trembling. "If you're really sure."

"I am." I spoke confidently. I had just killed my younger sister because of Tranquility's mind sweep. I would not put myself in that position anymore.

"Understand that some memories may not come back. She has the power to block things even from my powers." Ceintra told me for the tenth time.

I was growing frustrated. "I know! Just do it!" I didn't mean to yell. I was still extremely upset, even though the fight was long over and the bodies had been disposed of. "Sorry." I mumbled.

Ceintra set her mouth in a grim line. "It is fine. Do not apologize to me. Now, close your eyes. Remember not to open them before I tell you to."

I shut my eyes tight, so tightly I saw multicolor stars behind my lids. Ceintra mumbled some chant under her breath and I could feel as her hand swept past my face multiple times. Nothing was happening. I wanted to open my eyes and tell her this but headed her warning instead.

Her hand went past my face, sweeping air past my bangs many more times before I finally saw a spark behind my lids. I focused on the silver orb with all my might. It swam in the rainbow tint and darkness.

It grew bigger and bigger until it took up my entire vision. I kept it locked in my mind, not letting it go. I focused as hard as I possibly could until images began popping up. They flashed by individually and I knew each one of them.

I knew the faces laughing and crying and talking. I could hear my mother's voice ring through my head. I wanted to weep. I could feel Ember as he pulled me into an embrace, and see Honour's excitement at having found a fairy.

And then I saw Juniper and I thought I would lose it all. She was in a white dress walking to William to be married. She was lying to me about being beat by her husband. She was laughing and running around our home while I chased after her.

Then she was dead by my hand. The second time I had seen my sister's death.

I sat up gasping. I couldn't catch my breath no matter how hard I tried. You don't have to breathe. I kept reminding myself of this but it wasn't working. Someone was touching me in the distance, trying to calm me down. They were mumbling in my ear that everything was going to be okay.

But it wasn't going to be okay. My family was dead! MY FAMILY WAS DEAD. At my hand! It was my fault! I brought the creatures into my home; I brought them around my frail sisters and mother. I was supposed to look after them. My father told me to look after them!

"Is she...?" I heard briefly in the distance from Ebony. I felt someone touch me again. Stop touching me! I didn't deserve to be alive. The cuts on my wrists should have worked. I should have been dead! I had been alive so long!

"She's having a seizure!" Someone yelled to my right. They were close, too close. Didn't they realize if they came near me they would die? I was destruction! I was pain! I was the end of all things! I had ruined so much.

My body was convulsing but it did not feel like my body. I could feel my head whipping back and my eyes fluttering open and shut, but I could see nothing but the faces of my past.

Where was Honour? What happened to Honour? I wanted my mother! Were they in a grave somewhere in London? I had missed out on Honour growing up! Juniper had never got to have her baby because of me! I had destroyed them all!

I fell off something. My body was in a heap on the floor and people were moving around frantically, unsure what to do. We do not save people! We kill them! We devour their insides and laugh at their fear. I had laughed at their fear!

How many lives had I ruined? How many people had I feasted on? How many children had come home to find empty parents and bloody beds?! All by my hand! To sustain my selfish life! They should have destroyed me. Why didn't they destroy me?!

Someone touched me again. STOP TOUCHING ME. Couldn't they see what I saw?! Didn't they realize the destruction they had caused? The people they had hurt?

I want to be dead.

I want to be dead.

I WANT TO BE DEAD.

"Victoria?" The disembodied voice was distant but I knew it well. I had grown to cherish it and love it, and find comfort in those syllables.

· I sat up but my head swam. I immediately lay back down. My head hit the pillow and I silently thanked whoever had put the soft cushion under me. I brought a hand to my forehead. I was hot. My body temperature was up. Was I running a fever?

Impossible. I was supposed to be cold all the time. I couldn't escape the cold.

What had happened?

"Victoria?" That voice again. "Open your eyes."

I did as I was told and looked around. Ember sat next to me on the couch. He was smoothing my hair away from my sticky neck and forehead. I was running a fever. He smiled down at me but it didn't quite reach his eyes.

I didn't want to smile back. I had nothing to smile about. I had been so caught up in my own world that I ignored what was happening right in front of me. Not anymore. I was well aware of what I was, and what I had been. I would never be the same again.

I used what little strength I had and propped myself up on my elbows. Ember shifted to allow me movement. "How long have I been out?" My voice was hoarse.

He looked up as if calculating then back at me. "Just a few hours. Are you okay? Ceintra feels terrible."

I coughed and gold blood landed in my hand. I wiped it casually on my dress. A worried expression crossed Ember's face but he banished it when he realized I was staring at him. "I told her to do it."

"Victoria, you had a seizure." He informed me.

I shoved off the couch and tossed my legs over the side. They had taken my shoes off. The floorboards under me were cold, it felt good. "I did not have a seizure. I had an epiphany."

"Oh." It was all he said. He stood and looked down at me like I was some small child. I suddenly wanted him to leave me alone.

"How do you do it?" I asked the floor more than I asked him.

He shifted from foot to foot for a second then asked, "Do what?"

I looked up at him, tears threatening to spill over. "Kill innocent people. How do you do it?"

He sat back down next to me and placed a hand on my shoulder. I shook it off. He exhaled deeply and let his hand drop to his own leg. "It's the natural order, Victoria. We kill humans to survive just as they kill animals."

"You feel no remorse?" I asked bitterly.

He reared back like I had slapped him. His eyes were full of shock and hurt. "Do you think I am some delusional monster like Tranquility?" he spit at me. "Of course I feel remorse! I wish I didn't have to do it! But it's required of me. I'm not going to die any time soon and I'm not going to torture myself just because I feel sorry for my food. Disengage yourself from what you eat; it'll make your life much simpler."

The response was cold. He knew as soon as he said it that it was the wrong thing. He stammered not making any coherent words then got up and left. I set my chin in my hands and rocked slowly back and forth.

I didn't know how I felt about any of this. Just a few hours ago I was killing ruthlessly and enjoying my meals. Now, I didn't know if I could ever eat again. The lingering taste of blood in my mouth made me want to vomit. I somehow managed to hold it back.

Ebony walked into the room. I could tell it was her by her shoes. She sat in the chair across from me and crossed her legs. I didn't bother to look up. I kept rocking and consoling myself the best I could.

"Listen, dear." She spoke softly, ever the maternal type. This made me look up. Her face was sweet and understanding. The look in her eyes told me she had been in my shoes before. She crossed her hands in her lap. "There is not one of us that doesn't regret our existence, I assure you. We all miss our families, we all curse our species, and we all hate ourselves for what we have to do on a daily basis to survive. But my dear, there is nothing we can do about it. Until the day comes when it is decided you should turn to dust and flee this planet, you are stuck among this race and with these instincts." She paused and smiled at me then continued. "If you are having trouble facing what you truly are, perhaps I can help. When I was only a century old I had this same realization. I did not eat for days. Tranquility had the guards force feed me and I would throw it right back up, hating the taste it left in my mouth. But I came up with a method, one that made me feel slightly better about what I had to do."

She stopped talking. I sat up, not wanting her to stop. She had looked down and was studying her hands. "What did you do?"

"I began only eating the organs of terrible people. I figured if I couldn't help myself, then I could help the human population. For centuries I have only feasted on the hearts of murderers, rapists, child molesters, and the like. Although I am still killing humans, I am not killing innocent ones."

The idea slammed into me like a brick wall. It was ingenious. The entire proposition made me feel a hundred times better about being what I was. I smiled at Ebony, thankful that she was back. I didn't know what I would do without her. But other things were still weighing on my mind.

"Do you think about your family often?" I questioned.

She nodded her head and uncrossed her legs. "Every day. But I have realized they are in a better place than I am. They got to live long, full lives of wonders and love. They died when they were supposed to. They ran their natural course and it has become clear to me that I should be happy for them. They accomplished what I cannot."

I stood without a word and crossed the space between us. Ebony stood, already knowing what I wanted. She held her arms out to either side of her and wrapped them tightly around me. I shoved my face into her shirt and inhaled her sweet aroma.

"Thank you." I mumbled.

She stroked my hair with her free hand. "You're very welcome, dear." She pushed me back to arm's length. "Do you feel better now that you truly know who you are?"

I thought over this question. It was loaded, that was for sure. Finally, I nodded my head. "Yes. I would rather know who I was and what I became then walk around blindly for the rest of my days."

She smiled, it reached her eyes and they lit up. "Good. Now that you're better, shall we go learn how to overthrow a queen?"

Twenty-Eight

"Back from the past, love?" Dravven giggled as I walked into the kitchen. He was teetering back and forth on an already unsteady stool and eating chopped up lung and berries.

I shoved him playfully and he almost fell off his seat. He laughed madly and went back to eating. I sat down next to Ember who seemed glad to see me in one piece and not mad about what I was.

Keelan was drawing a picture on a piece of parchment across from us and Ceintra was lying with her head down on the table. She looked up when she realized I had entered the room. "Oh, Victoria! I am so sorry!"

I waved her apology away. "Admittedly, that was horrible. But I think I'm alright now. Ebony put some things into perspective for me."

"I shouldn't have done it! I knew it would be bad!" Ceintra cried.

I scrunched my face at her whining. "It is over. I no longer care to talk about it. I am sorry for giving you a fright but also thankful for the gift you gave me. Now, what do we have thus far?"

Ember raised his eyebrows, impressed by my new in charge attitude. Something had come over me. Something Ebony had said had struck me deep, although I did not know what it was. I was somehow proud of what and who I was, and more confident about it.

I didn't feel horrible. I felt powerful.

"Keelan is drawing a map of the castle." Ebony said from the cupboards where she was pulling glasses down.

"Why do we need a map of the castle? We've all been there." I retorted.

"We figured we should mark the safest exits in case anything goes wrong." Keelan mumbled, intent on his drawing which I had to admit was rather good.

"We will have to dress in the correct attire." Ember said while warming his hands over the tea Ebony had just placed in front of him.

"Which will require what?" I questioned, sipping the tea and enjoying the warmth as it slid down my throat.

"It's a masquerade, love!" Dravven yelled too loudly. "Masks and gowns and... and hats!"

"The masks will make it easy for us to enter undetected." Ceintra added.

I nodded my head in agreement. "But where will we acquire such things?"

Ceintra and Keelan looked at each other in knowing. Dravven giggled and flipped his cup upside down, spilling the contents across the table. Keelan jerked the map out of the way and glared at him.

They were making fun of me, I knew, but I was still clueless. I looked to Ember for help but he hid a smile behind his hand. I was missing something obvious. Ebony set her cup on the table and leaned her elbows on the wood. She inhaled the scent through her nose.

Lazily she answered my question, "We have a tailor in our midst."

Twenty-Nine

Dravven was sewing and clipping fabric faster than an animal on the prowl. Ceintra had brought fabric from who knows where and set him in the corner of the living room. He laughed, his eyes gleaming brightly.

I sat on the chair closest to him, watching him intently. Every so often fabric would fly through the air and land in my lap. I brushed it off and let it drop to the floor. I could only catch small glimpses of what the others were saying beyond Dravven's mad laughter.

I finally turned to him, giving up on joining the conversation. "How long have you done work like this?"

He looked up momentarily then went back to sewing pieces of black felt together. The skirts of a gown were beginning to be visible under his grasp. "As long as I can remember, love."

I leaned my elbows on my knees and studied his rapid movements. The dress he was working on was gold with black felt flowers covering the bodice and skirts. "But what about when you were mortal?"

He pricked his finger which bled for a second then healed, not a drop of blood was spilt. "What about it?" he giggled.

His question was not what I had been expecting. I had thought he would simply answer me then go back to work. But instead he looked up, his eyes boring into mine, and his hand still moving without his notice. "What was your profession?"

"I..." he thought, "I had no real profession." He looked back down. The light had vanished from his eyes and he concentrated even harder on his work. He pulled the full skirts away from him and draped the dress over his chair. He started hemming the bottom.

"What do you mean?" I was relentless in my questions, even though I knew this was obviously a subject he didn't care to speak of. I was curious, he was hiding something.

"I was only fourteen, love. I was not yet old enough to hold a profession. I still had much to learn, although I was also the heir to a great fortune left behind by my parents." The answer was swift; I had to strain to hear all the words he said.

"You were fourteen without parents? What happened to them?" I was thinking over the loss of my father. It had torn my family apart for a time before mending it back together. I couldn't imagine losing both, especially at such an age.

He turned to face me once again. The glint was back in his eye and madder than ever. "I killed them."

The answer was so short and abrupt, so absolutely serious and his attitude so happy about what he had said that I was taken aback. I didn't know what else to say. I turned back in my chair and looked out the window.

I had known he was mad... but to kill the people who had given him life? I didn't know how I felt about this, but then again, it had been centuries. His parents would be dead anyway without his help.

I decided to let the subject drop and to not bring it up again. I would not base Dravven off of his past actions. There was more to the story he was not telling me. I managed to catch the conversation now that Dravven was no longer giggling. He was intent on sewing a man's outfit to match the woman's.

Ember's voice was harsh. "Are you a moron? We can't just waltz up to her!"

"Well, we can't exactly waltz into The Mayhem Realm either, now can we?!" Keelan shot back.

Ebony crossed her legs and coughed. She was detached from the conversation, like she had heard it all before. She drank her tea and warmed her hands on the sides of the cup, and listened halfheartedly.

"You can't cast some spell?" Ember spat back. "I thought you were filled with magic and powers."

"We have told you once," started Ceintra, "we would have to kill you, or very nearly. That's the only way you can get into the realm. Victoria is the only person I have known in centuries that made it back."

"Then I can go again." I piped up from my corner. They all turned to stare at me in disbelief. Ebony was suddenly attentive; she set her cup on the floor near her feet and leaned forward.

"What do you want us to do?" scoffed Keelan. "Rip your guts out? Tear yours limbs away?" He laughed at the proposal, thinking it was absurd.

I looked to Ebony and we locked eyes. Another wave of understanding passed between us. It was like electric behind my eyes, something clicking in just the right area of my mind. I felt more connected to her than Ember.

"No, nothing like that, but you can tear my heart away," I replied.

Ember jumped to his feet shaking his head. Keelan and Ceintra went into an uproar; their voices mixed and made everything they said unintelligible. Dravven hummed to himself behind me, obviously not paying attention to what I had said.

But my focus was not on the actions of them, it was on Ebony. She stayed seated with the same interested expression. She was still staring at me with a great force. It occurred to me that this was the only woman in the room that had been intimately close to Tranquility.

She had been her best friend and her mentor. She had been the only one there to give her advice at one point. She had known Tranquility's soft spots and deepest secrets.

Finally, she nodded her head in approval. That was all I needed to argue my case. I stood to match Ember and stared him down. "It is the only way. I know my way around The Mayhem Realm, have you forgotten in a second that I was there before? I can speak with whoever you need to me to, just give me an hour."

Ember strode across the room and held my hands in his. His gaze was caring and worried. "What if we can't bring you back?

What if something happens and you are forever lost to the flames?"

"Then I shall seat myself in the Realm and wait for you." It was the logical answer. Although I did not find being forced into The Mayhem Realm for all of eternity pleasing, I knew this was somehow our only shot.

Ceintra was now standing to the right of Ember. Her white eyes darted around their sockets, never focusing on one thing for too long. "She is right. She is our way in. She is our way to him."

"To who?" I let go of Ember and took a step back.

"We need you to enter the realm and take someone. He will be part of Tranquility's great undoing, a very important part. If you do not bring him back with you, our plan will be lost. A chance at defeat will be obsolete." Ceintra explained while using her hands to gesture wildly. She was clearly excited.

I shook my head in understanding. "Which one do you need? There are only two men."

She glanced back at Keelan, a momentary conversation taking place between them, then turned back to me. "Athan Erasmus."

"I did not think they could leave the realm." I said, standing barefooted on the frozen ground while Keelan and Ceintra raised the fire. Ceintra had insisted I only wear a flimsy white gown. It was almost see through. I crossed my arms over my breasts self-consciously.

"I have never been there." Ember confessed almost embarrassedly. "I would not know."

"You are not happy about this." I noted from the tone in which he spoke.

He glanced sideways at me. "Of course I am not. You are my partner, my mate. If I lose you, I will lose myself. What if these two cannot bring you back? It was rather simple with Ebony, she required a different heart. But with yours? They're taking out and replacing a heart already corrupted by Mayhem."

I rubbed his shoulder absentmindedly. I had to admit I was not paying much attention to his words. I was too focused on my second thoughts and the flames jumping higher in the air.

I knew he was worried, but I could not console him. I knew that until he saw my body rise once again from the flames he would not be content. He leaned into my touch ever so slightly and we both stood in silence.

Keelan and Ceintra hopped around the fire pit and shouted their chants. Everything was happening too fast once again. Did this race ever take a break? Did they ever lounge in their chairs and laugh about old stories? Unlikely.

Ceintra broke from her rounds and reached a hand out for me. I grasped it in mine with a fleeting glance at Ember. He had crammed his hands into his pockets.

Her hands were colder than mine and fragile. I felt if I squeezed too hard every bone would crunch. Ceintra stood me directly in front of the flames; the heat lapped at my skin, and set me aglow. Keelan had his arms raised in the air and was shouting.

Ceintra let go of my hand and stepped back. I waited her signal. The flames turned from orange and red to blue and purple. Heat washed over me more directly, my brow began to sweat. Keelan's voice grew louder and louder until, "Now!" Ceintra yelled behind me.

I jumped into the flames, ignoring the burning sensation on my skin and focusing on The Mayhem Realm. I pictured the red tint and broken wall, the four fairies floating absently in the air, the way Tranquility had been frozen in place. I kept the image locked in my mind until the flames ebbed away and the heat died out.

I opened my eyes.

"Welcome back," was chimed in unison.

Thirty

I opened my eyes to see I was yet again positioned below the four floating fairies. They all smiled down at me and welcomed me back to the Realm. They had not changed a bit since the last time I had been here, which had not been very long ago.

I ignored their questions and comments, and focused my attention on Athan. Like the others, he smiled down at me with a fake happiness. His eyes did not glow with joy and his position said he was actually very unhappy.

"Athan," I started, "I need you to come with me."

His brow creased with puzzlement. He folded his hands in his laps and chuckled lightly, as if I was joking. "I cannot leave."

"Yes, you can." I assured him. "We don't have much time. My body is burning in a fire right now and I have to get back before I'm damaged beyond recognition. But I can't leave without you."

He unfolded his hands and uncrossed his legs. He drifted to the ground gracefully and hit the stones with no sound. His wings were kept concealed in his skin and his satin shirt moved across his torso like water.

"What am I needed for?" he questioned, I had grabbed his attention.

I exhaled slowly and ran my hand through my bangs; they were growing quite irritating constantly hanging in my eyes. "We need you to help us defeat Tranquility."

He smiled widely; his white teeth glimmered in the dull cave. "Then I shall come with you."

It clicked with me that this was too easy. "You knew." I simply
stated. "You knew when I came here the last time that I would
need you."

He shrugged his shoulders and smiled again. "Of course I did."

"So then..." I paused to grasp my train of thought. "Why didn't
you tell me last time? You could have saved us so much trouble!
People have been hurt in our quest to overthrow her! You could
have prevented it all."

He did not have time to reply, Keelan and Ceintra's chants could
suddenly be heard echoing throughout the entire Realm. The walls
shook and stray pebbles fell from the ceiling. The other three
fairies floating in midair wavered a bit before gaining their
composure.

I reached my hand out and grabbed Athan's shirt. It was slippery
under my grasp making it hard to hold onto. He in turn clasped his
hand over mine and in a spin, and disintegrating sensation I was
back in the fire.

I screamed at the pain of the burning and leapt from the flames
in a quick motion. Ember draped a wet blanket over me and I
hopped up, and down trying to get the burning to go away. My
skin was dark and some parts were peeling away. My hair was
thankfully still intact.

I turned to watch Athan leisurely stride from the fire and stop in
front of Dravven. They regarded each other silently and Dravven
stepped aside. Something deep inside me told me not to trust
Athan. He had already hid information from me; he could surely
do it again. I silently promised myself to tell Ember this when I
had the chance.

I hugged the wet blanket to my hot skin while Keelan and
Ceintra extinguished the flames. Ember hovered close by and
Ebony was already moving back inside the small shack. Dravven
was trying to sneak into the woods but Ember turned to face him
before he could.

"Dravven! Don't you go running off, you have work to do! Get
back over here!" Ember shouted.

Dravven sulkily moved back into the meadow and towards the
house. Ember hung back to stay with him but I went ahead into the

small building. Athan walked close behind. His presence made me feel uneasy and I constantly felt he was staring at me.

I entered the house and slumped onto the couch, careful of my more gruesome burns. In what seemed like no time at all everyone was congregated in the living room again. Dravven was back to his sewing and Ebony had another cup of tea. It looked like nothing had changed.

Athan clapped his hands and we all turned to face him. "So what is the grand plan?"

I narrowed my eyes at him but did not comment. I would not let him know I was suspicious of him anymore than I already had. Ebony spoke up, "We don't necessarily have that much of a plan right now. We know we are going to infiltrate the castle while the masquerade is going on, and we know you have some part in it, but that is about it."

He leaned forward with his elbows on his knees. "That's it? You didn't even bother to come up with a plan before fetching me? You do realize every moment I am here is another moment I vanish into nothing, correct?"

"You... what?" I asked appalled.

He turned to me. "Yes. I am dead, dear. I am not meant to be among the living... or rather, the... living corpses?" he looked into the air as if searching for the right word. "Anyway, I no longer have a soul; I am just an empty carcass. The longer I am in this realm, the more of me that vanishes."

"How long would you say you have?" Ember inquired nervously.

Athan paused before answering. He counted on his fingers and once again swept his eyes through the air as if the answer would pop out of nowhere for us all to see. "I think about a week."

Ember clapped his hands together and startled me. I jumped slightly and my blanket fell off my shoulders. I surveyed my skin under the light. The burns were fading, leaving no trace of scars. But I would be slightly darker than usual for a while, which I had no problem with.

Ceintra shifted in her seat and turned to face our new addition. "I guess we had better work fast. We were Tranquility's second and third creation," she gestured to Keelan and herself.

"Something went wrong since she was still learning and we became seers. But not only can we see the future, but also the past. We have seen you as a significant person in Tranquility's memories."

He cut her off before she could go on by saying, "Of course I was! We were married for almost a century before the fall of Atlantis."

Ceintra nodded then continued. "You are her greatest weakness. She loved you so much she killed you to allow you to spend eternity with her best friend. That is true love. The type of love she has never exhibited before."

Dravven coughed in the corner and fabric could be heard scraping against the floor. I glanced back at him and saw that he was trying to focus on what he was doing rather than the conversation. He was acting quite peculiar.

"I do not see what love has to do with anything. Love is creation, not destruction." Athan retorted.

Ceintra shook her head and waved her finger in the air. "No, no. Love is both. You helped to make her a good person, you helped to erase her mortal ways of selfishness and greed, but you also destroyed her." She hesitated, "You actually broke her apart twice. Once when she thought you had died and again when she found you were alive and with her best friend."

I gasped inwardly, having forgotten Athan had fallen in love with Ophira. I wondered if this was part of the reason I did not like him. He had had the power to make Tranquility a great and powerful woman that loved instead of hated, but instead he broke her heart. Things were beginning to come into perspective.

"You can't help who you fall in love with," was all Athan said in reply.

"Yes, but you could have went about things very differently. You did not let her down gently and it only caused her hatred to grow and grow. It became something that overtook her inside and out, a disease that could not be cured." Ceintra replied.

Athan sighed deeply and ran a hand through his messy mop of hair. "What exactly are you getting at?"

She was becoming giddy, practically jumping out of her seat in excitement and hope. "You are the only being that possesses both the power to create and destroy her, Athan. You are the only one that can damage her with weapons and words. If any of us were to cut her or stab her, she would simply heal back. But not you. You have too much power over her. The wound would go deep and would stay. It would drain her of life and finally banish her from Earth."

"I guess true love really is killer," he joked. Nobody laughed. It was not the time or place for jokes. All of our lives hung in the balance and if he did not take it seriously, we could all be destroyed. He sighed, noticing none of us found him amusing. "So let me guess, we're going to get into this masquerade, somehow get me to her, allow me to cause some damage, then let Victoria take her place on the throne?"

We all nodded in unison, hoping the idea did not seem too far-fetched. He considered this a moment then stood. "Sounds good to me."

There was a collective sigh of relief and then a scrambling. Keelan and Ceintra began filling pouches with vials of blood and elixirs, while Dravven lined his work up near the hearth for us all to see. Things were falling into place; it was refreshing after the chaos that led to this point.

Ember crossed the room to where I was now standing and brought me into a hug. He rested his chin on the top of my head. "I was so worried about you, but now I finally feel like we have a chance."

I pulled back from him to look into his dark eyes. "I know, it's nice. I think this is actually going to work."

Athan broke our moment by walking up to us and standing uncomfortably close. We ignored him for as long as we could, but seeing that he was not about to move we finally turned to him. He stared directly at Ember and ignored my entire existence. "It is nice to see you again."

"Again? I thought you died long before I was even thought of." Ember replied.

Athan shook his head. "No, I was alive and well when you were born. I actually wasn't killed until right after you became a fairy."

"Oh." Ember commented. "I'm sorry, but I don't remember that much of my early Mayhem years. They're all kind of a blur thanks to Tranquility mind sweeping me and other things."

"That is understandable, but I believe you know me a little more intimately than that." Athan responded. "Does the name Edgar ring any bells?"

Ember froze and let go of me. His arms dropped to his sides and his eyes widened. His shock swiftly turned to menace. "How did you know Edgar?" he growled.

Athan laughed lightly and stuffed his hands into the pockets of his trousers. "You will learn soon enough. But no worries, I did no harm to your precious friend. I merely knew him quite well." With that he was gone. He strode towards Dravven and engaged in a fierce conversation. Dravven seemed no gladder to see him than anyone else.

Ember stayed stiff and rigid even after he had walked away. I massaged his shoulder with my hand trying to assure him everything would be alright. "Ignore him," I said, "There are too many things hinging on his existence in this realm right now to let him bother us. I do not feel at ease around him, and Dravven does not seem to either, we don't have that much time with him."

Ember softened under my grasp then turned back to me. "You're right." He rubbed a hand down his face and shook his head as if slinging all impure thoughts from his mind. "All that matters right now is killing Tranquility once and for all."

Thirty-One

We were lined up outside the castle in our outfits Dravven had created. They were stiff but gorgeous. I was given the pleasure of wearing the gold and black one he had been working on, and Ember wore the matching suit. Keelan and Ceintra matched in all white. Dravven wore deep red, Ebony purple, and Athan all black.

We each sported an intricate and detailed gold and black lace mask that covered the section around our eyes. It was itchy, it was all I could do not to rip it off and throw it on the ground.

My guts churned with nervousness at the idea of what we were about to do. Never in Mayhem Fairy history had anything like this been attempted. Laws and higher powers were always respected, even when they were wrong and far-fetched.

We were becoming intimately close with death.

The torches lining the wooden path were alight and had gold ribbons wrapped around them. The path itself had a long black carpet covering it, and if you looked closely enough you could see the imprints of others shoes.

Ember took my hand and we went first. I was not used to the customs of this event, but Ember had briefed me before we left. Fairies were to enter in twos, preferably with their mate, and introduce themselves when they arrived.

The masquerade seemed very formal and out of place in such a chaotic species. I walked hand in hand with Ember, while Keelan and Ceintra followed. Dravven was not going to enter with us but instead go around the back and into his quarters. I felt a slight breeze as he took to the air and left. That meant Ebony and Athan would have to be paired.

My stomach knotted with every step towards the glistening castle. Oberon came into view standing next to the door with another guard I did not know on the other side. They both wore suits of black armor with the helmets down and covering their faces. Their spears had gold silky ribbons tied around them and their armor had gold wings etched into the fronts.

They saluted by clashing their spears against the marble floor when we approached. Ember nodded his head to Oberon who didn't recognize him due to the flimsy mask and we passed them. We heard them salute Keelan and Ceintra then Ebony and Athan in the same fashion.

The main doors were standing open and the candles in each chandelier had been replaced. Everything was gold or black, as if our species was not already overly addicted to those two colors. Ember squeezed my hand in assurance and my stomach unclenched some but not much.

Immediately fairies came into view, more than I had ever seen before. They wore outfits of all sorts. The women decked themselves in vivid blues, greens, yellows, and reds. The men matched in top hats and exquisite coats.

Each wore a mask of some sort or another. Some had feathers sticking out from the sides, others were coated in glitter, and some were purely drawn on with steady hands. Mixed with the already perfect physiques of the fairies, the entire scene was quite mesmerizing.

I couldn't keep my eyes off them. Ember pulled me along reluctantly.

We made our way through the hall and towards the stairs in The Gathering Room to the Royal Rooms. We would be dropping Ebony off at the staircase to stand guard. She would be our closest agent to the main door. We passed the staircase, not bothering to glance at it, and I watched in my peripheral vision as Ebony moved from Athan and leaned against the banister.

The move was so fluid and calm, so precisely done that no one in the room questioned it. They saw no motive behind our actions.

Athan merged with Keelan and Ceintra, and we continued on into The Dining Area.

The fairies in this room turned when we entered. A gold carpet had been set down the middle of the room and the single long table had been broken apart to form two smaller ones. A throne sat in front of the main fireplace and in it was Tranquility.

Her long black hair was loosely curled and hanging in rivulets to her breasts, and her legs were crossed. Her dress was black with gold beads in the shapes of mini wings covering the skirt. The top was a corset that fit snugly to her thin frame.

She had one clawed hand draped over the arm of the chair and the other holding a goblet filled with blood and mashed organs. The mask she wore was black and glittery. It was simple and stuck to her face without strings.

She did not see our entrance. She was occupied by another set of fairies that entered before us. Their outfits were simply black and their masks were made of paper. She was smiling but scolded them for not trying harder for her event.

I exhaled slowly, trying to gain my composure. I had met this woman face to face many times before. There was no reason for me to be afraid of her now. I knew my powers matched hers in every aspect; a duel was unnecessary and produced no effects.

A man darted in front of us and we stopped abruptly. I did not see him at first, Ember had to pull me back. The motion caused me to almost fall but thankfully Ember stuck his arm out and balanced me.

"Names?!" the man shouted at us from behind his elaborate mask. I could not see how he managed to keep it perched on his face. It must have weighed a ton due to all the colored jewels, feathers, and glitter plastered to it. It was a shining star compared to his worn boots and simple black suit.

"Ember Sky and Victoria Renae." Ember responded gruffly. He was obviously not pleased with this man's sudden appearance.

The man turned and held out a parchment. He scribbled the names swiftly then cleared his throat. "Now presenting, Mayhem Fairies Ember Sky and Victoria Renae. Son of Ebony Vail and daughter of Queen Tranquility Erasmus."

The man bowed and ushered us forward. We continued our journey down the never ending golden path towards Tranquility's throne. Ember had told me we would be forced to bow in front of her as a sign of respect. As much as I did not want to do this, I also did not want to alert any of the fairies around us to our true intentions.

Each fairy at the tables turned to stare at us as we made our way forward. They were indistinguishable behind their masks; some even had their eyes covered in light fabric. My face heated under the lace and made it itchier than ever. It took all my power to not rip the thing off and rub my face furiously.

We stopped a few feet in front of Tranquility's throne. She glanced up expectantly, a smirk displayed on her face, and the air of power emanated from her every pore. I wanted to strike out at her, rip her perfectly done hair from her scalp and tear the specially made dress off her skin to expose the flesh beneath.

But instead I simply bowed along with Ember and forced a smile. It was like trying to choke down a food you obviously did not like. She approved of this because she nodded at us both in turn and held her hand out. Onyx rings lined each finger. I wondered how she managed to wear them when they were our only weakness.

Ember let go of my hand to kneel and kiss her hand then stood again. This time she stood and we did the sign of Mayhem by placing two fingers to our hearts and then our lips. We clearly said, "May Mayhem be With You," then turned to walk away. Tranquility took her seat as we searched for seats of our own among the mess of human entrails and fairies cackling insanely.

We sat ourselves at the end of one broken table near another fireplace decorated with more black and gold ribbons. Two black candelabras stood to either side of the roaring hearth with gold candles. As we sat we heard the man's voice boom, "Now presenting, Mayhem Fairies Keelan and Ceintra Sarpin. Son and daughter of Queen Tranquility Erasmus."

I snapped my head towards the man's voice, my heart leaping out of my chest at Athan's name being introduced next. But Athan was nowhere to be found. He had disappeared. The only figures standing on the gold carpet were the man who was bowing low and Keelan and Ceintra who were glowing in their white outfits.

Their blue wings fluttered silently behind them and their eerie eyes scanned the room looking for fairies they had known in a past life. They gave up the hunt and settled their gazes on Tranquility.

The Queen jumped up at their approach, her mouth was open in shock and her hands clutched the arms of her throne to keep her posture. We had guessed something along these lines would happen. Tranquility acted as if she had not seen her creations in centuries.

What we had not expected was every other fairy in the room to begin mumbling. Some yelped in delight and surprise, and others jumped from their chairs to get a better look. Keelan and Ceintra were quite the celebrities.

They did not seem to notice the commotion they caused. They gracefully made their way toward their creator. Ceintra's skirts swept across the carpet and Keelan's arm stayed tightly entwined with hers. They glanced at each other every so often, having a silent conversation no doubt.

They stopped in front of Tranquility but did not bow. Another wave of murmurs swept the crowd. They were openly opposing her, something no one else had the bravery to do. Tranquility let go of her throne and brushed her hands on her skirts to smooth them. Her posture suddenly became poised and straight.

The twins still did not bow. They stood facing her as equals. "Tranquility." Keelan acknowledged her with a slight bob of his head.

"We see you have not changed." Ceintra added with no sign of respect.

Tranquility's mouth set into a line. "You are forgetting something."

Keelan and Ceintra glanced at each other but still did not bow. "We will not bow to a being we are more powerful than." Ceintra confessed.

My stomach turned. This was not part of the plan. Ember gripped the table next to me, no doubt thinking the same things I was. They were going to ruin everything due to a grudge from long ago. Dravven startled me by throwing himself down into the chair on my other side.

I turned to look at him briefly. The light was gone from his eyes and his hair was disheveled. He was watching the scene near the throne as intently as everyone else. The clatter of utensils had disappeared and conversation had completely vanished. The room was utterly silent.

"I have not seen you since you left lifetimes ago and this is how you repay me? By disrespecting me in front of our entire race?" Tranquility questioned ferociously.

They shrugged but did not reply. Tranquility kept her composure but for a moment then shrieked. The room was filled with the vibrations of her high pitched voice. I flinched from the sound and Dravven covered his ears.

"GUARDS!" Tranquility screamed. Two fairies decked in the same gear as Oberon ran into the room. They armor clanked noisily in the silence until they stood directly behind Keelan and Ceintra. They bowed towards the Queen awaiting their orders. "Lock them in their respective rooms. It is beyond time they became acquainted with the life they were supposed to live."

The guards grasped the twins roughly and shoved them out of the room. They put up no fight and did not bother to give as a reassuring look. My heart was beating furiously. They were vital pieces to the puzzle. We were three fairies down and surrounded by hundreds.

Tranquility adjusted her mask and smiled at the fairies still staring at her. She held her arms into the air. "Do not fret my devoted fairies! They were but a scratch on the perfection of our annual masquerade! How about some music and the next course to lighten our spirits?"

Cheers met her question. She snapped her fingers and a hidden band I had not seen began playing a somber melody. Every key struck on the piano was in minor and the harp was played with precision and sadness. The tune dampened the moods of everyone surrounding us, which showed signs of being exactly what they wanted.

Several fairies opened the cages in the corner which I now saw were packed to bursting with whimpering humans. They pulled them out roughly, laughing at the ones who tried to put up a fight, and slammed them down on the long tables.

Fairies immediately dug into them. Their screams echoed throughout the entire room. Blood sprayed across our section of table, and guts flew into the air only to be caught in clawed hands and mashed into small gold chalices.

The behavior was animalistic and crude. I was not yet accustomed to such acts. Ember and Dravven did not seem at all phased by the brutality of it all. Along with the fresh corpses lining the tables, fairies burst from a hidden door to our right that led to the kitchens.

They brought with them immaculate platters of human food. Berries, cooked meat, vegetables, and pudding were among the few I caught glimpses of. They were set in between the torn open bodies of mortals and fairies dug into these too.

By the looks of it, they had been starved for decades. Although I knew this was far from true.

Wings flapped and eyes glowed in excitement. Some fairies were playing games where they scratched each other and timed how quickly they healed. Those that lost had to hand over the organ they had been about to bite into.

Other than the distorted ways they celebrated, the entire event seemed to be merry. The fairies around us were genuinely enjoying themselves. I realized with a start that not all of them would want the peace I could offer. They thrived in the disorder Tranquility supplied them with.

Tranquility was making her way through throngs of fairies. She was talking to several small groups at a time, and laughing at jokes made by her subjects. She was in her element, among killers that did not care how crudely she ran things. There was not a care in her mind.

She suspected nothing.

Dravven dug into the human that was set before us. The man shrieked but it was cut off when Dravven's entire hand sunk into his chest and tore down his middle. He pulled the heart out for himself and bit deeply into it. Blood gushed all over his outfit he had worked so hard on and splattered my dress.

Ember followed suit and pulled a lung out for his own enjoyment. I gave a small shrug and took the other one. It tasted delicious. The humans had been laced with something, fed something in particular that had sweetened them further.

I quickly devoured my first organ and reached for my next. "I have always loved this event!" Dravven told us rather loudly. Maximum volume was his norm.

"Honestly? I have too." Ember confessed. "In the mess of things as of late I had forgotten how much fun I had had here in the past. Tranquility may be a lot of things, but a bad party coordinator is not one of them."

Dravven nodded his head and blood seeped from the corner of his mouth. He threw his arm onto the table in front of me and raised his brow at Ember. "How about a game of Sever the Servant?"

Ember raised his hand into the air and his nails extended to sharp points. Dravven did the same with his other hand. Ember set his bare arm next to Dravven's and they both slashed each other's skin at the same time.

Their wounds healed in record time, but Dravven's was a second faster. Ember's arm had taken long enough time to spill a drop of gold blood. "Damn!" Ember exclaimed.

He handed the organ he had been eating over to Dravven then grabbed another from the almost empty body. Dravven giggled and pulled his arm off the table. "Still terrible at this game, I see!"

"You have many decades on me, it is hardly fair!" Ember shouted back.

I cleared my throat and set the remainder of the kidney I had been eating down. I turned to Ember whose face was alight with excitement. I hated to ruin his fun, especially after all we had been through, but we were here on a mission. "We need to go retrieve Keelan and Ceintra."

Ember let go of bladder he had just taken a rather large bite out of on the table. Blood seeped from it and stained the table runner. He leaned his hands on the table and stood. "Yes, I guess you are right. I let my mind go for a moment. Terribly sorry, dear."

Dravven and I followed his lead and removed ourselves from our seats. The fairies around us were so engrossed by the fun they were having that they did not notice us slip from The Dining Area and make our way back into The Gathering Hall.

We dodged flapping wings and small duels between fairies throughout the hall until we reached the staircase where Ebony was holding a chalice and speaking with another woman.

The woman's wings were also purple and flapped noisily behind her. Great thrusts of air swept my hair back. I studied the woman harder at our approach and realized she looked a lot like Ebony in almost every aspect.

Their hair was the same shade, their eyes were aglow the same, and their posture was so much alike I would think they were sisters. I scrunched my face into an expression of confusion. Did Ebony have a sister among our race she never mentioned?

Ebony saw us mid-laugh and straightened up. She took a sip from her cup and came up with her lips tinted red. The woman talking animatedly turned to stare at us. Her expression grew serious. She glanced from us to Ebony.

Dravven groaned to my left. "More people I don't care to see." He mumbled under his breath.

I almost lost my serious, in-charge composure to laugh at his comment but kept myself under control. "Ebony." I nodded at her in greeting.

"Hello, dear." She replied airily. This was a woman who didn't have a care in the world.

"Who is this?" Ember asked. He was always one to get directly to the point.

"Oh..." Ebony looked at the woman as if it was the first time she had noticed her, "This is Grendel Vail."

"Is she your sister?" Again, straight to the point.

Ebony threw her head back in a chuckle. Grendel did the same. The contents of their cups swished and spilled over onto the floor. I stepped back; I had been sprayed with enough blood for one night. "No, dear. This would actually be your sister, if we are going that route."

Ember's eyes widened. "But I have never had a sister. What have you been drinking? Are you drinking poison elixirs? Are you drunk?"

"Of course not! Not on such an important night! How dare you ask me such a thing, you should be ashamed of yourself." Ebony retorted rather angrily. Ember slunk back, his cheeks turned pink. "Grendel is another one of my creations."

"I didn't think you had any other children." I piped up, now even more confused.

"Of course I do." She smiled. "There was a point in time when we had to make as many of our kind as we possibly could. Tranquility put us out into the world for that sole purpose."

I now remembered seeing that played out in The Mayhem Realm. I felt idiotic for asking the question in front of other fairies that knew of these things well. None of them seemed bothered by my obvious questions.

Ember stuck his hand out. "Well, hello Grendel Vail. I am Ember Sky."

She shook his hand roughly and shrieked. "Ember Sky! Ebony has always told me so much about you! You are definitely her favorite creation. It is so nice to finally meet you! After all these decades!"

Ember had to force her to let his hand go. He rubbed it where a red mark had formed from her grip. He turned back to Ebony with a knowing glare. Her smile faded into a grimace and she turned to Grendel. "Dear, I have some matters to attend to." She patted her arm gently. "I will catch up with you again later."

Grendel's face fell. She was obviously disappointed by this turn of events. Dravven sighed thankfully at her vacating our presence. Ebony turned back to us expectantly. She was obviously annoyed at our rude interruption.

"Let me guess," began Ember, "You didn't see the guards bring Keelan and Ceintra through here because you were too busy socializing."

Her eyes became ten sizes bigger in horror. "What happened?!"

Ember stuffed a hand into his pocket. His mask shook as he spoke, "They wouldn't bow down to Tranquility. So she made the guards take them to their old rooms. You probably could have stopped it if you weren't so infatuated with Grendel."

She waved his words away and rested her almost empty cup on the end of the banister. "I couldn't have stopped it if I had tried.

One of me against two or more guards? Don't be so jealous, Ember. I did not raise you that way."

"You also didn't raise me around any of our other created children, but that's no matter. We need to get Keelan and Ceintra. We are running out of time," Ember spit at her.

I didn't want to hear any more of their bickering. I stepped away and began ascending up the stairs. Our plan was unraveling. I knew I had to take the throne, that her overthrow had to be completed tonight. Something inside me was keeping a constant clock ticking away the minutes until something horrible would happen.

I lifted my skirts so I didn't trip in front of everyone and embarrass myself, and ran up each carpeted stair as fast as I could. I heard the others hit the stairs below me and tried to slow down , but it was no use. I was moving unnaturally fast.

I reached the top and made my way over to heir doorways. There were no guards outside the doors. I hesitated. How strange. There was no way Tranquility would leave them to their own devices. I waited for the others to catch up. They all stopped dead when they saw the lack of protection.

Ember turned his head to sweep his gaze over the fairies lingering in the hall. They were all too engrossed in their food and discussions to notice our group standing absentmindedly in the middle of the hall.

"You don't think their inside the rooms, do you?" Ember questioned.

"Oh, dear. I hope not." Replied Ebony.

That was all it took. I closed the remaining gap between myself and the door and turned the handle. It was locked, of course. Ember came up next to me and waved his hand in front of the knob. It clicked softly and swung open. We both entered Ceintra's room.

Dravven and Ebony did the same with Keelan's, hoping that we would be able to retrieve them both in half the time. We still had Athan to track down and find.

Ember closed the door behind us so no one outside would expect anything. We were immediately engrossed in darkness. I turned to see Ember's eyes glowing and I did the same. My vision came more into focus.

Someone was whimpering on the bed. The sheets were crinkling and moving in distress. I half ran the distance across the room and threw the blanket back. I gasped in horror at what I saw. Ember came up next to me and grabbed my shoulder to prevent himself from collapsing.

Ceintra's eyes had been torn from their sockets. She held them steadily in her hands while her entire body quaked and trembled. Gold stained her entire face and was pouring from the fresh holes in her face.

I leaned onto the bed and wrapped my arm around her frail shoulders. She jerked back trying to figure out who I was. "Leave me alone!" she screamed and pulled herself from my grasp. She shoved herself into the fetal position in the corner of the bed.

"Ceintra, it's me, Victoria. No one else is going to hurt you." I cooed.

"V-Victoria?" she stumbled over the words and slunk back towards me. I once again placed my arm around her and rubbed her shoulder.

"There's only one person that can fix this." Ember pondered aloud.

"Who?" Ceintra and I both questioned.

"Dravven. And I don't know if he can do a successful job. He's used to sewing wings and fabrics. He may be able to mend the nerves and such." Ember spoke softly.

As if on cue Dravven and Ebony burst into the room. We tensed expecting it to be a guard until Dravven's manic laughter filled the space. It bounced off the walls and echoed through the almost empty room. They held Keelan between them, his eyes also missing. Blood dripped onto the carpet.

"We need to get to my Quarter's!" Dravven exclaimed.

I pulled Ceintra up, guiding her off the bed and helped her to find where each foot should go until we had crossed the room and were standing in front of where the two of them held Keelan.

"Ceintra?" Keelan called into an empty space.

"I'm here!" she called back, throwing her hands into the empty air. I guided her palm to his cheek.

"I can't hear you in my mind." He whimpered. I felt immensely bad for them. This entire night was becoming a disaster.

"Because we have no eyes! We won't be able to see!" she cried.

"Do not fret!" Dravven assured them. "I believe I can fix this! We need to get to my room quickly."

Ember pulled Ceintra from my grasp and picked her up with ease. Her body somehow seemed even smaller and fragile in his arms. Dravven did the same with Keelan and they were out the door before anything else could be said. Ebony and I looked at each other, our eyes brimming with worry.

We didn't say a word. She shook her head and we chased after Ember and Dravven.

Thirty-Two

Keelan was screaming like his guts were being torn from his body while he was still alive. Dravven held the smallest needle I had ever seen between his index finger and thumb. He worked slowly, which was more than unusual for him.

Ember and I sat with Ceintra in between us on a pile of discarded fabric. She cringed every time Keelan's voice ripped through the silence. Chatter and laughter could still be heard coming from downstairs. Ebony had left us earlier to search for Athan.

Dravven whispered into Keelan's ear as he worked. What he was saying we did not know. I could only hope it was words of encouragement and not his insane babble. Keelan's nails were tearing into his pants and his teeth were gritted in agony.

Dravven finished with one eye and stepped back. I leaned forward to get a better look. It looked to be fully functional. There were no stitches showing or ripped skin. The blood had subsided and been wiped from his face. Once the remaining socket was filled I was sure he would be back to normal.

Dravven started on his second eye. Keelan's screams erupted once again throughout the room. My mind was spinning with what had happened. This was not at all how it was supposed to be. This was supposed to be an easy job.

We would bring Athan to destroy Tranquility, Ebony would keep watch at the stairs, Ember and I would make sure no other fairies got in the way, and Keelan and Ceintra would continue to look into the future for unknown obstacles.

This sparked a light. "Why didn't you two see this coming?"

Ceintra turned her head to my general location. "Like all other seers of the world, we cannot see into our own futures. It is blocked from us. It is a general rule among our power."

I scrunched my nose. "A rather bad rule."

She considered my comment. "I think it does more good than bad. It prevents us from knowing when we will die, or when something horrible like this will happen to us. It saves us from being frightened for our safety at every moment of every day."

Dravven finished with Keelan and stood back once again. I did not rebuke Ceintra, I knew she was right. I had no idea how horrible their power was to bear. I could not even get my substantial powers to work.

Dravven flicked his wrist in front of Keelan and a white smoke entered the air. It formed around Keelan's newly constructed eyes and evaporated into them. I watched in anticipation, hoping this magic would work and they would get their abilities back.

Keelan's eyes closed and he stopped moving. Dravven giggled and covered his face completely with his hand. His needle was still held in the other. Keelan's body went slack and he slumped out of the chair.

His body lay crumpled in the floor. Ember stood, letting go of Ceintra. His entire body was rigid. Dravven took a couple more steps back in shock. None of us had been expecting this. Ceintra sensed something was wrong from the abrupt silence.

She pushed herself to her feet the best she could but stumbled over a stray piece of fabric and crumpled to the floor. She reached her hand out on the wood panels searched for the chair Keelan was supposed to be in. Instead she touched his leg.

She screamed but the sound was cut off. She too crumpled into a mess of white in the floor, her head resting on her brother's leg. Her body went limp and the life drained from her.

I covered my mouth with my hand. I was trembling and tears were erupting without my consent. Our two most valuable players of the game had just died at our feet.

Dravven finally let go of the needle and it tinged on the panel under his feet. "I... I didn't mean to... I swear I didn't."

Ember rested a hand on his back. "We know. This was not your doing. You were just trying to help."

I stumbled off the pile of fabric and made my way to Ember's side. "But why did Ceintra die?!"

He turned to face me; tears were falling down his face too. He swiped them away, trying to act as manly as possible. "They were connected in every way. Mind, body, and soul. Keelan died and so Ceintra went with him."

We stood in utter silence examining their bodies. I felt responsible for their deaths in every way. I had been the one that wanted this so badly. I had put all the people I loved in danger for a moronic reason.

"Now we really have to overthrow her." Dravven whispered in complete seriousness.

Both mine and Ember's heads snapped to the side to look at him. "What do you mean?" I demanded. "If this is another of your insane suggestions, I do not want to hear it."

"No, love." Dravven assured us. "They died trying to defeat her. We must continue on without them out of respect."

Thirty-Three

We found Ebony sitting defeated on the stairs. Her head was in her hands and her shoulders were slumped. When we told her of Keelan and Ceintra's deaths she sobbed hard and fast. As fast as her tears were there, they were gone. She agreed with Dravven wholeheartedly.

"You have found no sign of Athan?" questioned Ember.

She shook her head, her hair had fallen loose and her mask was coming untied. I had completely forgotten I had a mask hiding my identity. "I have looked everywhere from the dungeons to the Royal Rooms. I am guessing he is in one the hidden rooms. After all, even if he did not spend much time in this castle, he would know Tranquility better than us all."

I looked between Ember and Ebony. Dravven had decided to stay behind with the bodies of Keelan and Ceintra. He didn't want anyone else disturbing them, even though no one was technically allowed in his Quarter's.

"How are we supposed to find him if he's in a hidden room? Isn't the entire point of one to hide things?" I inquired them both.

Ember shrugged. He was out of ideas and felt defeated. I could tell by his expression alone he wanted nothing more than to leave and never return here. I knew the feeling.

Ebony threw her hands into the air and sparks ignited from her fingertips. "Magic, of course. I will simply trace my hand along the wall and wherever my magic ignites there is an opening."

We followed Ebony, starting from the topmost turret and making our way towards the dungeons. We found nothing on every level. With each wall clean my heart leapt from my chest. We were definitely running out of time now.

We needed to find him soon or all hope would be lost.

As soon as we stepped onto the grimy floor a shudder passed through me. I associated bad memories with this part of the castle. I could remember the feeling of my wings ripping as I pulled myself away from the wall, of the joy that swept over me when I found Ebony and Dravven.

That had only been a week ago. I realized this with a start. I felt as if I had lived centuries. I turned to Ember and whispered, "If a week goes by this slowly in our world, how slowly does a century go by?"

He glanced at me but kept most of his attention on Ebony. "Agonizingly slow."

"They're here!" Ebony called, her hand was glowing along with a perfect square on the wall. She pulled back and pushed strongly on the marble, the section swung open with ease.

She looked back to Ember and I for assurance, we both nodded our heads then followed her into the dark room. I could see absolutely nothing, even with the rims of my eyes glowing. I held my hand out for Ember and he took it with ease.

"Hello?" he called into the empty air.

We waited for a response we assumed would not come. We were proven wrong. "Hello?" a croak came back from the silence.

I listened as Ember ran his hand along the wall looking for a candle or some other light source. He obviously found one because a flame was lit to my right. Everything came into focus.

The room was small with several doors at the far end, unlike the rest of the castle; the walls were worn stone and grimy. Athan was tied up in shackles in the left corner, his head was hung low and he was crying.

I let go of Ember and ran to the wounded fairy. His wings were torn to pieces and his face was scratched up. I almost could not recognize him. Ebony was whispering something to Ember behind me but I paid no mind.

I rubbed Athan's cheek with my hand. "What happened?" I whispered.

He lifted his head and tried to say something but all that came out was air. His throat had been cut and was not healing as quickly as it should have been. Ember knelt down next to him and placed his hand over the wound. A shudder went through the room and when Ember pulled his hand away the cut was gone.

I looked at him in disbelief. "Out of all the times we could have used that."

Ember grimaced. "I forget sometimes I have this ability."

I shook my head, suddenly annoyed with him, but banished the thoughts from my mind. There were more pressing matters at hand. I turned back to Athan. "What happened?"

He rubbed his hand across his throat and coughed. "She... she..." his voice was still raspy and hard to hear and he seemed to be having a hard time speaking.

"She what?" I questioned, already knowing who she was.

Athan's eyes turned to me, they lit up in comprehension and he slunk away from my touch. "You need to leave." He choked out before going into another coughing fit.

Ember stood and looked back at Ebony; I did the same but kept my eyes trained on Athan. "Why do we need to leave?"

He looked up at me; his eyes were brimming with tears. He lifted a shaky finger and pointed behind us. "Too... late..." and his head collapsed. We all turned to look where he had been pointing. I gasped, startled by her presence.

"You killed him!" Ebony accused Tranquility.

Tranquility smiled then shrugged nonchalantly. "I only did to him what you were trying to make him do to me."

I had had enough, my cup was full. This woman could not keep terrorizing us like this. I inhaled sharply trying to retrieve my calm but it wasn't coming. Ember tried to grab my hand, obviously seeing my distress, but I shook him away.

Tranquility turned her playful gaze to me. She was not fazed by any of this. This was all just a cruel game to her. She placed her hand on her hip and smirked. "What's wrong, love?" she laughed.

She wiped the lipstick at the corner of her mouth and giggled some more. What was wrong with her? I had never done anything to her! She was the one that had taken me from my home, she was the one that had assigned Ember to me, and she was the one that had ruined my life! It was not the other way around!

A growl erupted from deep in my throat and my wings flew from my spine. They hit the stone walls and slid easily into the rock. My fingers went numb as my nails pierced through the skin and became black and my eyes reflected in hers.

"What have I done to you?!" I half snarled and half yelled.

She flipped a stray curl behind her ear and grinned again. "I have a very valid reason for not liking you, Victoria. You may think you know more than me, you may think that because you retrieved your memories from Ceintra and because you woke up before you were supposed to that you have the upper hand, but you do not." She had folded her hands in front of her and was intently staring at me. I held my ground. "There are memories that even Ceintra could not recollect, and there were things that you were part of before you were a fairy that you had no idea about."

I was taken aback by what she was saying. She was making no sense. Ember and Ebony were tensed beside me, obviously awaiting a fight to break out. But I knew if I started something in this cramped space they would be hurt in the process.

"Quit speaking in riddles and just tell me what you want to." I growled.

She tapped a finger on her lip and considered how she was going to go about explaining whatever it was she needed to explain. Finally, she got it. "I am assuming you know that I have Royals, my most loyal creations." She shot a look at Ebony. "Well, at least they are supposed to be." Ebony looked down to hide her disgust at the comment. Tranquility continued, "What you do not know is that my fourth Royal is a very close person to you. You knew him almost your entire life, and I think it is time you two become acquainted again."

She stalked between Ember and I, her shoulder brushed against my wing but left no mark. We turned to watch as she stepped carelessly over her husband's body and opened one of the doors behind him. She entered and disappeared into darkness.

I looked at Ember and slid my wings back into my skin. Before he could make any suggestions I was through the door and following blindly. As I had said before, I was no longer scared of her. Merely annoyed.

Ember and Ebony followed without comment and when the only candle in the entire room was lit my blood curdled. The walls were once again white marble and the floor was black carpet. The entire area was lined with shelves which held potions and elixirs of all sorts.

Some hissed and fizzed while others bubbled and gurgled. A single desk sat in the middle stacked with books and empty vials. A small candle that was down to a lit nub sat in a gold tray on the corner. I looked at the fairy for a long time then forced myself to look away.

Tranquility stood next to the newly lit candle examining some of the potions and laughing to herself. Ember's brow was creased and Ebony made no comment. I dug my nails into my skin and looked up again to make sure what I was seeing was real.

The fairy pouring over his work as he spilled purple liquid into green to form a hissing black had silver wings that pointed down. They were average size and had no interesting colors mixed in them. His hair was dark brown and pulled back with a cream ribbon at his neck, and his eyes were glowing orbs of silver.

Small black framed glasses were perched on his pointed nose and his black blouse had colored stains covering it. He hummed to himself and ignored our presence. I turned on Tranquility with a ferocity I did not know I possessed.

"How long have you kept him here?!" I demanded.

She turned holding a vial of gold tears. She shook the shimmering gold around and checked it then placed it carefully back on the shelf. She dusted her hands off on her skirts. "Kept him? I have not kept him. He has been one of my loyal subjects since before you were born."

My mind spun. It was not possible. The man before me could not be who I thought it was, but who else was it? I knew the crinkles around those eyes and the lingering smile better than I knew my own. Ember was looking at me in puzzlement.

I turned to him with tears in my eyes. "That is my father.

Thirty-Four

Ember opened his mouth like he wanted to say something but no words would come out. Instead his mouth opened and closed several times before he decided to rub my arm instead. I felt no comfort in his touch. My body felt like ice.

Tranquility clapped her hands together excitedly. "Yes, yes! I'm so glad you didn't forget what your own flesh and blood looks like. Riah has been one of my faithful servants for... well, as long as I can remember!"

I felt faint. I grabbed Ember's arm in an attempt to keep myself up. "But... how?"

She crossed the room and rubbed my father's shoulders. He did not seem to feel her touch. He was still intent on mixing his potions and doing his work. "He was assigned to your mother. He never truly loved her! And when I had realized he had three children with her, well, I just had to do something. So I had him fake his death. I put a spell over him immobilizing him and you fools buried him and wept." She patted his shoulder and picked one his books up. She flipped through the pages halfheartedly and threw it back down. A puff of dusk exploded into the air. "But matters became more complicated, you see. I realized not only did you have Mayhem Fairy qualities, but so did your sister.

"What was her name? Oh... yes! Juniper, that's it. The one you killed, yes, thank you for that. She was a pain from the moment I had her created. Anyway, when I realized you were hybrids, I assigned Ember to you. You were so vulnerable, it was really quite easy. To think that you had contemplated and attempted suicide, what a shame. Didn't you ever wonder why you never bled out? Or why you somehow always landed on your feet when you tried to plummet to your death?"

She paused to let this soak in. I had wondered these things. The problem was, I always assumed it was just a sign from God that it was not my time. I was shivering in disbelief and shock. I had never been normal. No matter how hard I had tried to fit in and go along with what my peers did, I was never like them. I had been doomed from the start.

"Oh, and Juniper." She continued, obviously not caring about how any of this made me feel. "She was quite the beauty. Eerily beautiful, wouldn't you say? That definitely did not come from your mother or some distant relative; it came from the blood your father mixed into her when he decided that having children with a mortal woman was a good idea."

She continued, "I digress. When I realized dear Reyenne and Juniper were hybrids, I sent my loyal subject to turn you both." She looked at Ember whose eyes had widened to match my own. "Yes, dear. I swept your memory of that also. You did not go to merely create Victoria then leave, you were sent for them both, but you foolishly fell in love with the older sister and forgot all about your duty to the younger one. Naturally, I had to step in. When I came to retrieve Victoria, I also took Juniper. But because Ember was not in love with Juniper, I was able to hand her off to one of the others and let them create her. That part was really quite simple. StarFyre did a lovely job, even if her creation revolted against me and ate our own kind. Then, all I had to do from there was take Reyenne and turn her into you, Victoria."

Her mouth broke into a creepy smile of admiration and hatred. "But, of course, along with everything else in my horrid existence, there were complications. I found you had Kingdom Poison in your veins. A Potion Maker's daughter! Can you imagine my disbelief? And so I knew I had to have you destroyed. And now, now I see that we find ourselves here. In a complicated mess with no way out."

The room went silent; there was no sound except the faint chatter of potions boiling. My heart was racing and my ears were ringing. I had not expected any of this. I did not know how to react to this information. I had been a puppet my entire life.

I remembered Ebony's words. The conversation she had had with me about accepting who and what I was, and making the best out of my future. I had had enough. She had destroyed my family from the very start. I threw my wings into the air and they ripped through the shelves.

Potions went flying and liquid sizzled as it ate away at the wood and marble. Ebony bounced back to avoid a green oozing potion being dumped on her legs and feet. "I am going to kill you, and I am going to enjoy every minute of it." I snarled

She opened her mouth to give some sarcastic reply, but I did not give her the chance. I was so fed up with this woman. I wanted her in a grave and I wanted her there now. She had utterly destroyed every person I knew, including myself. She was a liar and a manipulator, and I was more than ready to take over the throne.

Something inside me snapped and the air around me fizzed and changed. White light emanated from my wings and they changed color. I turned and watched in awe, momentarily forgetting Tranquility was even standing in front of me.

The color of my wings slowly faded away and was replaced by white with swirls of gold. Ebony gasped to my right and covered her face. I could barely see her over the bright light escaping the feathers of my wings.

"What... what's happening to me?" I cried out.

"It's the prophecy!" Ebony shouted obviously appalled by what she was seeing. "You're finally fulfilling it! You're becoming the good to counter the evil! Strike, Victoria! Strike her down now! Your Kingdom Poison is ready!"

I took her advice and became a swirling tornado of wings and sparks. Glass broke and shelves went flying in every direction. I saw Tranquility through glimpses; she had elongated her wings and was doing the same.

The sensation was familiar, and when her wings met mine and the clashing began, I knew the sound well. Ember and Ebony had grabbed my father and were flat against the far wall. I tried to get away from the door so they could escape but Tranquility was eagerly shoving me into the wall.

My feather caught her skin and gold blood splattered over the broken glass and potions on the floor. Hope filled my heart and I pushed against her ever the harder. She shoved back, obviously feeling my hope and I skidded across the room. My wings unfolded and slammed into the wall where Ebony, Ember, and Riah were standing.

I had no time to check if they were okay. She was coming at me in full force with her wings spinning madly. I gathered my bearings and jumped up. I turned into a twisting tornado once again and clashed into her wings. For a while all that could be heard was the scraping of metal and our heavy breathing. Every now and then I heard a cry of alarm but I assumed that was from Tranquility.

I obviously had the upper hand.

I saw a piece of her torso was exposed between her wings in flashes as I spun. I knew this was my chance to end everything. My heart elated and my mind cleared of all other thoughts. I crouched and shoved the tips of my wings out then went in with a force I did not know I possessed.

The glowing had vanished from my wings but I saw perfectly as the white and gold tip slammed into her side and gold poured out along with pieces of broken rib. She stumbled and fell against the wall.

I stopped spinning and slid my wings back into my spine. I watched as she slid down the wall allowing the remaining bottles to break behind her and the jagged pieces of wooden shelf to dig into her skin. She clutched her side where my wing had bit into her skin.

She looked up at me with wide eyes then ran for the door. I didn't bother to stop her, she was not healing and that was obvious. She left a gold trail and she limped to the door and disappeared through it.

Had I won? Was I finally queen? If I was shouldn't I feel some difference? Some transition of power? She obviously was not dead yet, but she would be soon. No one could help her. If she couldn't heal herself, surely another fairy could not.

I turned back to Ember and Ebony, my thoughts happy but my stomach nervous. It clenched in disgust and anticipation. But when I turned to smile at them, my entire being disintegrated.

Riah was back at his torn apart desk trying to shove the contents of vials back into their original place. He was obviously under some kind of trance spell, more than likely as a punishment. I would have to learn magic before I could help him, but he was not the one I was worried about.

Ebony was crouched on the ground holding Ember in a heap. His head was completely disconnected from his body and he was bleeding profusely. Ebony shook with sobs and was whispering fiercely. She kept his head cradled on his neck so that it did not roll away.

I dropped to my knees next to her and grabbed Ember's hand. Tears rolled down my face no matter how hard I tried to conceal them. "D-did I... did I do this?!" I shrieked.

Ebony looked up at me; her eyes were covered in a thick film of gold. Her entire body trembled and she nodded, unable to speak. She held Ember's head and used her other hand to wipe her tears away.

"But... he has Kingdom Poison! He should be healing!" I shoved Ebony aside and tried to push Ember's head and neck together. But no matter the force I used, they would not go back together. If anything, I was making it worse. Blood spurted from the stomp and soaked my clothing.

I ripped a piece of my skirt and tied it around his neck like a scarf, hoping that if the two pieces stayed together they would somehow merge. Ebony had stood up behind me. She was kicking vials and potion bottles out of the way in search for tears. But every vial had been destroyed and the liquid had already soaked into the carpet.

It was no use.

"He will not come back. Simply because Tranquility is mortally wounded and only three with Kingdom Poison can be alive." Her voice was monotone, unfeeling. "I read all about it when you arrived. Ember has already died... that means she will heal."

As if on cue there was a great crashing from upstairs. The few bottles Riah had managed to fix broke apart again. He hummed happily and began mending once again as if nothing had happened. It was annoying given the circumstances.

I looked to the ceiling then back down to Ember. "Too many people have died..."

Ebony knelt next to me again and held Ember's lower half. Together we hugged him to our bodies. "I don't know what to do." She confessed. "I knew our race was complicated, but until you came along I had no idea just how much. If Ember is dead then only two remain in power and that is all the prophecy called for. What if we can never bring him back?!" She was growing more and more hysterical as she went on.

I racked my brain for ideas. None came. I thought over the deaths of Juniper, Keelan, Ceintra, Athan, and now Ember. I had lost so many people close to me. I felt like I was part of a horror novel. Would it ever end? Would I ever honestly be able to live a life of happiness?

My mind wandered to Ceintra sobbing in her bed as I rocked back and forth with Ember cradled to my bosom. An idea occurred to me. I turned to Ebony who was humming a child's tune to Ember's lifeless corpse.

"Keelan and Ceintra replaced your heart and you regenerated..." I began, "Could we do the same with Ember?"

Ebony looked up at me. "No, dear. I was missing a heart. I was not actually dead. Look at him, his heart is still there, he is not aging. He has already left us and passed into the Realm."

I deflated. The little hope I had managed to muster evaporated and I was back to misery. Ebony stood once again and dusted her skirts. I set Ember's body carefully on the floor, trying to avoid laying his limbs in glass the best I could and stood up to face Ebony.

She exhaled deeply and wiped the remaining tears from her eyes. I had to give her credit. Ebony may have been a lot of things, but weak was not one of them. I was still blubbering like a fool and gasping for air.

"I suppose there's only one thing left for us to do." She sighed.

"And what is that?" I was secretly hoping she had an idea that would bring him back and kill Tranquility.

She shook her head and shoved the stray hairs from her face. She straightened her shoulders. "Shoot him into the stars and give this all up. We tried, and I would rather live my life knowing that then continue this nonsense and kill more fairies. The least we can do is give Ember a proper funeral and go back to our respective lives."

I rubbed the tears from my eyes and looked at her in bafflement. "We're just going to give up?"

I couldn't believe what I was hearing. If we gave up now all their deaths would be in vain. They would be forgotten or talked about as the foolish fairies that tried to go against the queen and lost. I couldn't do that. I had to keep going, until I took my last breath.

Ebony threw her hands into the air and let them fall back to her sides. They slapped against her thighs in defeat. "What would you have me do?! I have lost my best friend, I have spent most of my time this past week with a lunatic, and now I have lost my pride and joy. That was my son! That is my son lying on the floor. As much as I love you Victoria, I cannot stick around and watch as the rest of my loved ones go down. I know you have had a terrible life but so have I. There is only so much a woman can handle."

I didn't speak, but I thought over what she was saying. I felt it was my fault all of this had happened. I could have easily ignored the prophecy and lived my days with Ember far away from here. Hell, I could have ignored Ember and stayed human and been dead by now, at least I thought I could have.

I nodded to Ebony. She smiled the best she could but it did not reach her eyes. The small curve vanished quickly and she knelt down to pick Ember's body up. I did the same and we carried him awkwardly from the room.

Thirty-Five

A few days had passed but I didn't feel one of them. My days ran into the nights and I didn't speak. A vital piece of me was missing. I didn't know how I was going to go on without him.

Tranquility was wandering the castle in one piece but she didn't bother to speak to me. I knew that no matter how hard she acted, a piece of her was missing too. She had lived so long knowing that Athan still existed in some realm that she had become content. But now that she knew he was really gone, a piece of her was gone also.

She had been the one to shoot them into the stars. Keelan, Ceintra, and Ember were laid out on gold slabs in order for us to say goodbye. Black candles flickered as we walked past them and I kissed Ember on the lips. He had turned warm. I inwardly smiled, he would have been glad.

He was no longer cold.

Ebony did not come to watch Tranquility go through the rites, she stayed locked in her bedroom playing with her garden snake. It was really quite beautiful, but I didn't stay for the entire thing either. I couldn't watch as Ember's soul left his body and floated up into the air to finally shoot and spark, then vanish among the millions of other lighted orbs.

I slipped out of the packed Dining Area after I had seen Keelan's soul vanish. Dravven had disappeared shortly after he learned of Ember's death. Ebony had said it was his way of mourning. He had obviously seen more death than any of us could imagine.

What really set me off was how normal everyone was acting though. Fairies came and went and ate at the huge table, they played chess, and they slumbered in their rooms. They were so used to how things ran that they didn't question any of it.

They didn't care to know why another of their kind had died. They were self-absorbed. And so with this information, I decided it was finally my time to go too. I knew I hadn't lasted long among this species, and I knew I probably had more to live for, but I wasn't exactly worried about it.

I had had my fill. And I knew I could not fail this time. I had the power to kill myself without anyone stopping me or bringing me back.

I sat in my misery on my bed in the Quarter's and expanded my claws and wings. My eyes shone involuntarily. My entire being was over spilling with self-loathing and pain. I couldn't keep up with this race. I couldn't keep up with myself.

I stood in front of my mirror and examined my appearance. My hair hadn't been brushed and my eyes were bloodshot from lack of sleep and food. My attire was plain gray and shabby from having worn it for days on end.

I pulled my jacket off and then my shirt over my head. I wanted to see my flesh being torn open. I wanted to feel maximum pain, I wanted to feel something. Even if they were only felt my last moments on earth.

I pulled my small vial out of my pocket and placed it below my eyes and forced myself to cry. A single tear slipped out of my left eye and dripped into the bottle. It was all I had left in me. I was already a walking carcass.

I took a deep breath and shoved my index finger into my chest. I gasped but kept going until I reached my heart. I was so used to pulling hearts from mortals that I knew exactly what it felt like to touch one.

My body started convulsing and trying to heal itself but I wouldn't let it. I kept twisting the claw in my wound until I was lying on the floor. I quickly pulled my finger out of the wound and let the drop of my tears fall into the small hole.

I closed my eyes and waited but nothing happened. I exhaled slowly. I thought this might happen. What had worked on Cleopatra with Tranquility would not work with me. So I went to option B.

I sat up and crossed my legs, still staring at myself in the mirror. I kept my eyes open no matter how much the frightened person inside of me wanted me to squeeze them shut. I shoved my entire hand into my chest, and kept my lips firmly closed so I did not scream out.

I drug my clawed hand down my torso and my gold guts spilled onto my lap and carpet. I was growing weaker and weaker. I fell forward and watched with my drooping eyes as my wings turned from white and gold back to black.

I wanted to laugh at the absurdity but did not have the strength to. Perhaps I was not as pure as they all wanted me to be.

My eyes closed into darkness. There was a swirling sensation like I was falling. But it was not the stomach plummeting feeling that you got when you thought you were falling out of bed, it was pleasant. I gave myself into it.

Ember was all I thought and then my conscious left me.

Riah

Thirty-Six

I had heard everything, but I had been too much of a coward to do anything. I could have easily thrown some sort of acid onto Tranquility and prevented her from slashing at my daughter. But like I said... I was a coward.

It was what had gotten me into this situation. I could have defied Tranquility and stayed with my wife and girls, but I was too scared of her wrath. So I went along with the Queen's idea to fake my death and then come back to the castle.

That ended up getting me places. I was forced back into this dreary Potion Room in a hidden department of the castle and for the first fifty years I was under a trance. What Tranquility didn't know, was that I had spilled an elixir on me and it had caused the trance to subside.

I had been prowling the castle at night for decades. I had even left a few times, making sure I was back by morning for Tranquility to check on me. As long as I kept up the dummy act in her presence, she didn't suspect a thing.

So much for being the all-powerful.

But now was not the time for me to tuck my tail between my legs and run for the hills. My eldest was in trouble. She had killed herself, I knew because I had unfortunately found her body. I had been on my way to tell her I had heard everything and I thought I had a solution, but instead I found a corpse and pile of rotted organs.

That was one scene I could have lived the rest of my days without seeing. Wasn't it bad enough that I had watched my dear wife grow old and decay? And my youngest daughter get older, marry, and have a family of her own?

If I had known what my actions would have caused, if I had known I would have created three beautiful children with a gorgeous wife when I took on the task of being assigned to a human... I never would have agreed.

It would have saved us all so much heartbreak. Oh, the nights when I used to watch Juniper cry at my empty grave. My heart would twist and clench, it would take all my strength not to march over to her and grasp her in my arms. But at the time she didn't know what I was, and when she came to visit me after she had been fully turned, I was still under the trance.

But forget all of that, now was my chance to make things right. I couldn't bring my wife or Honour back but I could bring Victoria, Juniper, and their loved ones back from the Realm. I had been perfecting forbidden potions and elixirs for years.

I was sitting on the floor in the Potion Room mending glass bottles and using a charm to suck the spilt liquids out of the carpet. I couldn't salvage them enough to put them back into their respective bottles, but I could easily remake them all.

But now was not the time for that. I would fill a few bottles to show Tranquility that I was diligently working but on the side I would be mixing the potion I had created to bring Dravven back from The Realm years before. Tranquility had banished him out of anger.

She had been so surprised to see him again, but he had followed my rules and told her he did it himself. She had thought he was even more powerful than she originally assumed. Little did she know it was her closet secret that had helped him.

I needed him again, this much I knew. He had had fled the castle after the death of Ember, and no one had seen him. But I knew where to look for him. I checked my watch and stood buttoning my cloak.

It was half past midnight; Tranquility would be in bed by now. She wasn't acting like her normal self. She usually rarely slept and spent her nights writing or harassing someone, but lately she had been going to sleep and barely speaking.

No matter, that meant the odds were in my favor. I set my latest mended bottles on my fixed shelves and slipped out the door and through the black rooms until I was standing in the dungeon. I looked both ways to make sure there were no guards lingering about and pulled the hood of my cloak up.

My silver eyes would give me away in an instant, so I kept my head down until I had safely made my way through the castle and to the front gates. Oberon was standing guard outside as usual. He nodded his head at me and kept his spear still. I had helped him once mend one of his wings with a forbidden elixir. He had forever been in my debt since.

I nodded back and made my way down the marble steps. Once I was on the wooden path I expanded my wings and took off into the night sky. My wings flapped noisily due to my not bothering with flictating.

I had always hated the act. Leaving the atmosphere was a bit too out there for me, even though I feasted on organs and had wings coming from my spine. I drew my line at following a path made of stars.

In no time I touched down in the town of Hardwick. I had been here so many times due to Dravven running from his responsibilities. I always thought fairies didn't take him seriously enough. They forgot that behind his mental issues, he was still a moving being.

I strode through the roads, still keeping my head down, until I reached the broken apart manor. It was really nothing but a foundation now. The few spare walls were still standing, but the rest had been knocked down due to storms.

This was Dravven's comfort zone, the place he came when he needed to think. I trudged through the stones and debris until I reached the cellar door. It was shut and locked with random scraps of wood thrown over it in an attempt to hide the only intact room of the building.

I bent down and threw the wood off the door then unlatched the lock and climbed in. I used my magic to lock and cover the door once again and made my way down the narrow staircase. I grunted at the effort, I was getting old... even for a Mayhem Fairy.

Dravven was perched in his usual spot among his favorite fabrics and sewing away. He hummed a spooky tune under his breath but stopped when he saw me. I flicked my hand and lit another candle to give us more light.

He set the blanket he was working on in his lap and smiled and giggled at my appearance. I sat myself down across from him among his scraps and needles. A pair of scissors stabbed my leg and I threw them away from me.

"Dravven." I acknowledged him by nodding my head and doing the sign of Mayhem.

He cackled. "What brings you here, Riah?"

"I thought you should know that Victoria, my daughter, has gone to be with Ember." I hung my head low in sadness. Saying it out loud made it somehow more real.

Dravven tsked and picked his sewing supplies back up. His hands moved in rapid motion. He was completing an orange and yellow blanket with intricate embroidery of black wings. "I am sorry, love. But why come all this way to tell me?" he went to laugh but slammed his lips together to stop himself.

I pushed the hood of my cloak down and flattened my unruly hair. It was the same color Victoria's had been when she was little. I suddenly remembered her playing with my hair and telling me all about how we had the same hair color. I smiled at myself then straightened my posture. "I need you to go back into The Mayhem Realm and retrieve her. Also, Ember, Keelan, and Ceintra."

Dravven didn't bother to look up. He stayed focused on his hand as the needle wove in and out of the fabric, creating the tip of a sharp wing. "I can only do that with a potion."

I nodded my head. "I will make it."

He glanced up and giggled, his eyes were glowing brightly. "And what do I get in return, love?"

"Whatever you want."

I fidgeted nervously, awaiting his request. With Dravven it could be anything. I only hoped it was something I could supply him with. I hoped he realized how important this was to me.

Dravven set the blanket down once again and twirled the thick needle in between his fingers. He tapped his free hand on his chest and pulled at his hair a couple times. I was used to such behavior from him.

"I want you to make a potion for me, love." He looked back down and continued to sew, "I want it to be a poison... one that has aspects of Kingdom Poison and Athan Erasmus' tears."

I was taken aback by his request. "Why?"

Dravven arched a brow and smirked. "Now that wasn't part of the deal, love." He held his hand out and I shook it.

Epilogue

Ever since the deaths of Keelan, Ceintra, Victoria, and Ember I felt free. I officially had no more enemies in the world. Those of my kind that despised me were too cowardly to do anything about it. And yet...I was not happy. The third death of Athan had hit me harder than I thought it would.

I knew that this time he would never be back. I would never see him again. But did I really want to? He had betrayed me by loving Ophira after all. Every time the thoughts invaded my mind, I tried to push them out.

But the harder I tried, the more forcefully they came. I tried to act as normal as possible. I kept up my front of cruelty by berating random fairies as I was passing them in the halls, and savagely digging into my humans in the Dining Area when others were about.

Yet I could not ignore the fact that I felt empty. My journal had stayed in its drawers for days and I hadn't gone hunting in what seemed like forever. I went to bed at dusk each night and arose at dawn each morning to walk through the forest.

Despite my sorrow and state of mourning for Athan's death, I also felt something else. I felt like the Mayhem Fairies were on the verge of something big. That something was going to happen and it was going to happen soon. But what it was I did not know.

It was the first time since early in my reign that I wasn't holding all the cards. Someone had stolen my Ace. I was wandering through the forest lining the castle when a thought occurred to me. I had never sent a single fairy into the stars. That meant, Victorian and Ember were still alive... just in purgatory.

My heart beat wildly. Would they be able to find a way out? Surely not. But then again, Athan had managed to leave. I shook the worry off. Athan had the assistance of Keelan and Ceintra, and now they were stuck there too.

They wouldn't be able to use their powers in The Realm, they were dead! Their bodies were here, buried on the castle grounds.

I ran through the trees to the spot where I had my guards bury wrapped up fairies after I pretended to do the funeral rites with magic and some fairy dust. So far no one had noticed that I wasn't actually shooting stars into the sky. And if they did, they didn't say anything about it.

My guards thought I was discarding the remains of human bodies after feasting times. Little did they know, they were burying the empty shells of their brothers and sisters in Mayhem.

I knelt on the ground next to the freshest grave. Keelan, Ceintra, Ember, Victoria, and Juniper were all in this one, wrapped up in black cotton blankets. I wanted them all in the same area so if anything were to happen; I could destroy their remains easily.

I ran my hand through the fresh dirt and wiped my palm off on my dress. I exhaled deeply. I was acting like a fool. Of course they weren't coming back! Nothing was going on. I had nothing to worry about; there was no one to oppose me.

Except, of course, Victoria and Ember's child. But they had no idea she existed. I made sure I put a double mind sweep on that small detail in Victoria's mind, and Mystic thought her parents were a human male and a female fairy.

It had been embedded in her head since birth that her mother was foolish and her father had died years ago due to his mortal lifespan. The female fairy, Grendel Vail, that I had put her in was an idiot. I made sure of that.

She knew she had given birth to a hybrid, but I had implanted the memory of her having a fascination with a male human. As far as she was concerned, Mystic was her child. The child she had absolutely nothing to do with.

The idea of her consorting with a mortal sickened her so much I thought she was going to abort Mystic. I had put a quick stop to that. Then when Mystic was born with the power of seeing, that was it. There was nothing I could do. Grendel threw the baby to the wolves and I was forced to clean up the mess.

Luckily, I found a nice coven that accepted her and didn't ask questions. And what do you know? She became the leader of the imbeciles. So that was that. There was no living threat. I was the most powerful creature alive.

Nothing could stop me now.

I stood back up, still examining the shallow grave. Honestly, having no one to fight against quite bored me. I had never lived a life where there weren't people trying to go against me or trying to destroy me. There had always been action and adventure in my life, always someone for me to one up.

I hadn't been stuck in a seemingly normal life since I was human, and I saw where that got me. Dead in my father's throne within a few months of taking it.

No, boring was not my thing.

I needed to find someone to go against me. I knew exactly the person. I trudged through the fields and back into the castle. Fairies bowed as I passed, I gave no acknowledgement of my existence. I almost wanted to scream at them to do something! To go against me! To try to fight me! Something!

They were all so damn complacent!

But then again, hadn't I made them that way? It had been taught to them since the very beginning, they were to follow all orders of their ruler without question. It was my fault they were so ready to do my bidding. I sighed deeply as I made my way to the dungeons.

I still did not know how Ebony had managed to infiltrate my hidden area. I had specifically blocked magic, which meant someone had taken it down. Perhaps I had and had just forgotten. After all, no one knew of this area except me and one other. And the other was in a trance.

I opened the secret passage and made my way through the first dark room and into the next. Riah was sitting with a single lit candle mending his broken bottles and filling the ones with ancient tears back up. He had done a fairly good job, considering it hadn't been that long since the room had been destroyed in my battle.

He did not look up when I entered. He was used to my visits. Due to the trance I had put on him he moved mechanically and never strayed from his work. He kept an organized log of all the tears we possessed and documented each bottle of potion he created.

He had even developed new potions and elixirs that had never before been thought of. He was a good puppet.

I examined the shelf holding tears from each fairy in existence. Vial after vial was crammed in the ceiling to floor glass case. Each vial had a small strip across it's center with the specific fairy's name etched into it.

It was a wonder this case had not been broken in the battle. We would have lost centuries of documentation. I scanned the rows of gold and names until finally I reached the top where mine sat by itself.

The name "Tranquility Erasmus" was printed largely on a small gold piece of parchment and carefully wrapped around the vial. My vial was bigger than the rest and held more tears. It was one of the only ones which contained Kingdom Poison.

On the second shelf sat Ember and Victoria's. Their vials were the same size as the hundreds of others, but had been brought to the front due to their high levels of Kingdom Poison. I gritted my teeth.

I crouched down to look at the bottom shelf. This was where the tears of fairies from Atlantis were stored. My father's and Ophira's were among them. Although I made sure they were kept towards the back so I would not be forced to look at them when I entered this room. I let my eyes linger over each name, bringing back a specific memory.

I reached the end of the row and saw that Athan's had been moved to the front. I put my palm against the glass then stood and turned on Riah. I walked over to his desk and stood in front of it, menacing and evil.

He did not look up. He was mixing green colored contents of one bottle into the clear contents of another and it was fizzing and bubbling out of the vial. "Riah."

He still did not acknowledge my presence, he never did. It was not part of his trance. His job was to make potions and organize the already made ones. "Riah, look at your Queen." I demanded.

His head snapped up but his silver eyes were glazed over in his trance state. His hands were still deftly moving to mix potions, even though his eyes were not watching what he was doing. Somehow the liquid did not spill over his desk.

"Riah, why is Athan's vial moved to the front? I thought I told you his vial was to stay in the back with the rest of the people's I did not want to see. Have you been in the cabinet?" I questioned ruthlessly.

He blinked absentmindedly but did not reply. That was another flaw in my trance. I did not give him the ability to speak. He was like a horse. All he knew was potion making and organizing. I decided to bring him out of his trance. He had been in it for decades and all his loved ones were dead.

I snapped my fingers and waved my hand in front of his face. His eyes immediately sprang to life and he jumped from his seat. The vials he had been holding smashed and the green liquid ate through the desk. He looked around with wide eyes, obviously confused.

I smirked and folded my arms across my chest. "Welcome back to the world, Riah."

He blinked rapidly and stared at me. "W-where am I?" he patted his clothing to make sure he was still intact and stomped his feet which had obviously fallen asleep.

"You are in the Potion Room. It has been your domain for over a century." I grinned evilly.

"Oh." It was all he said before he pulled his chair from the floor where he had knocked it down and sat back down. He picked up the now empty vials and waved his hand over the desk. The contents gathered and put themselves back into the glass bottles and the desk fixed itself. He went back to mixing the potions.

The movement took me off guard. I had wanted him to be furious, but instead he was content! The green and clear liquid finally mixed and turned gold. It bubbled and he corked it. The vial was sat in a holder on the edge of the desk and he picked another vial up.

I could stand it no longer. "I killed your daughters!" I blurted.

He looked up and for an instant, I thought in anger, but it turned out to be curiosity. "You did? I assumed they would have died a long time ago." He went back to his work.

I bit my lip. "You are not angry?! You do not want to fight me?!"

He shook his head in disbelief. "Why would I want to do that? I went against you once and it got me torn away from my loved ones. I will just go back to my work. Thank you for taking the spell off, it feels good being in control of my limbs again." He flexed his arms and rolled his head on his neck then concentrated on pouring another green liquid into clear.

I stomped my foot in a mini tantrum and left the room. I stormed through the castle and into my chambers where I slammed the door and pulled my journal out. I wrote furiously about all that had happened. It felt good to get it off my chest.

When I was done, I clutched the book to my chest and wept. I finally had everything I wanted, and I had never felt so defeated.

www.ingramcontent.com/pod-product-compliance
Lightning Source LLC
Chambersburg PA
CBHW020058180626
46812CB00006B/2378